Other Titles by B. K. Sweeting

Bubbly By The Sea

○

For a preview of upcoming books by B.K. Sweeting

visit Bksweeting.com or find her on Facebook.

Learn more at www.Bksweeting.com
Printed in the United States of America
First edition 2021
ISBN: 978-1-09839-780-7 (print)
ISBN: 978-1-09839-781-4 (ebook)

PEARLIZED
B.K. SWEETING

DEDICATION

For a few high-quality and genuine gems in my life:

May your light beam on forever.

Sizzle, Mary, Amanda.

o

PEARLIZED

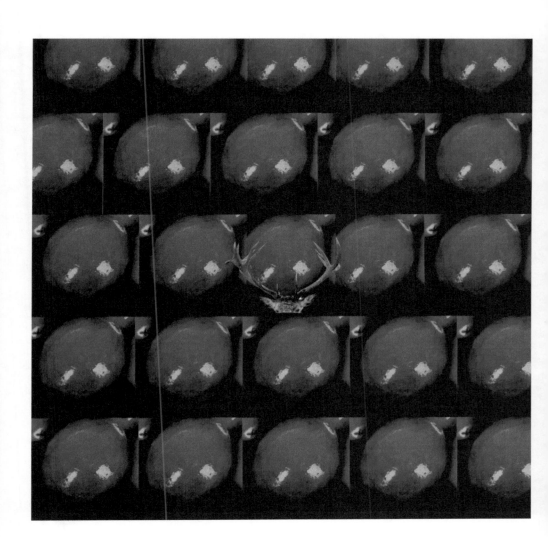

"Vengeance is in my heart, death in my hand, blood and revenge are hammering in my head."

— William Shakespeare

"Life can only be understood backwards;
but it must be lived forwards."

— Søren Kierkegaard, 1843

THE ART

FOGGERTON, A SMALL town in Upstate New York, involuntarily provided a frozen crescent-shaped bay as a canvas for the day. Home to ring-billed gulls, trophy small-mouth bass, roses of spectacular varieties, and an abundance of fragrant fir and spruce trees. The eastern bay of New York, shore to Lake Ontario, occupied a population of 1,258. Within that population, a malevolent artist, carefully carried out an action with an aesthetic purpose, displaying natural elements against a natural platform to express an idea. A deadly idea.

Crystalized bursts waltzed off the ice with each whisper of wind, exposing a deep cabernet medium that was pour-painted over a barely-there pale blue with white veins. The rich red pigment led to a classic gem protruding from the liquid, next to an exposure on the surface. Brackish water kicked up to lick thick jagged edges of ice, teasing the blood above as a threat of washing away its sins.

The painting stood alone, with no one to claim their handiwork. The gaping hole was all that remained. In the afternoon on December 12th, 2002.

000

ICE SCREAMS

December 12th, 2002

A BLACK AND YELLOW bus made its last stop of the day, rounding a neighborhood that had a one-lane, dead end road trailing from it. A 12-year-old boy hopped off the bottom step of the bus, into grimy black slush, and began walking down the middle of Silver Beach road. Past a line up of Red Maple trees that fenced the front of his neighbor's homes, to his right. To his left was the woods, where he frequently played in with his best friends. The last house before a dead-end, a weathered red brick ranch-style home, with a matching brick chimney, white wrap-around porch, and a cherry red door. Snow trickled off branches as he passed them. The movement released the fresh scent of earth and a hint of dust. A familiar and comforting aroma to him. The smell of home.

Glittered flakes funneled upwards after each of Oisín's boot prints in the snow. A five-minute walk in negative six degrees Celsius with a lake effect breeze would make anyone shiver. Not Oisín, though, not today. He could see the snowman that he built the previous day, standing at a little under five feet, just like Oisín. His ears stung upon the sight of his lime-green earmuffs he forgot about on the compact round snow head. He picked up the pace. His soft and mousey brown hair, shaped into a bowl haircut, flowed in the wind. The boy possessed a lingering weight of exciting news to announce, news that he clung to with both of his mitts, a school talent show flyer.

Butterflies soared in his little belly as he entered his home, fully decorated for the holidays.

"Mom, I'm home!" he yelled out.

Oisín threw his blue and yellow canvas backpack over the couch with his mitts, kicked off his saturated boots, and hung up his red, white, and blue *New York Rangers* coat on the hook bar.

"MOM! We picked out a song for the talent show!" he shouted, louder than the first announcement.

He rounded the floral sofa couch that separated the foyer and living room. The middle schooler set the talent flyer on his piano music rest, between one brown bear *Beanie Baby* wearing a Santa's hat and a tuxedo penguin *Beanie Baby*.

"*Mom?*" Oisín inquired.

The boy exited the family room to the kitchen. Where wood-panels befriended eggshell painted walls and where coconut carpeting met geometric solid wood. Oisín's blue and brown eyes practically popped outside of his head when he saw the newspaper *Toys 'R' Us* catalog sitting on the kitchen table. As he approached the magazine, he wondered what pages his mom bent over and how many more minutes alone that he had to figure out what he was going to get for Christmas.

"Ugh, what is this?" he griped. He lifted his foot up off the dark parquet flooring to observe his oversized white holey socks and recognized that it was just water. Well, cold water, that was inconveniently forming mini puddles from the back French doors to the carpet he just left.

Oisín grew impatient. His mom, Claire, always greeted him when he came home from school. Their weekly routine involved playing the piano together and chatting until his dad got home. After that, the boy did homework with his dad, Aidan, while Claire fixed up dinner for the three of them. Claire spent her week-days developing specialty pastry recipes for her second edition cookbook. The lack of sweet-smelling and yeasty aromas showed Oisín that she had not baked today. After the boy took his past-their-prime socks off, he made his way down the hall.

He called out once more for his mother, "Mom! Where are you? And why is the floor all wet?"

Silence.

In fact, more silence than the house has endured in a long time. The Murphy household typically ran a chorus of family sitcoms, piano keys playing, game console sound effects, and chatting amongst the family. The blondish hair on Oisín's arm pricked up from both the stillness and the chilly air on his naked feet.

He chucked his dirty socks in the corner of his predominantly navy-colored room. His nautical room was a collaborative effort. The family of three wakes up early every weekend to spend half of the day at the local flea market. Oisín scouted out the vintage lighthouse lantern on his desk from an outing a few weeks ago. Aidan helped Oisín build the mini fleet of wooden sailboats on his desk. Claire taught him to organize his belongings at a young age. She showed him how to make a space both functional and fun. They picked out his navy twin sized bedding together. He favored the comforter with white anchors that paired with his orca stuffed plush. Inspired by his favorite movie, *Free Willy*, he insisted on the nauti-cal theme and vowed to study marine life someday.

Oisín pulled his prized possession out of his jean pocket, an engraved brass compass that read, *My Little Deer, May you find yourself on the path to righteousness. Love, Mama.* Shadows developed across the walls as the winter sun disappeared. This stressed Oisín's already unsettled expression. He put the compass on the desk tabletop and turned his lighthouse light on. He put on clean whole socks and layered his favorite ivory Aran sweater over his cartoon graphic tee-shirt. He left his room to seek his mom in the primary bedroom further down the hall.

Still no Claire.

His dad doesn't come home from work for half an hour. This recognition of this sent the pre-teen sprinting to the garage door to check if his mom's car was present. It was. Oisín slammed the garage door shut and sprinted back to the breakfast nook, where the wet puddles first assaulted his foot. He grabbed the pale-yellow phone off the plastic wall holster and dialed his mom's new *Nokia* cellular phone number. Each unanswered ring sent an unpleasant pressure from his belly up to his chest. He held the phone away from his ear, in efforts to hear a cell tone ring or buzz from inside of the house.

"Hi, you reached Claire Murphy. If you're calling about a baking and pastry order, please leave your name and a good number to reach you. I will call you right back. Have a beautiful day!" Claire said in a clear, light, and pleasant voice.

Oisín hung up the phone on the wall. A tension in his head developed, resembling a trash compacter, squeezing out the little hope that he had left for a response. He believed for a split second his mom could have gone for a walk. But he recalled the door was unlocked and there were wet spots on the floor. An anxiety developed further, after the thought that maybe there could have been a break-in.

He dialed once more.

"Hello?" Logan answered.

"Can, can, ugh!" Oisín stammered.

"Murphy? Is that you?" Logan asked.

"Hi Lo, Logan. Can you get your dad? I can't find my mom. I'm not sure if something happened," Oisín said, trembling.

He slumped forward to glance out the breakfast nook windows, squinting hard as he brought his eyebrows together. He dropped the phone; it recoiled upwards, then down, avoiding the kitchen floor. It swayed leisurely on its cord.

"Hi Oisín, it's me, Detective Dawson. What's going on?" a man voiced.

Oisín pressed his hands up against the glass window on the back door. He tried to make out the sizable disruption on the ice, near the snowy shore.

"Mom? MOM!" he squealed.

Like an air-hockey puck, he bounced back and forth between the front and back doors. Carelessly stepping over the puddles in a race for his boots back by the foyer, stumbling to pull them on, he pushed his little feet in and flew back to his kitchen. He threw open the unlocked French double doors that preceded to their wooden conservatory.

BANG! BANG!

Oisín repeated the action with the conservatory set of doors. His knees flew high as he trotted through the foot of powdered snow, scanning the area for any sign of his mom, for anyone. The temperature was dropping. The gust nipped at his lobes, a whirring from the wind scorched his ear canals.

Arriving at the shore; he noticed movement with his peripheral vision, to the right of him. A woman, Oisín's neighbor, was standing behind a window on the side of her home, about fifty feet away. Her kitchen ran parallel with the Murphy household's double-sash family room window. Oisín waved his hands at the first glimpse of hope, eager to get his neighbors' attention. She was expressionless as she glared out the window, moving her arms in a scrubbing motion. In return,

Oisín's brows wrinkled into his little porcelain forehead, and he grit his small, straight teeth together. Little fists formed at the ends of the merino wool sleeves; hands keeping their balled-up shape as he performed a jumping jack motion to get her attention.

"HU, HELP!" Oisín yelled frustratedly at Sandra.

Sandra cocked her head to the side interestedly; short, straw hair met her shoulder as she continued staring. Confused now, but politely, Sandra brought her hand up, waving slowly back at Oisín. He shook his head furiously at her misunderstanding. He desired her attention. But he reserved his energy. Oisín wasn't confident in his actions, but he felt in his gut that he had to act fast.

Pursuing with caution, he made the first step onto the ice. It gave out under the hundred and ten pounds of weight, cracking instantaneously. The water from the slosh and splashing was much colder than he had imagined it would be, but it did not stop him from continuing. Eager for a more stable surface to stand on, he stomped until his boots finally met a promising solid surface. Oisín lowered down onto his knees and laid down on his belly to distribute his weight. Just as his father had instructed him to do every winter, if he ever found himself on thin ice.

Beads of sweat developed on his lightly freckled forehead. He pulled himself forward, unhurriedly crawling toward the hole to avoid too much pressure on what he knew was a sensitive floor below him. The rescue act damaged the skin on his hands. He felt a piercing pain from each of his little fingertips as he inched forward. Blood vessels near his skin constricted. Oisín approached the hole from a safe distance away. The curious inky liquid was close enough for him to register that it was blood. The only time that Oisín had seen this amount of blood was from watching *Jaws* on *VHS*.

His jaw dropped; he gasped for air. Unable to move an inch further. The stillness, the scene, the pounding in his chest. It heightened a fear that he had never known before. The horror distracted his focus from the excruciating pain in his hands and ears. A tear formed at the corner of his left eye, where he had segmental heterochromia. An island of smoky topaz flourished against the cerulean blue at the bottom of Oisín's iris.

He fixated on a curious attraction, a finger-painted symbol on the surface. Oisín thought to himself that it appeared to be the letter X next to two vertical lines. A gleaming orb demanded his attention. He tapered his eyes in on a pea-sized white bead sitting in a miniature pool of coagulated blood next to the hole. The pre-teen had never seen the pearl before, but a deep intuition screamed that there was a significance to it.

Oisín inhaled deeply and breathed out deliberately, building the courage to grasp the gem. He reached his right arm out in front of him, stretching it with all his might, though he struggled. His fingers moved at a sluggish pace, numb. At last, a thick, tacky crimson glue pulled up with his prized pearl.

A booming thunderclap erupted below him. The pressure of his movement and heat transference from his body disturbed the ice. Before he could scream for help, the ice separated, escaping beneath him. He closed his eyes tightly, as the water splashed upwards like a thousand tiny liquid daggers. Oisín's body lunged forward over the chunks of bloody ice and jagged edges, into the piercing polar and murky waters.

ooo

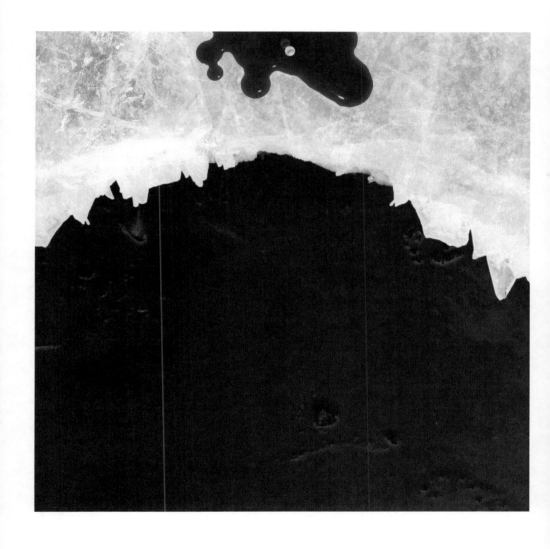

THE JOURNAL

September 3rd, 1988

HELLO NEW JOURNAL. Had brunch at Rossi's Eat O'clock with Sofia today. I'm so glad that the Summer is over! I longed for fall because that means school is back in session next week! Sofia spent most of the summer partying with the popular click, Jackie, David, and Mike. Gag me. She's probably working them for something. But it will not press a negative effect on our friendship. Sure, she's not wild about my grungy, thrift-store digs and shit talk about Mike's brown-nosing. But we're still meeting up for our weekly weekend breakfast. Something we started freshman year. It's a way for her to share all her problems, wants, and needs outside of school. I don't care, I'll take it.

Mike Johnson hit on her today. Staring down at her jugs from the restaurant window, cupping his hands to his chest and making kissy faces... a real Romeo. I offered her my black leather bomber, but she insisted on letting the barf bag drool over her. She says he's a Toy Boy, but 'not like the song'.

This café is the only decent place to eat and hangout in Venoice, Pennsylvania. Best food that my father's stolen money could buy. I love me a hot Italian meal to enjoy with a hot Italian girl. Mr. Rossi had just renovated it. Dark ambiance, lots of wood and leather, killer lighting, and the rad five-foot working clock sculpture. Painted-black wood with stainless steel. I want to steal it so bad. But I won't, don't shit where you eat. I guess I could, though. I could steal it if I wanted to. Or I could recreate my own.

Mr. Rossi doesn't tolerate stoners or troublemakers inside. And I'm the only one who still gets in with combat boots. Dolores always chases the airheads with a tiny pecker head out the front door when we sit down. She's a rad person, always waits on Sofia and me and puts our order through before we even sit down. All the football jock straps line up outside to be tortured by Sofia's bombshell blonde hair, high white socks, and a plaid mini that could give an old geezer a heart attack on the spot. It's funny. But I have to exhibit extreme self-control. I see what they see. I know that she's become more bodacious over the past few years. She's homecoming queen every year. She hangs out with the cheer bears more but won't officially join the cum guzzling cult. She enjoys feeling wanted, but she's a virgin. A tease to the maximum. When I see them making jokes about her, violating her with their eyes.

I want to break their ugly faces in. Smash them in until they can't look at her any longer. Self-control.

And that is why she's not invited over. Father thinks I'm a loser with no friends. He insists I socialize more, but he's putrid and not the person who I want to seek suggestions from. He sees what I want him to see. Mother adores Sofia from afar. She knows her mother, Mrs. Colombo, well from their lady lunches and the neighborhood picnic parties. Sofia and I have built a friendship from a foundation of me tutoring her since freshman year. We decided this year to just give up on the lessons and she'll copy all of my work, or we will just trade it to make it easier on the both of us. I've been a sound board for her so-called issues for the past three years. Worth it? Hell yes. To be close to her. She never asks about my problems, but I know everything about her. That's what

I have John for, but he thinks I'm high for not seeing that she's wasting me. He's wrong. Nothing to spaz over, though.

Also, Missy, our puppy died, Father almost had a heart attack at the sight of its intestines spread out by the tree in the backyard. I didn't think it would be that funny, but it was. Father's face was skeptical and repulsed. I wasn't able to hear what he muttered from behind the bushes, though. Popping out from behind kids' lockers in the hall has nothing on this scare level. I thought he would have a cow, but he just cleaned it up. I imagined that this would have given him a heart attack. Heart attacks are the perfect murder. I thought that the old asshole would fall over. Instead, he remained balanced, tight, and upright.

Balls. Mission 109:8 is a complete fucking failure. I'll work on that, in between fixing up the truck with John. We have so many places to go, go!

Senior year is going to be a party!!!

ooo

RIGHTEOUS RUNS

October 13th, 2020

THERE IS SO much darkness that I can't even tell if my eyes are open. It feels like I've become a benthic species, experiencing the harsh despair existing as a fish out of water. I wipe my clammy hands across my forehead; it forces drops of saline-like water to build and drip down into my eyes, delivering a sharp stinging sensation. Blinking hard, I try to rid of the burn, but it only forces impatient tears out. Perspiration drips down my temple, over my square jawline, forming droplets of sweat at the bottom of my long facial hair. Briny and wet, washing over me continuously. It won't stop. Trickling down my Adam's apple onto my exposed boxy chest and sliding over once-defined abs. I attempt to peel my eyes back open; the bite is still present. Defeated in the dusk, alone and in pain. There simply is no way of wiping it all away. I'm drenched in memories.

Sometimes, as I'm dying in my dreams, I see her face again and it's worth it. But in this dream, I was back in my child-like form, lying still on the ice, watching a dark figure lurk back at the shoreline. Not just any figure, but a baneful, black-hearted human, holding up a six-inch dagger as blood drips off the blade in slow motion, like molasses. They are the Pearl Point Murderer.

"I'm awake!" I repeated to myself aloud, sitting up fast.

A series of loud bangs resembling gun shots made me jump, breaking up the sweat fest. I sprung out of bed. I desperately sought change to the darkness. Crouching down to feel for my baseball bat under my king-sized bed, but still blinded by the unlit room. Now pissed that I placed my phone so far from my bed to sleep better. The five o'clock alarm hasn't gone off yet, which is a sign that it's earlier. Smacking my hand ferociously around the carpet, I finally feel the bat handle and rip it out from under the bed frame. I get up and run to my desk to face the door. The hall light flickers on, exposing a silhouette of two pairs of feet before the door. My heart lunges forward, while my body remains.

Two men burst in and the taller one flips my light switch on, which exposed their grins as wide as the ocean. I lower the bat immediately upon recognition of my roommates. Logan and Brent.

"HAPP-YO, what in the?" Logan bellowed.

I was speechless, gawking at them, staring back at me.

What a sight for them.

Drenched, pale skin in a pair of sopping wet gray boxer briefs. Clearly ready for the ballgame of the century. Both Logan and Brent turn to face each other. Logan extends his muscular arm out to lean on Brent, with one hand on his shoulder and the other on his own stomach. He erupted with laughter, cracking up so hard that I could see both his toned arms flexing and his muscular curves bending in his thin white tank top. Brent joined in on the hilarity.

"Oh, shit, Murph, we scared the piss out of you! Sorry man!" Logan howled.

He let out an even deeper genuine gut laugh. Logan had one of those laughs that could make even the most stubborn of people chuckle, just from the sound of it. Including myself, I let out a scoff that led to unintentional chuckling.

"What a scaredy-cat you are, *oh sheet*!" Brent hooted at me.

"Ah ha yeah, sorry guys, my bad. Brent, I told you to just call me Oisín. It's *OH-SHEEN*," I annunciated back to him.

Brent dropped his smile, closed his eyes, and opened them back up in an annoyed fashion. He threw the prematurely let-off party poppers on my embarrassingly wet bedding and left my room.

"Uh, okay, thanks Brent, sorry Brent!" I yelped out after him.

"Don't worry about him, he's butthurt because I requested him to keep the video games to a dull roar yesterday. I don't want to parent the guy, but *damn*," Logan complained. "Nightmare again?" he continued.

Logan pulled the corner of his full, peakless lips to one side.

"Yeah, it's nothing, though. Some birthday surprise, talk about a *real* dirty thirty."

"It's all good... Welcome to the club, man! Let's get some liquid gold in us and hit the tar!" Logan cheered. "And also, maybe throw your sheets in the wash, because you stank."

All I could do was smile and put my palms up to him, to which he got the hint, and left the room.

I could already hear the coffee grinder going. The bean connoisseur was creating his daily crafted coffee for us. He does this each morning. In efforts to avoid our use of the auto cup machine, it also serves as a solid wake up call. It hasn't been easy working from home, mostly because of the trust fund baby who got stuck renting here during school when COVID-19 hit. He would have been home by now, but

his family is using the quarantine excuse to keep paying for him to remain here...
He's taken over our living room, with his gaming and video-chatting with random
girls. I avoid him at all costs, which means I'm pretty stagnant in my room *every*
single day and night. It's been rough. Even worse, knowing that Logan coerced him
to surprise me, that had to have been a tremendous effort on his part.

I knocked on Brent's door to invite him to our run.

"Murphy, I don't even get up this early to pee. I will lay here in pain. Go,"
Brent replied.

I wanted to apologize for the weird morning scene. I know this guy wants to
get out of here enough as it is. Annoying him is also a guilty pleasure.

ooo

Feet fast on pavement, our only social interaction, that also keeps us mildly
in shape. Considering our lives have become a game of musical chairs, from our
bedroom desks to the kitchen table and back. Managing the boat dock from home
isn't difficult, it's just isolated. We switched to the *Dock Master* system, allowing a
seamless transition from being in the office to working at home. With my dad's help,
before he left me, I gained a solid rapport with his friends at the wharf. I started
working there at an early age in high school and earned a management position
soon after graduation.

Logan leaves the house just as much as I do, which is extraordinarily minute.
He lands more than a few photography sessions every month. They are high-quality gigs and high in demand enough to allow him to thrive. Somewhere amid these
dark times and doing less, we ended up losing our appetite for food. Replacing
that hunger for a coffee addiction to get through all the computer work that we
are doing.

Our winter Thailand trip isn't happening anymore. We don't have an impending necessity to get ripped, like we planned. We still keep up with the running that we started in March regardless, otherwise; I was never a runner before this, just enthused about abdominal work. I was looking forward to *finally* traveling. Now I sit in regret living out a tiresome sequence of staring at the computer to facing nightmares, over and over.

Memories have anchored me to Foggerton since I was a teen, hoping that my mom's body would wash ashore, or that she would come back in perfect health. Preferring the latter. But at least having a routine of going out with the guys to the Irish pub after work and playing football on the weekends kept the memories vague and less vivid.

"Yo, so are we going to talk about this?" Logan inquired in a deep voice.

I knew I was about to get a heaping dose of Logan's logic, so I picked up the pace. Running ahead of him in my black spartan pants and black cold gear tech hoodie.

"Ay, you can't run away from this. Drop the male bravado stuff," Logan insisted.

"Now?"

"Yes, *now*, nobody around. Just us, some romantic fall leaves, a little cardio. It's a two-for-one therapy date. With a limited-time offer."

I couldn't help snickering back at him. It left me out of breath. I slowed down, letting him catch up to me. It's fall alright, crisp air and chilly mornings leave us snorting and striving to breathe throughout the route. Our run transitioned to a full stop at the corner of Seafarer and Appleton road. I put my hands on my hips, trying to catch my breath and articulate this better.

"I'm not above admitting anything. I've just been, distracted," I disclosed.

I scanned the neighborhood in procrastination; it was quiet and not just because it's a Tuesday. The tall post lamp speckled light down between the wrestling tree branches above our heads, and down onto the dark amber and russet leaves that blanketed the road beneath our running shoes. There were rows of two-story Victorian-style homes with abundant space between each homeowner's yard. Middle-class cars in every driveway, while residents sleep in, only to wake for *Zoom* meetings and online learning. The fall foliage and the low-lying fog are both unnerving and tranquil at this time of the year.

"The dreams, that I have, ya know? They're occurring less, which is cool. But the intensity of them, they're becoming so, disturbing. It feels weird saying that out loud. I feel like a kid. We talked about this about a decade ago," I acknowledged.

"You think you should talk to someone professional about this, maybe?" Logan questioned.

"Uh, I think we're past that. But I should have, a long time ago, yes," I huffed.

Logan rubbed the exposed nape of his neck to tugging the short black hair on his chin. They trailed up to his clear, warm brown skin. He had one eyebrow raised.

I don't need a speech on my birthday.

"I know a thing or two 'bout you, we've lived together forever, man. Ya kind of wear your pain. Do you remember that summer that you and some of the other kids at school would swing from a massive oak tree into the riverbank? I always hung back and basically played with sticks in the mud. You told me that when I was ready, you'd teach me to swim, *only* when I was ready. You continued to say that my life would be happier if I were ready sooner than *later*. It goes the same, bud, when you're ready..." Logan said deeply.

A white sedan entered the intersection. We moved over to the sidewalk. The run is over, but I know this conversation isn't. The sun is rising, which means walkers will be out soon. We put our masks on to avoid a surprise attack of mask shaming over social media posts. This neighborhood is far ritzier than ours and the residents are obnoxiously conscious of those who live amongst them and don't. We head back in the direction we came from.

"Yeah, I remember that. *Good times*. You are right. I gotta dive into those fears and address them. I just don't know what I'm facing because it's still so mysterious," I spoke.

"I'm no professional but writing or talking out your thoughts, man. That might be a start. Healing, it has to be intentional. You might even have to get to know yourself again," Logan responded. And served me with a major side eye.

Logan's logic is always on point, that's what makes it hard to hear.

"This morning was crazy. Any relationship I've had up to this point has been temporary. How, how on earth is an invested girl supposed to react to that episode? I'd scare the shit out of her. I want a wife and a family. But I don't know. Not that we can get the ladies outside of the Bumble bubble *now*," I said, detouring around the subject.

"*Alright*, dude, that is deflection. I know this is more than just about the ladies. But on that note, speak for yourself. I'm meeting a Vanessa for a cocktail before your dinner party tonight," Logan said.

I shook my head as he outlined an exaggerated hourglass shape with his hands, secured in the thumbholes of his long sleeve black half-zip fleece. He put his hands back on his hips, red training shorts over black compression leggings.

"*Psh* okay, right? You mean virtually?" I retorted. I bobbled my head and rolled my eyes back at him while smirking.

"I *would* take her downtown, but the whole must order a meal to have a beer deal. That locks me in. Gotta feel it out beforehand, am I right?" he explained.

"You mean to say that you want to see how she looks beforehand. It is *so* clear now. I get why we are the last singletons in our class," I replied.

"Nah. Nah, that can't be right. Is it? Shit, whatever. And don't play, you know I'm the first to open the door. I always pay, I'm happy to wine and dine an interesting woman. But, if it's a game of catfishing, or I'm about to get ghosted, then I want to know who the hell I'm dealing with. Especially now that the entire world is online. Anyway, I gotta go submit my portfolio from the last photography sesh. Catch you later!" Logan yelled. He crossed our lawn and jogged up the steps to our home.

A text from Brent distracted me from his rant. But I knew what Logan meant. I opened the notification and read.

Brent: Card for you on the table. Someone knocked a million times just for that. Stupid stray cat won't leave stoop, make it.

Honestly, who hates cats this much?

ooo

THIRTEEN TICKS

October 13th, 2020

GLORIA, RETIRED DETECTIVE Charlie's wife, sure turned their home around since I last saw it. He deserved her, and she deserved him. I admired the new gallery art over their wood-burning fireplace mantel, exceptional photos of their wedding outfits at the courthouse, from the summer. All of them taken by Logan, of course. He was the only one invited under strict protocol. Their joyous union is the positive that we all wanted to see for a significant amount of time. The world has been upside down since March. But this marriage is a blessing for Charlie, it's a marker of his finally moving on and accepting the love he that merits.

Logan's dad, *our* dad, raised us three. I was thirteen when I nearly entered the Dawson family, that's still a huge duty to take on for a single parent. Especially since my dad gave up after my mom disappeared into thin air. Three successful bachelors with decent paying careers, passions, not perfect, but happy, *mostly*. Charlie did well, so well that I sometimes forget details about Aidan. My dad gave up on searching for his wife and left me for a job overseas. There isn't a lingering resentment, but he was my only family... Everyone else couldn't bear to see me, without being reminded of *her*.

"Hey Murph! Happy birthday, baby!" Gloria said excitedly.

"Gloria! Looking gorgeous as ever!" I said, elbow bumping with her.

Dressed to impress in a fitted purple pant suit and black pointed heels. Normally she rocks a jet-black afro blow out. Beauteous tonight with thick, long, and layered braids, she pulled in a half-up hairstyle.

She observed my baggy blue and light brown flannel, blue jeans, and battered old boat shoes. Definitely the most underdressed, at *my* birthday party.

Thankfully, she can't see my cheeks faltering from humiliation under this mask.

I recognized two family friends that declared space in the corner of the great family room. Rich mahogany furniture, regency era art, and a large French blue rug that spanned the dimensions of the room. The rug itself is a piece of art. It makes me shudder, walking over it in my shoes. I could hear music playing, rhythmic melody from saxophones with accenting upbeats, that had me involuntarily tapping my foot.

"Thank you so much for putting this together. It's amazing to get out of the house. Um, should I keep this on? I don't want to get anyone in trouble or sick," I queried.

Gloria replied, "No baby, no trouble. The party is at the back. We have heaters on, lights up, drinks out, social distancing. You can keep your mask on. I made your favorite, just for you. Charlie and the guys wanted to do a cookout with burgers and hots."

I tailed behind her as she danced to the kitchen, towards the far back left portion of the house. Gloria, a retired history professor, had a potent influence on their older home. She transformed it into a luxurious wormhole, into the past. From the intricate carved details on dark wood door panels and the fireplace mantel, to the faux animal print upholstery, rich gold accents, historic paintings, mirrored surfaces, and bold print sculptures. There was also an antique walnut running bookcase that led from the family room to the back sitting room. Extravagant but homey.

The odds of getting sick here seem slim, but I am still in contact with potentially contaminated paperwork or packages at the dock from time to time. I don't want to spread an exposure to my friends and family. To anyone.

Wow, no mask could mask the smell of perfectly cooked chicken French in a buttery lemon pan sauce. With the home-made dough essence of a sweet potato pie.

My heterochromia blue and brown eyes lit up. My stomach growled. She even has my favorite local beer in glass bottles on the counter. The dinner spread is overwhelming, in the best way.

"All of this for me? Gloria, I don't know what to say. What did I even do to deserve this!"

"*Murphy*! Thirty is a milestone and we're family, baby. It comes with the territory, but we're only glad that restrictions have lessened, and we could get together for a short while. Speaking of, did Logan come with you?"

"No, I ordered a ride. He said he had to pick something up on the way. Maybe a bouquet for me," I kidded.

"Delivery for the one and only, Mr. Murphy," said a familiar voice. Devon came around from behind me. He stood before me with a wide grin, exposing large, straight white teeth.

"Oh man, Dev! It's so good to see you!"

I accepted the wrapped gift that he extended towards me.

"Not a bouquet, ay. Might be a new Laker's cap, though. The proper gift is me. I'm actually here to stay for a while with pops and Gloria. Now come on in, brother, you ain't getting out of a big ass hug from me," Devon said.

He pulled me in to pat my backside with might, then pushed my loose shoulders away to look down at me. He peered down at my boat shoes and crinkled his nose, shaped like a funnel, where his nostrils pass over his bridge.

I should have known better. We haven't cast our eyes upon each other for months, and this is the gritty ensemble that they get from me.

"Hm, I got tested before coming up here. Were we supposed to wear one of those?" He asked, concerned. Nosing towards my face covering.

"Oh, no. Gloria said it's up to you, we're all supposed to be outside. I'm just, you know, cautious."

I pulled my mask off, smoothed my light brown comb over, and tugged at my medium-length beard to adjust the unruly hair. My long sleeve flannel is more of a curtain than a fitted shirt. I look like a frosted hobo up in here. I scratched the back of my head and stuffed my mask in my back pocket.

"Aight. You're looking... good. You good man?" Devon queried.

He's manicured from head to toe, looking the best I've ever seen him. He wore tailored flat front wool trousers that matched his black cashmere sweater. Adorning a short gold chain around his neck and a chunky gold watch on his left wrist. He had the same defined jawline as his younger brother and clear brown skin, with warm undertones.

"Uh yeah, good as, as one can be. But dude, *you* look amazing. New York City has been treating you good, I see!" I croaked.

I crossed my arms to pull on my flannel a bit. Hoping that he didn't acknowledge my mortification. Devon is used to this though, quarantine or not, he's older by three years and had it all figured out, even back in the day. An old soul who could cook a Michelin meal at eighteen. It was outstanding for Logan and me until Devon left for culinary school. Heavy shoes for Charlie to fill while being dragged away for copious amounts of cases building at work. We basically ended up scarfing down pop-tarts and grilled cheese throughout high school.

"Well, not *too* well, considering our restaurant still closed down. Doesn't seem like any business, five stars or not, is safe from the pandemic. I'm just grateful that I received a lump sum and a prestigious letter that could take me anywhere. I been doing this for fifteen years. Honestly, my dream has always been to open up a bougie style delicatessen and bakery. I love Michelin world, but it's the comfort food that is thriving now. I don't foresee it slowing down from here on out. Any who, happy freaking birthday, my man! We have much to catch up on and even more time to do so. Good lord, Miss Gloria, does it smell divine in here!" he said.

I grinned and let him pass me to reunite with Gloria. Clearly, our greeting entertained her. She was moving to the rhythm of a song called *Counter Clockwise* by *Sonny Stitt and Gene Ammons*, while grinning at my awkward nature. After that shit show, I grabbed two *Genesee Beers* from the maple top island, one for me and one for the nerves.

ooo

Gloria and Charlie's large fenced-in yard is spacious enough to have a small gathering. I stood on the deck to appreciate the ambiance. Charlie set up three bronze seven-foot-tall umbrella heaters on the natural stone patio and red rustic garden lanterns on the family-style tables. The light from the lanterns and heaters flickered off the mostly masked faces of my friends and Charlie's colleagues. Everyone gathered around the benches and sat down for dinner. Gloria handed each person a single-use paper plate and plastic utensils.

A campy, piquant scent fanned over from the grill that Officer Rocklin was manning. I washed my worries down with another gulp of deep-golden lager. I heard the screen door slide open behind me. Logan dashed out to my side, displaying his famous dimples. The dimples that got him out of mostly any trouble as a kid.

"Thanks for grabbing me a cold one. Here's your gift!" Logan said animatedly.

He exchanged the full beer in my hand with a bottle of *Midleton Irish Whiskey Very Rare Vintage Release*.

"*What*! Dude, thanks so much!" I shouted.

"You're welcome, man. I had to go pick it up from a delivery locker. I know it's not the same as going to the Irish pub anymore, but hey, it's damn good stuff. I heard that it's going to be released to be sold in the United States next year," Logan crooned.

"Oh sweet! That is going to be awesome, thank you for this!" I rejoiced.

I fist bumped him with knuckles wrapped around the half empty beer bottle.

"So, I got a new joke for you. An Irishman walks into a bar and asks for two beers," Logan began, interrupted by my hand.

I turned to face our group of friends and family, holding up the beer and bottle of whiskey.

"Hey everyone, I just wanted to say thanks for coming out and for being safe. It's so outstanding to see friends and family after so long. I'm incredibly grateful to Charlie and Gloria. You two are heaven-sent. And it's nice to meet everyone else here. I just wanted to say since twenty-twenty is clearly more drunk than *I've* ever been, consider me still in my twenties!" I shouted, grinning widely.

Charlie stood up in his black V-neck sweater with a white dress shirt underneath. He lifted his gray herringbone wool cap from his head with his left hand and raised his beer in his right. Charlie chanted, "Here, here! Happy birthday, ma boy!"

ooo

I tripped getting into my room; I lost my footing and slammed to the ground. It felt like someone bashed me in my skull from behind.

Maybe I should call Lexi.

Standing uneasy, before my bed, I tried hard to focus on the sponged dark gray paint that held Logan's candid photography. He framed each photograph in a modern brushed gunmetal. Logan shot the photos here in Foggerton, some in Rome, and elsewhere along with his travels that I wish I had joined. There's an emptiness within these frames. I don't have my own photos to fill them out with *my* life experiences, *my* family, at least biological, or any of *my* passions.

What am I even doing? I feel like some lonely, lost chump from an abandoned story. Where the writer intended for me to have a fulfilling life. How they started out typing about my triumph over past traumas, with intent to inspire others. Riddling me with depth, entertaining dialogue, and wholesome accomplishments. But we write our own book, and I wrote mine to succumb to deadly routine.

A trench in the bottom of my stomach widened. The void expanded. I squinted down at my large bare feet, standing on the eight-by-ten asphalt gray rug with an ebony border that protected the hardwood flooring from my granite king-sized bed frame. I grunted at the distressed black and white panel headboard and stumbled backwards, reaching back to grasp the top of my desk chair to steady myself.

Tick, tick, tick.

Still staring ahead at the two simple contemporary dark nightstands on both sides of my bed, the scattered water bottles on them puzzled me. The only décor that I kept from my childhood was a series of mini sailboats. They sat on floating shelves just above each shadowy nightstand.

Why are all the lights on?

I could see from the corner of my left eye that the hallway light illuminated into my room, but I couldn't face it. The hanging metal light fixture swung above my bed, back and forth, inducing me into a dizzy spell. It continued swaying from side to side, from my bookshelf wall with mind improving books, to the windows that stretched across the entire front wall. From the corner of my right eye, I could tell that my long black curtains were wide open, letting the light in from the front porch.

Tick, tick, tick.

A deep sense that someone was watching me made my skin tingle. My tattoo raised. I could feel the itchy sensation of it leveling with my scar. Burning. I had a deep urge to rub my wrist and crawl into bed, but I could barely move my weary eyes.

Tick, tick, tick.

It feels like someone took red hot chili peppers and rubbed them against the lining of my stomach. Losing muscle control, mouth dry and unable to ask for help. The lights, blindingly bright, blurred and distorted my vision.

Tick, tick, tick.

The small stand-up analog clock on my desk marked each second that passed. A persistent sound pleaded for me to make a move, insisting that I break free.

Tick.

And I'm collapsing.

ooo

ROUGE RECALL

October 14th, 2020

"WAKEY, WAKEY, EGGS and bakey."

I pulled the gray comforter away from my face, trying to block the light with my hands. Struggling to make out the figure above me, even my hearing is off.

"What time is it?" I grumbled. I attempted to lubricate my chapped lips, though my tongue was dry as a bone.

"Time for you to get up and eat, my man," Logan said.

"Oh shit, I'm going to be sick!" I blurted out.

I jumped out of bed and tripped over a clutter of jeans, hoodies, and one dozen bread slices thrown about the room. I made it to the shared bathroom closest to my room. The deep yellow abstract bath rug bunched up under my feet as I scurried across it. I had to grab onto the bathtub wall and the porcelain toilet seat for stability. An involuntary pressure forced me to throw up bits of chicken, water, and alcohol into the toilet. The ghastly smell forced me to vomit more, until I was dry heaving, hacking up green bile. My head fuzzy and thumping. My stomach muscles ached. Acid scorched my throat. I remained hugging the toilet as if it were a lifeline. I could hear a voice from back down the hall.

"OH LORD! If it isn't a party up in here!" Devon yelled.

"What the hell happened last night?" I questioned.

Logan was above me, holding me up by my armpits, trying to lean me back against the bathtub.

"Bro, you scared the shit out of me. You, okay?"

"I feel like death," I replied hoarsely.

"Aight, friend, let's get you back to bed. I'll put a can in there for you."

My dehydrated lips trembled.

ooo

"Hey man, here are some extra strength pills and some *Pedialyte*, it's *the* cure," Logan said.

I sat up in bed to retrieve the hangover remedy from his hands. I was still holding a mild headache. At least the room wasn't spinning any longer.

"Um? How much did I drink?"

"That's the thing, bro. You only had a few beers at pops' house. We had dinner, and we came home. I saw you had one more beer here, but you didn't even break into the *Midleton* whiskey. But after that *last* beer… It went downhill. It irritated you that none of your clothes fit. We tried to convince you not to call Lexi for a booty call. You did anyway. You even did her dirty by putting her on speakerphone out in the living room. Dude, she basically said that she was dating someone else now.

Following? So, that pissed you off more, somewhat understandably. You were all over the place," Logan explained energetically.

I gawked at him, unable to recall any of these single events.

"Yo, so it got worse. I think you were opening birthday cards in your room, on the floor, like a kid. Brent laughed at you, like the little asshole that he is. You came out blaming him for pranking you. Dude, you *punched* him. That kid straight up moved out. It took him an hour to gather the few things he owned, and he left. I put all these water bottles here and over there for you. I still don't know how you could be that drunk. I would think that someone roofied you. *If* it weren't for us celebrating amongst trusted friends and family. Devon got here early this morning to help. He's taking Brent's room now, which works out fine as a dime. Hope you don't mind?" Logan inquired.

I glanced down at my right hand, flexing my fingers to balling my fist, observing the light damage on my knuckles. They're bruised with a few rouge red cracks that ran between my pale skin like the lines that run through broken ice. I must have hit Brent's jaw. I winced, not at the evidence, but at Logan having to put up with this.

Logan's diamond stud dazzled under my hanging light. He put his hands up and raised his brows. Making a flat line with his full lips, his sharp jawline became even more defined. He rubbed the micro hair waves on the top of his head that faded down to the perfectly angled line on his temple.

"I never seen you this messed up. It ain't a biggie, just maybe get that hangover in check," Logan concluded.

It's like being told a story about yourself for the first time. Hard to trust this because I can't even picture or place myself in those moments. I could hold my own. I've always been able to out-drink the guys and still not end up this bad. Friends and co-workers praised me as the *infinite* Irishman at the local pub. What a shitty move on my part. Especially after all they did for my birthday, while the rest of our friends had order-in pizza, alone, while streaming *Netflix* for their hefty three-oh. Not an awful way to celebrate, but not the special effort that Charlie and Gloria congregated.

"*Sorry*," I said. It *was* all I could muster up.

"It's okay, for real. Get cleaned up and head to the kitchen, after. You might not feel like it right now, but Dev's concoctions are a true revival." Logan elated.

ooo

Logan and I invested in this fixer-upper eleven years ago. It was the year that they declared my mom legally dead, the year that I received life insurance bene-fits, and the same year that my dad had left town. We went half in on re-modeling costs for one room per year. And now it looks like an entirely renovated modern mid-century home with a contemporary minimalism style, except for the basement.

I saw Logan sitting on one of the five metal chairs at the round marble-top kitchen table, with a single walnut veneer pedestal base. He shook up a protein shake in his blender bottle and placed it back down next to his open laptop. Logan has had better business in twenty-twenty as a freelance portrait and landscape photog-rapher than ever. With everyone stuck inside, the local and county-wide businesses reached out to him for COVID inspired photography. And they're paying well for professional shots, to draw people to their social media and websites alike.

I get that. It's like we long to see that we are not alone in being alone, that we share this inevitable seclusion together.

I can't fathom being retold of anything else from last night, but I'm still so confused. Instead, I slid the island barstool out over the smooth hardwood floor and sat down. Devon was fixing up some eggs on the other side. He had a variety of ingredients spread out on the pietra gray polished marble countertops across from me. He must have gone shopping, because it's the first time that I've seen someone use this kitchen, aside from the espresso machine.

"Earth to Murph?" Devon quizzed.

He leaned over the counter and waved the silicone spatula in front of my face.

"Oh, sorry. Just thinking about last night," I griped.

"Don't be so hard on yourself. We all have those nights. Here is my mushroom omelet with gruyere on top, some greens on the side, and a Bloody Mary with a candied bacon slice," Devon proclaimed. He slid over the full plate of food and the ornamented drink to me.

It looks like something that you'd admire on the Food Network.

"Damn Devon, you delivered," I muttered between impatient bites.

I stirred the tomato-based cocktail with the celery stalk and pulled it out to lick it.

"Bro, I have no clue where Stew, the stoop cat is. I put a new can of food out this morning but, he's been missing since early yesterday," Logan said from behind me.

"I'm sure he'll turn up. He always does. I love that little guy. Devon, this is, this is crazy good," I complimented, between rushed bites.

"Just wait, it's brown butter squash ravioli with sage sauce tomorrow. Going to come through with all the top fall dishes this season. Gotta keep my chef knife sharp, ya mean? Maybe fill your cheeks out again too. It ain't Halloween yet, Murph," Devon joked.

"Cool Dev, he lost weight. We get it. But our casa is your casa, have at it in there. There should be plenty of room for all of your equipment. We didn't remodel this place just for resale value, *and* we definitely will be your taste testers," Logan said thickly.

My head felt fuzzy again. Logan closed his laptop to join Devon in the kitchen, giving an official tour of the space that he could make use of. He went from the dark flat panel cabinets to the black modern cabinetry above the range and cook top. He pointed to the floating shelves above the single basin kitchen sink that held a variety of coffee mugs from his travels. Devon proposed he could get us a discounted professional gas range here in no time. He went on about how much he admired the contemporary touches of the black hanging light fixtures above the island and the Moroccan tile backsplash along the main cooking wall. He jested about bone-white tiles matching the *Casper* in the house.

Damn. I get it. I don't even recognize myself.

Usually sporting a farmer's tan by now, from being out on the dock during the week and spending all weekend on the field subbing for football games with the teams, Buffalo Ballas and Totes Goatez. None of that happened this year, for any of us. I screwed my balance up with the changes, and last night was a bloody wake-up call.

Blacking out and assaulting someone just about does it.

ooo

I searched my room for what evidently sent me into a fury. Brent was mostly harmless, just a nerdy and annoying twenty-something. But he never instigated violence before. I sifted through all the birthday cards, but there wasn't a vulgar note from Brent. Only pleasant words from friends and the Dawson family. My dad sends a card every year, but he must have forgotten this time. Found some cash that I forgot to collect, but nothing appeared to be out of the ordinary. I picked up all the clothes off my floor. I must have been trying to look good for Lexi. I can't believe I messed that up, too.

I noticed a white envelope peaking out from under my rug. I dropped the pile of monochrome clothing on my bed and bent down to pick up the card. Something deep red stuck to the back closure. *Wax?* There was a broken rouge wax seal. I opened it to reveal the contents; inside was a small white square card with typed words that read,

Twelve pearls of mine.

Mommy floats in time.

Seek hell, south of home.

Where the key lies in the stone.

I felt each assailing word strike me, twice.

ooo

"Murph, where are you going? I'm making white hots in truffle mac and cheese for dinner," Devon called out to me. I was half-way out the door.

It was frigid, clouded, and dreary out. I ran back into the house to throw on a gray cardigan over my baggy white tee-shirt. Logan met me at the door that I threw open and forgot to close behind me. He picked up the outdoor felt pumpkin wreath that fell off the hook. He scowled as he eyeballed me, sprinting back past him. Logan barked, "Dude, what's wrong, where on earth are you going?"

"I have to see Charlie. I gotta go. I'll be back for dinner, though!" I replied.

I rushed down the steps.

"Well, hold on! You need to wear your mask, just in case. I talked to dad this morning. I kind of let him in on what happened. But he couldn't talk long, he said he wasn't feeling too well!"

I halted just before the midnight black eight-cylinder pony, parked in the drive-way. A fall wind propelled a freshly raked pile of leaves from the corner of our lawn.

Ovate-shaped leaves swirled from the pile into a gust above the blacktop, releasing an earthy-sweet scent from the bottom rot. A large black raven landed beside a tall, blazing red and gold maple tree that faced the house. The bird produced a chilling, gurgling croak.

Kraa-kraa!

"Oof, okay. I really have to go, but do you think it's, you know?" I hesitated.

Logan shrugged and replied, "We aren't sure yet. I pray not. Just be careful, *regardless.*"

I cringed and nodded back in concern. If Charlie is sick, to any degree, I have to get to him now more than ever. I need answers.

ooo

MAD WORLD

October 14ᵗʰ, 2020

GLORIA GREETED ME wearing an orange and purple mask this time, her eyes blood-shot and puffy with dark circles just below them.

All I could think about on the drive over here was the Pearl Point Murderer.

"Welcome baby, the boys gave me a heads up you were on your way here in some kind of rush, but pop isn't feeling too well. He's been up all-night coughing," she said.

"I don't mean to just show up like this, it's important though. Please."

"Murphy? Is that you?" Charlie called from the second story.

Gloria waved her arm out for me to proceed up the stairs.

"Just, keep a distance, baby," Gloria called up.

I ran up the stairs in a frenzy. I pulled the card that was secured in my sweatpants out and held onto it. My heart raced as fast as my car did to get here. I didn't even have time to prepare a logical explanation for this.

"Hey Murph, I'm not as bad as Logan may have said. Just have a little cough. Might just be a cold. What seems to be the problem, though?" Charlie asked.

No words would escape my naturally pink mouth. Even if they could, I would end up saying them out of order. I surveyed the dim room. I turned on the little lamp next to his bedside and handed him the most distressing birthday card that I have ever received.

"What is this? I can tell you ain't right, even with that mask on. You can take it off, just hangout over there, on that lounger."

Charlie shook his head at my awkward disposition. Holding a handkerchief up to his mouth to cover his dry coughing fit. He turned the blank envelope over to open it. His jaw dropped immediately upon viewing the seal. His thick salt and pepper eyebrows burrowed deeply into the middle of his wrinkled forehead. His face flushed from an umber complexion to a splotchy sepia clay, beneath the stubble on his cheeks and chin. His eyes grew so wide that I could see the blood veins practically multiplying around the pale hues.

"Oisín, who did you say you got this from?" Charlie asked firmly.

"I, I, didn't say. You think it could be the Pearl Point Murderer?" I insisted.

"Lord, son, he is dead, and you know that. I can even recite his last words and last meal."

Charlie opened it, holding the small, square-sized card with the threatening words. His body jolted up from his slumped posture in bed. His jaw closed, tight-lipped and still frowning. He shook his finger rapidly at the card with his other hand as if he could banish it, though it remained.

"Uh, so, my roommate, or our ex-roommate, Brent, he said that someone brought it yesterday morning. He said that whoever it was, came over during our run, knocking on the door a lot. Apparently, I opened the card last night and *may* have punched Brent, thinking it was from him. Charlie, this has to be about my mom, right?"

I know I sound whiny, but the look on his face is far more chilling than the troubling artifact of literature that I received.

"I've seen this wax seal before. But look, Murph, your birthday is on the thirteenth and its almost Halloween... people are stir-crazy and itching to mess with others. Misery loves company," Charlie speculated.

He let out a few more dry coughs into his white handkerchief, continuing to scowl down at the card.

Gloria brought up a wood serving platter with hot tea and a glass of water for each of us. She glanced at Charlie, folding her lips over one another with concern. But Gloria didn't interrupt his thought process. She knew *that* look. It was the working mind of a retired detective, examining something. The lines on his forehead formed highways of concentration. Gloria is Charlie's rock and although they only got married this year after his retirement, she has always been in his life. She knows him best. Understands his mannerisms most. So, I followed her guidance to remain quiet.

"Before we get ahead of ourselves, it is a seal that the Pearl Point Murderer used, but it is widely known. It is a mechanical clock design. Initially, it was mocking at the fact that there would be another victim, in a matter of time. The position on the clock would show which number the victim was. The first time I saw it was back in the early nineties. Our department received a few empty envelopes with the wax seal, and we had nothing to make of it at the time. And then our friend, Sergeant Michaels, he mentioned a letter with the seal a few years later. He grew up here, we went through the academy together, and he eventually moved his family down to Sapphire Glass Beach, Florida, near Naples. You probably don't remember, but he's been to a few of our cookouts when you were kids. Hold up, didn't Logan install the new doorbell cameras that I got for you guys?"

"I uninstalled the old one and was going to get to it, *soon*," I answered.

Gloria rose from the other side of the room; her black pantyhose silent on the clouded gray carpeting as she inched towards the enormous bed that she shared with Charlie. The impressive bedroom size nearly occupied the whole second story.

"Hunny, maybe you should give your throat a rest. I'm sure Murphy would be more than okay with waiting a little while," Gloria interjected. She nodded at me.

"I know. He is polite. But this is exactly why I want to explain this history, now. To comfort the kid a bit," Charlie remarked.

Gloria's skepticism softened. The wrinkles around her eyes relaxed as Charlie concluded his sentence. She turned away from us to stoke the logs in the wood-burning fireplace. The builders aligned it perfectly with the fireplace on the first floor. The raised and extended mantel shelf also served as a stand for their flat-screen television. Gloria turned the channel to a music station with piano covers. *Mad World* by *Brooklyn Duo* played delicately in the background.

Returning to the comfort of her tufted leather love seat, Gloria slumped down and threw an indigo posh blanket over her legs. This led me to believe that she knew this was going to be a long talk.

Charlie continued, "I appreciate you, baby. Just have to help our own when something arises," Charlie asserted.

Gloria smiled at the both of us, amiably.

"Now, where were we? This was my experience with a Pearl Point victim. Hm, November 29th, 1994. Inopportunely, I remember that day like it was yesterday.

It seared the images into my mind," he said deeply, staring into the fire across from his bed. "For one, a fellow inmate of Jeffrey Dahmer had killed him the day before. Deputy Robert Brown and I were chatting about it. It was a little after noon when the sound of the alert tone went off in our patrol car. That stopped the conversation and had us on high alert. We got the radio dispatch for a person bleeding in Cottage Wood Park, you know, by the birdwatch area. We knew something perilous had happened. We got there in maybe under five minutes. We pulled into the park entrance to the woods. There were a few cars and a truck in the parking lot. We saw two young men by the park sign, standing with backpacks on and those chunky flip phones in their hands. We could tell right away by the look on their faces, that it was bad. I'll never forget how truly terrified they were. They explained that there was a girl, covered in blood by the brook. We wanted to secure the area; in case the assailant was nearby. A small department meant that my partner and another officer had to remain with the young men. We hadn't eliminated them as suspects. I walked along the narrow path with my gun drawn; it was damp and cold. I remember looking to areas that someone could hide, a thick tree log or bushes, you know. With each branch that I stepped over, or small animal scurrying, my adrenaline was chugging right along. Because even during the day, it's dark with the density of the trees overhead and shrubs along the trail. It was her light blue sweater with white daisies that first caught my eye, at the end of the path, in a clearing by the water that breaks into a T. She was lying on her stomach, the left side of her face was down, with her legs straight out. I was the first to the scene and called over my radio to the other officers. It was just Dawn, me, and the burbling brook, for the longest minute of my life. The perp draped a section of her long black hair over the water's edge, it flowed in the brook waters. There was blood spray on the rocks and over the moss before the waterline. Her left arm was slightly parallel to her body. Someone positioned her hand with her middle, ring, pinky, and thumb fingers folded in. Her index finger pointed to the letter V, followed by two lines, in the dirt. Her throat had a deep and singular incision that trailed off at the end. There was a small pearl at the scene, in a puddle of blood by her mouth and neck. Our department developed the name, Pearl Point Murderer, even before the discovery of more victims. Was a lot of blood, lots and lots of blood..." Charlie narrated.

A powerful rumbling from the angry autumn sky shook the house. I leaped from my seat. Next, a loud rush of rain violently rattled against the bedroom windows. The fireplace hissed with movement from an upper log being split in two.

"Dawn had a cassette player and candy near her body. She was probably just enjoying some alone time and never saw it coming. She was a student where Gloria taught history. After that horrific day, I did a drop in for her class to explain personal safety tips. If you're alone, be aware of your surroundings. Don't zone out with your hearing obscured. Although, it didn't seem random at all, the killer carefully executed and staged that scene. In my entire career I, well, my heart sank for that girl. And that was Dawn Price, also known as number seven, according to William," Charlie said.

He traced his finger over the red, waxy seal, unphased by the storming disruption.

"Hunny, please drink some of your tea. I see it's helping your cough. Murphy, you can stay for dinner. I have baked ziti in the oven," Gloria insisted.

How could they go from a bloody body to pasta? I had to remind myself that she was a history professor. Blood is history. But I'm more disturbed now than I was when I first got here. More confused, and most definitely not hungry.

"Yes, thank you. I'll have dinner with you guys. I just need to text Devon. He was talking about grilling some white hots on his indoor grill," I said.

"*Mm* boy, can he cook. We should have a cook-off between the twos of you," Charlie said to Gloria.

"*Mhm,* baby, let's focus on you getting better first. Let me know immediately if you feel any different," Gloria said, on her way out of the room.

"As you know, I kept much of my work at work. And I apologize for not talking to you about this sooner. During your mother's investigation, we believed you saw the news report about William Campbell's execution, carried out by lethal injection. He was active between 1989 and 1996, with nine known victims, and not another murder with those specific killing cards, since. The report on all of this, aired the day before your mother's disappearance," Charlie recited.

"Well, that might be. But those killing or calling cards you mention, that is exactly what I saw on the ice. I saw that as clear as a quartz."

Charlie dipped his head down low, making a flat line with his lips.

"Murph, you suffered significant trauma from falling through the ice, the blood loss, and being shocked by Claire's disappearance. We believed that because of those factors, you repeated the killers' killing cards from the news report. We figured you were trying to make sense of things and cope by placing blame on the last dismal thing you saw. There simply was no evidence of Claire's blood, no evidence that she walked or skated out on the ice, or that there was even a disturbance on the ice prior to your fall. We were lucky that your mailman was so fond of you and checked around back when you didn't come to the door for a package."

"Trust me, it has been hard for me to forget it ever since. I relive it, sometimes. I know what I saw, and I know I didn't see the news report about William. My mom would never even let me watch anything to that magnitude. Remember, when she had a field day because you took Logan and me to that movie, *Signs,*" I urged.

"Ah, yes, I remember that. She interrogated me about how violent it was on a scale of one to ten. You kids ended up making those tin foil hats for weeks. Ah, but your mother was as sweet as the pastries she made. She was just looking out for you..." Charlie said, trailing off.

The warm crackling sound of fire comforted the silence between us.

"She *was* an amazing mom. I remember the blood and the Roman numeral though, and that's what haunts me. I wasn't aware of the stuff in the news, for real. Even when my dad went off the deep end, he kept me moderately sheltered after that," I responded.

"Your father had a troubling time adjusting to those unsettling changes. The entire town did. Not everyone is strong enough to defeat the power of booze and a broken heart. I was more than happy to take on that role for you when he couldn't. You're not *like* a son to me; I consider you a son. You're a grown man, I know. But as long as I'm alive, I'll do my best to protect you from whatever evils may rise. But this, this just isn't one of them," Charlie assured me.

I swallowed hard as I fought the sentiment that was building up in my throat. Charlie delivered the words that I wanted to hear for a long time. He has been a noble father to me. My being solemn over something that happened so long ago might not be fair to him. But someone or something has summoned me.

As long as I'm alive, replayed in my mind while he spilled a few wheezy coughs into his handkerchief.

ooo

"Gloria, two phenomenal meals in a row. Wish I could cook like this. I really appreciate the invite after I stormed in here," I praised her.

"Murph, you are too kind. It's the fresh homemade tomato sauce that makes a world of difference," Gloria explained.

"No offense. We were a little worried when we saw you yesterday for the first time in a while. You boys could learn a thing or two from Devon. It ain't a bad thing that the college kid is out of there. All my boys under one roof again, it's nice," Charlie said.

"It could have happened a little more subtle though. I feel pretty terrible about the way things *apparently* went down. But the kid was a growing nuisance to Logan. I guess, all happens for a reason. I am still curious, though. Charlie, do you have any explanation for the reason behind this card?"

"I truly don't know, Murph. Some kids or someone was inclined to mock such horrific circumstances. I can explain to you what I know about the past, and we can figure it out from there. In the meantime, you eat, enjoy the meal," Charlie said.

All I've done for the past twenty-four hours is eat loads of food, fight, get sick and eat some more. I haven't had an appetite since this pandemic, but with the recent events, it is comforting. There has just been *too* much time to overthink the past now. After my mom went missing, after my dad had left, and after Stella and her family moved away. It just feels like I'm stuck. The Dawson family had brought me out of my funk before. It isn't fair to let them be responsible for a second round.

But I have to know.

"As I was saying, son, our murder case, Dawn Price, in 1994, it was eerily similar to the murder of Brooke Walton in 1996, at Sapphire Glass Beach, Florida, which Michaels oversaw. The perpetrator posed this young woman near a body of water, pointing to a bloody Roman numeral. It was drawn on a flat muddy surface near a palm tree. She had a single white pearl placed under her tongue and is the last known victim," Charlie described.

I recoiled and shrunk into my seat. Staring down at my dinner plate, pushing the flesh-colored pasta around in the bright red tomato sauce. I felt motion sickness from shaking my head in efforts to avoid the sight of bloodied pasta. I put my silver fork down on the shiny, dark walnut dining table. I tried to contain my discomfort and smiled back at the both of them. They're definitely unphased and have a much stronger gut for the realities of life, which I could learn from.

"There was a letter sent to Sapphire News about a missing young woman, Brooke Walton. They sealed the envelope with this mechanical clock design in red wax. It was a whole hot mess, to put the community at unease with an announcement of a menacing criminal on the loose. The letter also mentioned a trusted officer being involved with the girl. I remember how chaotic it was. Michaels was venting to me almost daily. A week later, William Campbell phoned the Sapphire Glass Beach PD. He had crucial information about Brooke Walton's disappearance and critical knowledge that wasn't released to the public. William advised the police department to look for Brooke's body at Graveshaw Sands, along the shore. An area that is relatively remote. The department brought William in, and he confessed to murdering nine women, including Dawn Price, here in Foggerton. A third victim, Karen Collins. They found her skeletal remains near a short line up of palm trees near the Roman numeral that Brooke was pointing to at Graveshaw Sands. William disclosed Brooke's location, but never spoke of the other six women that he claimed," Charlie reported.

"It was a winner for the press, here in Upstate New York and Florida. Definitely the most unnerving thing to happen around here, well, since Shawcross. At least the poor parents of Dawn received closure," Gloria commented.

"Ah yes, you think Bundy had followers. There were girls as young as thirteen, the loads of 'em lining up round the court down there, wearing necklaces, bracelets, earrings, all pearl everything. It didn't deter people from buying pearls. In fact, jewelry business flourished. The fans of William Campbell were obsessed. They really fell for the narcissistic young man that confessed to making a shucked oyster out of young women and gifting them with a pearl. It was barbaric and repulsive. A complete disrespect to these families who lost a daughter, sister, friend, and girlfriend. And the only physical evidence for all three murders, was a single pearl left at the scene, no prints or DNA. The pearl left with Karen was mostly deteriorated by the elements. The confession was direct evidence and that led him to be convicted for the murder of Brooke, Karen, and Dawn. But he was ultimately sentenced to death in Florida for Brooke and Karen. We went off the theory that when a serial murderer has gone undiscovered for some time and is about to be exposed or they might be dying, they will go out with a bang," Charlie stated.

Charlie continued explaining different serial killers and their tactics. I went into autopilot mode, staring at the bright orange pumpkin centerpiece until he finished.

"Okay, this is uh, it's a lot to take in. You don't exactly sound like you believe William sent the letter, though. Maybe he wanted attention and falsely took credit? Do you think that the actual killer is walking Scot free? And could have sent this to me?" I questioned.

"No, Murph, no. I wanted to explain the backstory of why I *know* this has nothing to do with your mother. They executed William Campbell. He's gone. To tell you the truth, my brain is a little strewn at the moment," Charlie said.

His eyes were pink and worn out.

"I mean, she was a mom and not some teenage girl hanging out by the beach. I feel like this is telling us something," I insisted.

Gloria and Charlie said nothing. I shook my head, avoiding their eye contact. I observed the Halloween décor in the dining room. In the corner diagonal to me, a skeleton with a face mask was sitting on the extra dining-room chair. The hollowed-out eyes gawking back at me sent me into further aggravation. My stomach performed acrobat back flips. I could feel my cheeks burning up, imagining that they resembled clown makeup. Fire engine red over pasty white paint. I shielded my face with my hands.

"Maybe we should take a break? Baby, you can get ahead of yourself sometimes. We don't want to overwhelm," Gloria said to Charlie.

"You are right, Mrs. Dawson, as always, beautiful. Look, Murph, I just wanted to deflate this ideal and provide some ease," Charlie said.

I uncovered my face and blew out a tremendous breath between my thin lips.

"Sorry, I thought for a moment, that someone was hinting at her whereabouts. Even if the card sounded kind of, evil. I can't evade the long-standing question. Why would anyone want to harm her? She was *so* incredibly... ordinary. We were just like any other family, enjoying the holidays," I said, heavy and wobbly.

"It is understandable, son. Everyone is hyper-sensitive at a time like this. Stress and anxieties are high as it is. We at least know you didn't write it, but I won't disregard your concern. I have to call Michaels soon, about our retirement sailing trip with him and his wife. Oh baby, do we need this vacation in the sunshine. I'll see what Michaels has to say about your card. But, after a breath of consideration, I don't think it radiates real danger. Probably some bored kids, pulling Halloween pranks. Until then, we should enjoy each other's company and get ready for the holidays," Charlie said light-heartedly.

What is wrong with me? We're in a pandemic, it's storming outside, and he doesn't feel well. I want to evaporate.

The love birds were distracted from my sheer mortification. Gloria held Charlie's hand as they beheld each other's gaze, soft and devoted. He yanked away from his wife to cough severely into his cloth napkin and began wheezing for air.

ooo

UNDYING HALLOWEEN

October 31ˢᵗ, 2020

WOODSBERRY, A SMALL town in wine country, California. Near the Naso coast, where sea meets vine. Where winding roads snake and twist east to Bonnes Bay, south to San Francisco, west to the countryside, and north to the redwood and sequoia forests. A little sleepy, fairly artsy, and home to locally produced wines. As well as a variety of local, fresh soft cheese and scrumptious aged hard cheeses. All of which draw tourism to, from all over the world, during harvest. Just the way Ella liked it, the perfect setting for her professional artwork to prosper and still enjoy the perks of nature's bounties. An introvert at heart, but she regularly sought entertaining outings and new experiences to network herself. That is before the pandemic.

Ella moved to Woodsberry when she was a budding pre-teen, blooming into a wild and intriguing flower of her own variety. The exciting 'new girl' status certainly got her attention early. Without organic roots in the community, she used that attention to her advantage, establishing her place in the town. Coming from an entrepreneurial family, she learned from her mom and worked fast. Ella figured out whose parents owned the wineries, restaurants, lodging, and galleries in the county. Their daughters became her friends, but those girls were also a small part of her unhappiness too. She knew, even as a child, that they would never measure up to the natural relationships that she developed back in New York. And they never did. Lia, Ella's little sister, rejected this gamely notion and paved her own alternative way.

Ella clicked the play button on the new voicemail notification.

"Hey girl, I'm going to visit dad on the rez. He needs more supplies. Can you come with? I know your gallery is still closed and I have some time off. Let me know, love you," Lia voiced.

Ella tipped her head back in irritation and returned to face her new text message notification and read.

V: Hey ghoul fran! Happy All Hallows' Eve! Be there soon with the bewitched popcorn and pumpkin krispies. Can't wait to get our spooky movie night on!

Ella recognized she was still sucking on her bottom full lip. Her mother's voice invaded her thoughts. *If you keep doing that, they'll get flat, and no one likes that.* She shook the memory of her mom out of her head and pouted her natural lips out for a moment, still in belief of the fable. Procrastinating a response to her sister or V, Ella continued playing her music, *rue* by *girl in red*, over the Bluetooth speaker and flipped her phone shut. She swayed to the alternative pop song, reveling in relatability.

Ella hopped off the barstool, wearing an oversized faded sepia, long-sleeve tunic with exposed seams, and white lace boyshort underwear. Barefoot, she walked to the pantry to gather a scoop of dry dog food and said, "Pinot, dinnertime!"

A year-old, miniature blue French bulldog with a white patch on his chest, came trotting out from her bedroom, down the short and carpeted hall to the steel food dish sitting on the kitchen vinyl. She learned of a neighbor's distress with his bluish-gray coat. The neighbor wanted a purebred French bulldog, and Ella couldn't distinguish where the disappointment was coming from. Ella fell in love with the puppy and adopted him just after her relationship with her fiancé ended.

An *honest slip* is what Ella's ex called it. In reality, it was a pretty little realtor that slipped into his appliance shop. All it took was a single business card. He slipped in and out of the realtor's bed more than a few times. Pinot didn't replace the affection that Ella once thought she was receiving from her ex-fiancé of three years. However, the short-legged dog provided a reason for her to care deeply for another creature, when she thought it might not be possible again, after the scorching burn of infidelity.

The corner of main and twelfth housed Woodsberry's most popular Mexican restaurant, Ángel Tacos. Next to that was a historic building that was converted into apartments. The one and two-bedroom units were situated directly over the retail space Ella rented for her art studio. It was a lucky draw to land the discreet home and to keep it through the trials of the local economy for over five years. It allowed her to be as close as possible to all the local hot spots, to never be late for a gallery night, and to never have to drive home drunk from an after-show round of drinks. This also meant no trick or treaters, this year, or any year prior. It didn't stop her from decorating during her favorite time of the year. Autumn hues ran throughout the small interior of every room.

She is a pro at do-it-yourself projects. Most of the décor in her home reflected that. If there was something in-store that she couldn't find that she had envisioned in her mind, she would gather materials to make it happen. A contrast of muted earth tones, with a California bohemian vibe, offered a relaxed and aesthetically pleasing environment to Ella. An unmarked champagne colored mini gun surfboard leaned against the wall next to the gas-burning fireplace, which centered the living room. An arched, white wood mirror sat level on the center of the mantel, flush with corresponding hues. The array of short and tall glazed clay vases on both sides of the mirror held wheat, sepia branches, bleached pampas grass and golden leaf bushels. A series of carroty orange fabric pumpkins took their positions on Ella's coffee table and kitchen countertops.

Ella closed her off-white, extra long, vintage drapes and grabbed her remote to turn on the original *Halloween* movie. It played on the *Samsung Frame* flatscreen in the right corner of the room. She felt like the horrors of being chased with a kitchen knife were much less horrifying than being cooped up in an apartment for half a year. Ella also knew that she wouldn't be able to hold this space much longer. This gave her actual chills. Still, she couldn't focus on the stalker in the navy-blue garage suit. She snuggled up to a chunky, mauve rose wool throw and dialed her sister.

"Happy Halloween biatch!" Lia answered.

"Hey, sorry I didn't get back to you right away," Ella responded.

"It's cool. I was just watching *Halloween*, just a chill night in with butt loads of candy. So, about dad…"

"Ooh, same. I'm watching it too and V is coming by soon. I baked some amazing pumpkin pecan bread if you want some tomorrow morning,"

"Queen of avoidance. I *want* to talk to you about dad. Can you please convince him to move in with mom, at least through the pandemic. It is so bad on the rez right now. I wish these two would just get back together. They ask about each other, more than they even ask about us."

"What do you mean?" Ella asked softly.

"Girl please, mom raves about dad. Aditsan this, Aditsan that. I suggested to mom that it would be smarter business-wise and easier on her heart if dad moved here. Then he could just send the bead kits back to Uncle Alo. To which she replied, *I don't know if I could live with any man.*"

"Lia, you know she is super stubborn. I know they are crazy about each other. It would be healthier for him to just come back to California, even just for a little while. They make it harder on us by being apart."

"Um, *us*? I'm the freaking one who uses all my savings to fly back and forth to Arizona. I have to drive along all the long dirt roads just to get to him. You never have to see how drunk he gets. Also, he doesn't always have running water and has to go half an hour away to get it, but he can't when he's drunk. *Do you even care?*" Lia fumed.

"Of course, I care! Wow, Lia. First, how is he getting the booze? I thought you can't buy it there or have it transported. Second, have you been drinking yourself? I don't like when you get like this. I understand things are hard there. I'd like to do more than complain, though. *You* can't help anyone when you're this rude and wound up!" Ella said, her voice strained and raspy.

"Right, wow, okay. Stop being so judgmental and blameless. I'm sitting in a cozy ass skeleton onesie and have had about a thousand bubbly waters. Trying to get white girl rested, yo. You're the one who sounds *overly* fine all the time. You know, that's a problem too. Whatever, this is about dad. I'm not trying to fight but it would be just *super* if you stopped pretending everything and everyone is just, fine."

Silence crowded both ends of the phone call. The sisters lived just a few miles apart, which allowed them to listen to the same whistling wind outside of their homes. A synchronized, high-pitched scream made Lia and Ella jump at the same time. The sisters giggled at the horror echoing over their phone connection.

"Can we just bury the hatchet? I'm going to skip going out there this time, but I'm not trying to get out of helping him, it's just not my favorite place in the world. I haven't had the same experiences that you have there," Ella admitted.

"How? You've avoided going there, for forever. It's just annoying how I'm the one running around for mom and dad, yet they praise you. You've always had it easy. They act like I'm the help and you're the better of us. Their words, *so put together*," Lia replied sarcastically.

"I'm not better-look, dad already understands this. When we visited the rez more, you were too young to notice, but the girls called me Paleface. It's like I was *too* white. Move on to our private school and I had to shorten my name to blend in. I've never truly felt like I've fit in, except in Foggerton. At least here, I mimicked mom's network skills and was simply... friendly. I don't know, something that *you* yourself could try. It wasn't *easy* for me to get where I am, to make the connections and maintain them. Right now, I'm not really feeling myself or this conversation. And I don't need you harping on me for not being the exact version of Ella that *you* want."

"Okay, take a chill pill. There are other things you could help with, like at least the bead kits for the Diné girls. They aren't the bitches that teased you... *Ugh*, okay, now I'm the one who sounds like an asshole. I just never get to sleep anymore because of these college brats. And Tammy has been driving me nuts at work. She's diabolical as hell. Sucks you're not feeling right. Is it being mostly alone or?" Lia speculated.

Thick droplets of rain pelted against Ella's tall arch-shaped windows, her favorite sound and favorite part of the building architecture. It calmed and centered her.

"No, I'm sorry, this *is* about dad. And you're right, it's the least I can do for the girls, so they can at least be happy. I'm good, I'm happy," Ella choked up.

"Stop saying you're sorry all the time. I *knew* something was wrong. You're not happy, you just fake it well. Whatever it is, I'll do less chatty and more listening. What happened?" Lia squeaked eagerly.

"Sto bene, Lia! I'm going to make it work. I have nothing going on in November. It will be a ghost town over here. Let's get together and I can do a mass production of the kits. I'll talk to you later, ti amo," Ella replied, sniffling.

"Ciao amore. And for the record, you should know that you could always stand under my umbrella, Ella, ay," Lia sang.

Ella patted Pinot's miniature head. He stirred upon the contact. The flat-faced dog rose from his nestled spot on the couch and climbed down the cherry-wood pet steps.

During the quarantine, Ella started off wading in ambiguity to later drowning in anxiousness. She contemplated if her independence was the driving gear that steered her into dark, unfamiliar waters. Her phone call with Lia led to an unintentional breath of admission, a confession of being in a slump of sorts. It enthused her to hear that her family thought so highly of her. She wanted to be what they thought of her. *Strong and put together*. Ella believed, for the first time during the undying Halloween of a year, that she could get through it. At least until winter, when she would receive her bonus. Her largest oil painting is being sold to an established hotel in New York City. The payment would keep her afloat until her lease ends.

Ella followed behind her short-legged dog to the kitchen, where she lit her favorite black cauldron aromatherapy candles and prepared two collagen moon milk lattes. Shrieking and B minor piano keys played gravely in the background. An intrusive buzzing noise followed. Ella stood taller, walking from the tiny kitchen to the building entry pad and granted V access. She continued back to her dusty blush velvet lustre sofa. Cupping the warmed moon milks, she sat down, joined by her trusty companion.

She spoke to the television, "Aw Laurie, we got this, we'll live."

ooo

THE JOURNAL

October 31ˢᵗ, 1988

GROUNDED! BUNK. I know Mike told Mr. Renata that my sick notes are fake. Real tough, always surrounded by his little minions, Jackie and David. They're still harboring over last summer when I picked up Sof from Jackie's lake house. I only stole a few Matt's Beerballs... COME ON. Ratting me out has now cost me my precious freedom from this hellhole. Hardly worth a few nights of getting plastered with John for this bullshit. I can't go out with Sofia to the party now.

Mike is a dirty little bitch. He knew we coordinated our costumes. I was going to be a ringleader, and she's going as a sexy tiger. I'm hot just thinking about it. I helped her find her costume at a thrift store, a tight orange and black catsuit. Totally want her to look as hot as possible, but she's trying to impress the popular jock straps. I stole some military epaulettes from my father's shit in the basement and attached them to my costume. I also found a whip down there, he's never used it on me, so I know he won't miss it. Was looking forward to this ALL year!!!

Sneaking out could cost my life, but I only need a little while. I have to give a little gift of appreciation to miss Jackie for Mike's ratting me out. A fat skinned rodent will be the perfect addition to her new blue Beamer. It's off campus and Halloween. Anyone could have left it. John and I found an abandoned cabin by the river, it's been a haven of sorts, plenty of rats to pick from out there.

Alas, how could I forget the most important part of the day. Father also took away my boombox and found my Loompanics, because of his talk with Mr. Renata. He shredded them! He's such a Nazi, he would wear his replica Waffen-SS uniform tonight if he could.

He screamed, "You should do better, be better, stop being weak!" Nothing like an inspirational lecture followed by a heinous corrective action to put me in my place.

He ripped my shirt off and bent me over while mom just rolled her valium laced eyes at me. He traced the back of my boney spine with the thick bottom handle of our kitchen chefs' knife, over and over. Shit hurt like hell. It was by far the strangest domineering act of punishments as of late. I thought I was artistic out in the wild, but he is straight up DEMONIC. He always finds an alternative way to keep me on my toes. If I could, I'd take that silver knife and shove it up his ass. I'd ask him if his holy self was grateful for the penetration that he so willingly bestows upon everyone around him.

I guess, if I were snarky, I could quote something a little more literate after, from Shakespeare. We went over greed for power in class the other day, a similar lesson father likes to preach in bible study, interestingly enough. It would be bitchin' to quote the play writer over his guru in the sky. Oh, how he would fall over. It would surely get his balls in a knot.

My parental psychos are dressed elaborately in their 50s sitcom masks, their natural state. They refuse to hand out candy for the neighborhood kids that they despise... A little contradicting. They are the evil clowns. They are the ones that bring forth the clouds of doom. This is their fucking holiday.

"Hell is empty, and all the devils are here."

Shakespeare

ooo

THE JOURNAL

November 5ᵗʰ, 1988

BRUNCH WITH SOFIA was weird. She was kind of quiet aside from asking what college I'm going to. I'm going where she is, but that has to be here. It wasn't even a proper question though; it was an opening to talk about her desire for the University of California, a real shocker. She's silly and doesn't understand. The work she trades with me is trash. What happens if she even got accepted into college? I'm embarrassed to turn half this crap in that she gives me. Which is fuel for father to unleash his wrath on me.

"My dead dog ate the homework" doesn't fly. And now, I have to worry about her finals and getting caught cheating. I love watching her dark cherry lined lips move and how her eyes light up at the most miniscule and simple of things. She's just so totally bodacious, my personal little Debbie Harry. That's who she says she wants our peers to see her as. Sofia says she wants to resemble Virna Lisi to her mother and family.

Who is she impersonating for herself? At least I get the true Sofia, no lies.

Father knows I'm doing someone else's work and keeps quoting, "Do not give what is holy to dogs, and do not throw your pearls before swine, lest they trample them under their feet, and turn and tear you to pieces." This could ring some truth, old man. But I ain't got no pearls, and Sofia has already been tearing me to pieces ever since we met. Every moment that we spend together, a piece of my soul breaks off for her, leaving nothing, only the bad parts of me for the rest of the world. She has my heart.

Father's stupid high and tight haircut, peanut-colored stache, and black wayfarers. It looks better in my mind, dripping with claret juices. How can mother even stand him? Her blonde bob, big bangs, and fit bod. She could have anyone. Oh, right? She doesn't even attempt it because she's always sedated. Highschool isn't hell, home is.

I will not run away, though. How far would a beater truck and a stolen wad of cash get? Father won't let me get arrested, that's a reputation booboo. He would be so embarrassed in front of his military buddies. Mom could not tell the nose-up Bettys she lunches with. In the end, father would make sure that I was dead before admitting he bred a failure. I can't survive without them; I also can't survive with them.

ooo

THE JOURNAL

November 15ᵗʰ, 1988

DEAR MOTHER,

   I figured out that you were in the basement this afternoon. I put one and two together, as I was staring at the cuckoo clock, singing its stupid song, ringing the charms, and chimes for me to realize. Father was standing over me, insisting that if I couldn't do my homework, he would find some work for me to do. He had a thirst in his eyes as he squeezed your pearls in his hand, mom. The fine Akoya gems that you practically treasured more than me. The ones that you tugged at when you couldn't bear to witness punishment for the total time. When you had to look away, as I reached out to you with my begging eyes.

   While he recited useless bullshit from the bible, blah blah blah remember?

   Father threatened I would get an enormous gift for Xmas. Grody to the max. Might I be the only kid on the block who doesn't want their father's gifts. He's burning my favorite time of the year, the holidays. He's like a dragon emerging from the hills, burning the towns below, bit by bit. A dragon leaves a few villagers for feeding on later though. You wouldn't eat an entire pantry of food in one sitting, would you? So, he leaves me barely alive, to feed on me, easy.

While all the other happy, shiny people get to go home and enjoy their normal lives, decorating, building gingerbread houses, wrapping gifts, playing games. I want to rip the freckles right off their cheeks. To burn their smiles right off their faces.

It isn't just father's fault; it is your fault too, mother, for leaving us. For leaving me. You must have flirted with the pizza delivery boy, the neighbor, or someone else? You had to have betrayed father to put us all in this position. Ruining our family forever, just for simple pleasures. I don't actually believe that. I wish it. I wish you had some desire to escape or bout for a better life.

Now, father doesn't look away when he rips me apart behind the glass of his wayfarer frames. Instead, he pierces me with his eyes, as to say, "Villain, I have done thy mother." A Shakespearean horror turned into reality. He fucked you up. He must have killed you while I was out. I would have stopped it, mother. I still would have done that for you. Unlike all the times, you refused to help me. I still would have...

I used to hate when you were here. Now, I hate that you're gone. Because I wouldn't have to endure this unnatural exploitation. At least you listened to me a quarter of the time. If only you would have fought back, for Christ's sake.

The mystery is how no one questions your disappearance. Now THAT makes for a good mystery. One that I didn't deserve a game of. I didn't sign up for this shit.

Why aren't the ladies who you lunch with, coming by? Why aren't your bake sale friends calling? He must have said you were sick... The excuse he gave me when I interrogated him about it a few times. You know, I was on thin ice with that.

I think... That I can smell you now, though. I know the smell of death well. The wife of a Lieutenant Colonel... missing and not a soul to question this? Or will question it? I want to shatter this bogus world.

I'm left with the only motherly advice you gave me, "God only helps those who help themselves." I'll help myself alright.

I've got a plan that will separate me from father's failures and from your failures, Mother.

No pains, no gains.

ooo

THE JOURNAL

November 24ᵗʰ, 1988

TURKEY DAY! THIS morning I helped Sofia's mom. She really didn't need it, but I can't help being a lush for Italian food and talk. Sofia was trying on a new hot pink mini dress with puffed sleeves and shoulder pads; so spoiled and so pretty. Everything looks great on her, and she loves when I tell her that.

Mrs. Colombo eyed me from across the kitchen and looked at me like I was a wounded animal. She clearly has never seen one. I stopped canning the pumpkin to prevent a waterwork show. I can see where Sofia gets her bod. Mrs. Colombo has been wearing a too-tight purple turtleneck lately. Showing off those sexy curves.

Mrs. Colombo stopped beating something savory at the counter and welcomed me in for a hug. She then began to speak loudly, using her hands a lot, saying, "You've been so strong through this. I'm so sorry about your parents, your home, everything. I know you're 18 now, but you are welcome to stay with us throughout the school year. Because

Sofia can certainly use your help with school. We expect a great deal from her, as you know. And she isn't, well, she isn't the brightest tomato in the garden. We're grateful for you hun, we'll take care of you too." Mrs. Colombo held on to me and displayed deep pity across her tan face. I wanted to tell her to knock it off, that things were as they should be. That this experience would translate to a blessing in her vocabulary. But it's sweet devilish pleasure that I've got now.

Mrs. Colombo offered a place in her home, a place at her table, and a place in their hearts. This is the nurturing I mocked my mother for lacking. How it could be both charming and bothersome? A fine family that doesn't beat the shit out of their kids, a full pantry, and being within ear shot of Sofia. Everything is just as it should be. Except for the nauseating, gaudy floral wallpaper that covers all the walls, the matching drapes and tablecloth. And the asshole family dog. I can fix these things in due time.

The house fire was juicy justice. A gift for both father and mother. Father insistently talked about getting into the pearly gates of heaven. My naughty father would always say...

"The kingdom of heaven is like a merchant seeking fine pearls."

Well, I'm the merchant now, bitches. And I'll decide who can pass or go.

Father was getting further from perfection, each day that mother was not present while he remained. Replacing her touch with mine. The fire department found mother's body in our burned down home. That's the day that father's valor also became deceased.

My spit sits pretty on your graves.

It smells like a damn bakery in here now! I can not wait for Mrs. Colombo's breads, cookies, and dinner soon!

ooo

DECEMBER DESCENT

December 10th, 2020

ENGLISH, NORTHERN ITALIAN, and a hint of Indigenous heritage are the source of Ella's toasted almond, high cheekbones that are the same width as her sharp jawline. She swept a pouf blush brush across the top of each cheek with a peach powder. She sucked her cheeks in and pushed her plump lips out to sweep a caramelized bronzer just below the middle part of her cheekbone, and upwards to her hairline. Ella used a smaller brush to place a matte dark fawn powder between the crease of her almond-shaped eyelids. Next, a metallic pink gold over her large eyelid hood, adding black liner along the waterlines, clear gel to her thick but neat brows, and added another coat of deep black mascara to her naturally long eyelashes. The range of cosmetics made her hazel eyes stand out extraordinarily, the feature she focused on whilst wearing a mask. She pulled lightly at her thick and lustrous coffee suede locks, with an argan oil serum for shine.

Ella displays striking facial features that kept people guessing her nationality since she was a child. A gesture that both annoys and amuses her. Ella's little sister, Lia, kept a bit of her baby face into and through adulthood, with a few freckles on her pierced aquiline nose. Ella contrasts with a straight, broad, and narrow nose. Lia grew to be four-inches taller than her older sister, who stands at five-foot-three. Both of Lia's arms are layered in a sleeve of black tattoos, while Ella's remain bare. She also rocks an opposite edgy flair from Ella's romantic blouses, skinny flares, and jaunty blazers.

Ella turned on relaxing holiday piano solos to set the mood for her premature present unwrapping. She began humming to the piano tunes and picked up the large square box from the foyer bench. An early holiday gift from Lia. The sisters developed a closer relationship since their argument in the fall and aimed to reconcile differences, to enhance communication. Ella sat down on her abstract carpet with Pinot and contemplated what was inside. Impatiently, she pulled the red satin ribbon off and ripped the black paper that wrapped the box. She pulled the box top off and peeled back the black tissue paper. A pair of over-the-knee boots with a pointy toe and four-inch heels. Her stomach fluttered as she beamed at the soft black suede high heels. It thrilled her to have something to finally amp up her style to sexy, even just for an evening. She wanted to stimulate her long-awaited date. It impressed her that the guy she kept at bay with text messages and occasional video-calls, throughout quarantine, was still interested in meeting her with a shelter-in-place order.

Ella made her way to the kitchen, where she picked up her check off the counter. The hotel made it out to Stella Russo-Redhouse, for $2,500.00. The largest amount that she had ever received for one of her oil canvas paintings. A painting that was difficult to part from, for any dollar amount. It was her absolute favorite piece out of all the work that she had created over the past ten years of her career. The 40 x 20 canvas had abstract cool tones painted eloquently in such a way that each person who passed by the retail windows would stop to admire it. She observed the street audience from her living room and wondered how it made each person feel. But in a pandemic world, she couldn't see facial expressions under masks. She produced prints for her own space, but it just wasn't the same. The way the flecks of gold reflected in the light, the intense phthalo blue textures that were noticeable even from across the room, and the original signature that Ella felt proud to display. Ella believed this payment was not enough, but for sentimental reasons, not professional purposes. She maintained a humble presence, always.

Ella exited the elevator and wobbled for a moment, not completely used to the skinny four-inch heels. She lived within a three-minute walk from her credit union and used the deposit errand to adjust to the new fit before her date. Ella wore a short black pleated skirt, a gray plaid boyish blazer, and a fitted white graphic tee-shirt that she tucked neatly into her skirt. She adjusted the silver crossbody chain to her black marble resin clutch. And exited her building to brave the walk across downtown Woodsberry.

Click, click, click, click.

Ella's heels announced themselves with conviction. She moved confidently, past the cemented and desolate downtown square. Ella pulled her mask down for a moment to absorb the honied cider and herbaceous scent from the late fall wind. There weren't many people for Ella to compare herself to, but she was positive that she overdressed for Woodsberry and didn't care. This new high lifted her off the pavement and closer to the last of the stunning and vibrant orange and yellow leaves that remained stubborn on tree branch tips.

A powerful sanitizing scent blasted Ella as she pushed the dark glass door open to the bank. It threw her off, and she tripped inside the small credit union.

A pudgy, private security guard to the right of her asked, "Are you okay, miss?"

He reached his hand out, secured with a blue sterile glove.

Ella giggled, nodding up and down quickly. She replied, "Yes, thank you. Sorry, that fan is, *strong.*"

She stood on the tape-lined square over the grainy white commercial vinyl. Only one teller station remained open because of business being remarkably slower this month than any year prior. Unusual bouts of crime throughout the state of California also pressed small businesses to reduce hours or shut down entirely.

Ella observed a tall woman with shoulder-length brown hair standing at the counter. The woman concluded her business with the bank teller and walked past one man in slim, tailored dress pants and another gentleman, dressed in a baggy sweat suit, both men seemingly in their mid to late twenties. They moved forward, keeping a six-foot distance between each other. Ella followed behind them.

The sound of the obnoxious air curtain installed above the entrance doors went off again as the woman left. The security guard held the tinted door open for a petite senior woman with thinning, short, and fuzzy white hair. She wore a pink floral snood covering over her face. Ella curved to the woman, who was moving at a glacial speed and clinging to her aluminum medical walker with wheels.

Ella offered, "Hi, miss, you can go ahead of me."

"Miss? Dear, aren't you so kind *and* so pretty? I'm Gertie," the senior customer replied in a croaky voice.

Ella giggled. She was in no rush and felt jubilant.

Another rush of air, but Ella didn't move from her spot. She was within feet of the door. There was no extra room to move aside. She thought it was unusually busy now. Her thoughts disrupted by a hard shove against her back, knocking her forward into Gertie, who held onto her walker tightly upon the force. Ella shifted at the angle of her stiletto heels. They gave out from underneath her, and she fell to the hard floor.

"Ugh, oh no, I'm *so* sorry!" Ella apologized to Gertie.

Jumbled with a tardy reaction to her assault, Ella remained on the ground. A woman's piercing scream came from the front of the room during Ella's ungainliness. Ella leaned her upper body and head to nod around the customers before her. She re-directed her focus from Gertie to the screaming bank worker.

"EVERYONE GET DOWN ON THE FLOOR, GET DOWN!" a man bellowed above Ella's head at the entrance. The shock solidified her movement.

"YOU, GET YOUR HAND OFF THAT!" the man continued.

The man shot off two rounds from a black pistol directly behind Ella. Two bullets entered the bulging belly of the security guard. The pressure from the shots forced blood to squirt from his gut, spraying the right side of Ella's long hair and the back of her plaid blazer. The ear-splitting bang noises from the gun shots left her even more immobile, accompanied by a deafening ringing in her ears. One man twisted the basic lock to the front entrance, the pair then passed the customers quickly to take control of the room.

Ella's skirt pulled taut, as she was uncomfortably side sitting on the ground with the other customers. She twisted her body around to face the entrance door and placed her small hands on the ground for stability. The blood from the guard had been pooling fast, spreading out in her direction. In a deep shock, Ella couldn't comprehend that the warm liquid skimming her skin was blood. It formed a dark red outline around her slender beige fingers on the vinyl. She released the breath that she was holding in and raised her hands, shaking them before her face. Ella shrieked as she wiped her hands off frantically onto her short black skirt and exposed skin on her thighs.

She whipped her body back around to face Gertie, noticing her khaki pants and beige comfort shoes still holding an upright stance. Ella shifted her eyes to the men dressed in all-black clothing, black ski masks, and homemade camo armor. She could tell that they were white by the little skin exposed around their eyes and hands. They aimed their black pistols at the customers and workers. The second man sprinted to the front counter where two bank tellers and the manager huddled together, holding their hands up.

Ella's hazel eyes widened from the shock, her mouth agape. Each breath sucked the mask fabric in with the little air that she desperately sought.

"I SAID GET THE FUCK ON THE FLOOR, NOW!" the first robber screamed at Gertie. He motioned to the floor with his gun.

Gertie remained standing in fear and deep confusion. Aware of who the man was screaming at, Ella tried to get Gertie's attention discreetly. She eyed the senior woman with desperation. Without response, Ella resulted to tugging on Gertie's beige sweater vest with her bloody hands. She whispered, "Gertie, *please*."

"Damn you, for making me do this!" said the first bank robber. He smashed the butt of his gun against Gertie's wrinkled, pale, veiny temple. Gertie let out a feeble cry as she crumbled to the ground. Ella placed her right arm out to prevent the old woman from rocking backwards and potentially damaging her head further. Gertie was in a distorted sitting position, half lying down. Ella placed her hand over the woman's bleeding forehead to comfort the pain. But it only made Gertie wince and recoil into a ball on the floor. Ella unintentionally left smears of blood, from her hands, onto Gertie's light clothing, face, and hair.

"*Now* that we have your attention! You comply, or you die! You four, throw your cell phones towards the center of the room, now!" screamed the first robber.

The blood from Gertie's injury trailed down the side of her lobe. She shook with grief. Ella tapped Gertie's arm and lifted her index finger to her mask. And then swung her black marble resin clutch onto her folded lap. Ella quickly snatched her black clamshell folding smartphone out of her clutch and slid it on the floor towards the middle of the room, exactly as they were instructed. Her compact and square smartphone played bumper cars with the other two phones near the deadly and vicious robber.

Looking around at the absurdly dated and trivial room, Ella blinked her eyes rapidly, trying to rid of the nightmare. She set her sights on the second robber at the front. He collected thick wads of cash from a teller and placed them in his backpack, while the manager lethargically opened the vault. Ella prayed in her mind that they wouldn't procrastinate and get this over with. One life taken is *too* many. The scene revolted her.

"You! Throw your phone to me, now!" the first robber screamed at Gertie.

"Look at her! Does she look like she owns a cell phone? *Please!*" Ella shrieked.

Ella stared up at the tall and medium-built robber with pleading eyes.

The masked man bent down before Ella, forcing her to scoot up, still side sitting. He placed the tip of his pistol on her black boot, and grazed it over the soft suede, from her bent knee to her upper thigh and then against her dark mini skirt. His eyes sharpened on hers with an intense, withering stare, his pupils so dilated that she wasn't able to make out what color they were. She whimpered as the robber pulled her mask down below her chin. He traced his gun barrel along the outline of her swollen, naturally rounded upper lip. Tears rolled down Ella's cheeks, creating lines of ebony over the light powder that she applied earlier. Her natural medium-light skin tone radiated through the trail of tears.

"*Yummy, Pocahontas.* You look like my next dead girlfriend," the robber hissed.

"LET'S GO! She's opening the volt!" the second robber screamed to his partner.

"But boss would love this one! Let's take her."

"NO! Hot, but too old. Stop screwin' around!"

"I saw your kind along the pipelines. I bet you taste as sweet as the berries you pick, bitch. I'd like to see what you've got under there," he grumbled, eyeing her skirt.

Quivering with horror, Ella could feel her bowels loosen. Her bladder reacted unreservedly to the overwhelming fear. Her cheeks burned scarlet as she witnessed the trail of urine streaming towards the first robber.

"What the-nasty mother f-*OH*, you're definitely coming with us now!" the robber screamed in a booming and doomful voice.

He backed up on his toes, squatting before her. The murderous man pulled his pant leg up with his fingertips, still clinging to the gun that was now pointed towards the ground. Gertie inched towards the wall behind the robber, without being noticed.

At that moment of the robber's distraction, Ella felt as if her life was on the line. Her pent-up rage compelled her to lean back and swivel her legs lightning fast in front of her, towards the bank robber. She pulled her right leg as close to her chest as possible. Opening her mouth, Ella released a deep, hoarse cry with all the strength of her core. The robber lifted his gun towards her chest, but before he could pull the trigger, Ella rapidly thrusted her stiletto boot up into his unprotected throat. The four-inch heel entered his skin and tissue with ease, while the flat toe box of her shoe smacked his jaw.

A simultaneous squish and crack noise petrified Ella's ears.

Squeezing her eyes shut, Ella faced the front entrance doors to her left. She pulled her boot heel out of his neck and back towards herself just as fast as she drove it into him. Blood gushed out of the gaping hole. His trachea was severed. The robber struggled for oxygen, but instead of the relief of an anxious breath, he inhaled thick blood. This caused a drowning reflex. A gurgling noise surfaced as he gagged and choked on his own crimson liquids. His eyes rolled to the back of his head as his hand remained gripping the black pistol, but immobile.

The second male customer in line, raised his hands up. He spiraled into a state of terror and further distress. The man attempted to create distance between himself and the horrifying scene, crab walking his way back to the security kiosk. His sweatpants fell from his hips, with the baggy hem between his sneaker and the smooth vinyl floor, he slipped, falling back a few feet near the dead security guard. He sat up and hugged his knees with his eyes shut tightly.

Concurrently, the first man in line wearing dress pants, raised himself and charged towards the threat. The first robber was paralyzed, but still alive, and maintained his grip on the loaded gun. The well-dressed patron pounced on him with force and smashed the robber's wrist on the ground, with intent on freeing his grip. This asserted his finger to pull back on the trigger. A last bullet sped past Ella's face. It ricocheted off the kiosk counter behind her and into the patron's back, who sought security during the chaos.

The second robber at the front climbed over the teller barrier with a backpack full of green paper, comprising of seventy-five percent cotton and twenty-five percent linen. A monetized paper that he violently sacrificed the life of others for.

Racing towards the entrance, the robber flashed his handgun at Gertie sitting against the wall, the brave patron who clung to his partner's handgun, and finally, at Ella, a crimson statue.

Before he exited, he screamed, "God damn it!"

The bank robbery lasted seven minutes, from beginning to end. Ella felt like it had been an eternity in an alternate, ruinous universe from her casual life. Blinking rapidly and teary-eyed, she could barely make out her bloody palms, shaking belligerently before her.

A calamitous triangle of deceased men surrounded the ravishing thirty-year-old woman. They dressed Ella with their blood and dead stares. Carmine syrup dripped from her hair and clothing, down onto the developed puddle of gore. Her heart thrashed violently against the walls inside of her chest.

She wept, "Call the police, call the..."

ooo

THE JOURNAL

December 12ᵗʰ, 1988

BEST DAY EVER. Sofia Marie Colombo kissed me! I'm pathetic, but clearly not that pathetic. A raging ball of fire has filled that pit in my stomach. She popped into my room earlier and brought me a brand new Loompanics mag and went to kiss me on the cheek, but I moved my head to face hers. She looked at me strangely and said it was "just because", but it feels like a damn early Christmas. I know it's because her parents have been praising her test scores and my work that she has turned in. Good scores for her is totally a score for me.

People are STILL coming by to bring me flowers, sweets, and casseroles. By people, I mean mother's friends. Father's people want absolutely nothing to do with me. Thank Satan. These women believe that they're doing holy work by bringing charity to me. Right, I'm not charity though. Whatever. I think it's an excuse for them just to come over to see the Colombo's. A family that is hellaciously banging. I am, without a doubt, their new black sheep. What the hell am I supposed to do with flowers? I give Sofia all the red roses and Mrs. Colombo the carnations. Oh, how they love it. Mr. Colombo can afford the new Motorola, but not a bouquet for his bitchin' babes? I have to keep reminding myself that this is real. Journaling and taking a fleck of flesh with my father's knife does the trick, oozing the most rad color in the world.

I am alive.

Only down a single hall from those sweet cherry red lips and sexy maple syrup stems. I listen to Sofia shower on the other side of my guest room and touch myself, imagining that it's her hands, her lips. Where I find the will to not take her into my room, rip her robe off and have my way, is extraordinary. I HAVE to play this right if I want her to be mine forever, not just for a night.

I'm giving her mother's pearls for Christmas. I've had them polished to clean the dirty deeds so associated with them. It's certainly no La Peregrina, and it's not rare, thanks to Mikimoto. But hey, they are true saltwater Akoya pearls. Father got them in Nam. From my research in the library, I learned that the smallest of pearls are even better than some famous colossal gem. An Akoya pearl's supreme being reigns from a combination of culture and nature. Like me.

I would like to forget everything about life at home. But both sets of grandparents keep insisting that I come live with them down in Florida. What in the hell would I do in Florida? I could beg Sof to come live with me, start a new life in the sunshine. But she would weasel in the California talk. Their old and decrypt faces would remind me of the heinous incessant contact I endured by the ones that they made, the ones who made me. I dreamed of them again. I've lost count how many times that I've had this same one since father died, but here goes it...

I am standing behind my mother and father, their bodies like statues, in some trance. I can see the back of their heads, tidy hair, neatly dressed, the both of them. We are in a small bright room, four walls, one window and a single tub in front of it. My parents kneel before the large white bathtub in mirrored motion. I hover over the tops of them to see what they're observing. It's a baby version of me, splashing about in a filled tub. They titter like twins, exact tone, exact length. Mother says, "There's our little devil." She pinches my ruddy cheeks. Father shifts his body at her unmatched actions to his. He's livid. Breathing heavily, he remains gawking ahead, at the major attraction, me. A white and stainless-steel folding knife abruptly appears in the back pocket of his slacks. My father deliberately reaches his arm around his back to grasp the top tip of the knife. And POOF, the baby version of me, vanishes. My parents remain. They snigger as the water transitions from crystal clear to wet bark brown to sundried tomato red. Mother drops single white pearls in the fluctuating tub, one by one. One, two, three. Seven, eight, nine. Eleven and twelve. All into a now maroon liquid, it stirs and flows until it rises and consumes the entire tub itself. Next, it consumes my mother and father. Blackened crimson water consumes everything in the tiny bathroom until we are all warped into a dark obscurity.

Some dream. I gotta stop eating so much damn candy before bed. But I can't resist taffy. The temporary rise and shine antidote is Sofia's cute face, her sensual bare legs, even in the winter. Her batting eyelashes and her uncertain voice when she tries to appear tough. Plus getting to see her before school, though we don't go together. It helps at least, for me to forget, until I'm forced to go through it again when I close my eyes at night. I'm hunting for a comfortable life for us, something better than this shit.

Seek and you shall find indeed...

Sofia won't need me once school is over. So, I need to have something to offer her. I have to seduce her. My inheritance will come in a few months. I've got my eye on a jet-black luxury sports coupe with a smoothed rear bumper, tail lamps, and a lay-down spoiler. Not my first choice, but she'll totally dig it and that's all that matters. I cherish how our lips met, but I still want so much more. I can't wait for the day that I don't long for her and have her, permanently. Together forever.

ooo

STARRY-EYED SERENDIPITY

December 12ᵗʰ, 2020

DEVON HAS COMPLETELY transformed my body. Pretty damn blessed to have a chef and personal trainer, all-in-one. His workout plan includes a variety of weighted upper and lower drills, consistently five times a week, every week. He has omitted cardio for now. I'm not tripping over the runs, though. The last time that Logan and I went, someone wearing a black face mask and dark parka kept driving by us, ominously in a beat-up red pickup truck. The country bumpkin might have been lost, but that's a positive assumption. It was aggressive and put us on edge. Devon installed a squat rack in the garage. We basically converted the space into a gym. It has become a refuge for me, to let off steam from the rage and desolation that built up since my birthday.

"Alexa, play *Question!* by *System Of A Down*," I said.

I stepped up to the rack and rested the bar between my neck and my upper chest. I placed my hands underneath it, shoulder-width apart, gripping with my fingers around it. I lifted my chest to support the bar and stepped away from the rack. Keeping my back vertical and my feet a little wider than hip-distanced apart, I lowered my body into a deep squat. Maintaining balance and centering weight, I repeated the exercise with three sets of ten repetitions. After a while of unraveling the meaning about berries in SOAD's music video while lifting, I pondered about afterlife, which led to thoughts about my mom and the Pearl Point Murderer.

ooo

I immersed my lower body into the full bathtub of ice and cold water, sucking my stomach muscles in to avoid the inevitable. I can't help that this activity puts me at a greater unease than the average person. Especially today, the twelfth is *still* harrowing. The hairs on my arm raised like falling dominoes in reverse, first at my wrists, up my forearms, upper arms, and up to the back of my neck. Next, a raw frostbite, not from the bath, but the recollections. I dipped my left wrist in the freezing water and lifted it back up to watch the water drip down from my raised, pale, thin line of skin. My scar.

Devon says that ice baths reduce inflammation and damage to the muscles. He also says that abs are made in the kitchen. He has me eating six times a day. It became easier with his meal prepping skills and shake recipes over the months. The meditating deal I'm working on. It's harder than I thought because my mind always trails back to deciphering the card. Motivation has never been more dominant; it stems from receiving the wax-sealed envelope with the square card. It lit a fire within me. But reading the letter that Charlie mentioned, it ignited a scorching desire to unravel the past.

I sat up in the tub and lengthened my long and heavy arm to the bathroom bench. Picking up the letter, I read.

Addressed to Sapphire Glass Beach, Florida News-Journal

9/6/96

Hello. I'd like to introduce myself. The irritant to society, the parasite that you never knew you needed.

How the sweet decay of rotting leaves beneath the trees brings me back to life. With death comes beauty in the fall. Similar to the fall of an oyster. An organic life is taken... Bred and killed to reveal the infamous gem. A pearl. Divulging the naturally occurring Symbol of wisdom, a representation of justice, the Adored and timeless charm. Some things are meant to be undone to become whole. To imply underlying beauty, to purify what was.

You focus on thugs, but these bitches that use, take, and break others to get what they want are no better. You don't fear them because they're so alluring in the hot weather. Lusting the lustrous, naughty, Naughty Sgt. Ramirez. Do you miss Brooke's breasts? Because I know where they rest... Sapphire PD Do tread carefully where thy senior princess parties with the best. Within deep waters lies deep vengeance.

This continues as they continue to lie, they're so different from you and I. You've got your set of skills and I've got mine. If you were as good as me, though, she would still be alive. Better open up your eyes. Or the shore will lick her thighs. It is only a matter of time...

Tick-Tock-Tick-Tock

This is hard to read, every time. And it hasn't been easy to take the time to think about it straight. Ever since I received the square card, my gut tells me that someone is there. When I blare *Dropkick Murphys* and early Y2K rock during weightlifting. When I'm in *Zoom* meetings and working on marina management on the computer for up to eleven hours a day. Even while I listen to calming ocean sounds and meditate in the evening. *It's there*, the lingering doubt that I am alone.

Shortly after my birthday, the hospital admitted Charlie, he had to be put on a ventilator. A few weeks after that, he had a tracheostomy. The surgery involved a hole in the front of his neck and a tube had to be inserted into his trachea. It was crazy challenging to not be able to visit him and comfort him, the way he has always comforted all of us guys during tough times. Charlie Dawson is a solid badass. If he can survive the most notorious virus of the decade, followed by a major surgery, and recover from that. I should be able to survive my thoughts and get things straight.

I pulled myself out of the tub, stepped onto the bathmat, and wrapped a bath towel around myself, securing it just below the visible edges of my muscular core.

ooo

We have an hour before we head to Foggerton Hospital. Afterwards, we are heading to Gloria's for a socially distanced dinner in their massive great room. Just the five of us, under Charlie's request. I relaxed in the black reclining lounger and turned the television on to check out the weather and news. I noticed a red flashing line on the bottom of the screen for national news that read, "*Woman saves lives during deadly bank heist with boot.*"

How would that actually play out?

Intrigued, I moved from the living room to the kitchen, where Devon was preparing a range of appetizers for the welcome home dinner, one being a chilled asparagus soup with tarragon crème fraîche that I'm stoked for. I searched for the headline on the internet and selected the first news link that popped up. A gorgeous girl was front and center on the news page. Leaning forward in the barstool chair, I gasped upon recognition.

Damn, this is why I couldn't find her on social media before. Stella is Ella, and she cut the hyphen from her last name.

I muttered, "Dude, holy shit, look, it's Stella. Something crazy happened..."

ooo

PEISKOS PACT

December 14ᵗʰ, 2020

"**E**LLA! OH, MY lord, oh my lord!" V said as Ella welcomed her into the foyer.

"V! Thank you *so* much for coming!" Ella elated.

"You do not need to thank me! Where shall I put these down?" V questioned.

"I'll take your bags, if-*ooh* thank you for the beautiful poinsettia, if you could put that on the kitchen counter," Ella said. She disappeared down the narrow hall.

"Oh, my goodness, the fresh pine and orange smell incredible. This is the most adorable little holiday wonderland that I've ever seen," V mumbled.

A few minutes later, Ella came back from setting up the spare room to find that V had taken her boots off and was playing with Pinot on the chocolate and cream abstract rug. She leaned against the hall wall to take in the scenery. Fake snowy blankets accented plain surfaces. Yellow and orange flames flickered steadily, illuminating V's round and freckled face. She was imitating Pinot's stance. Her slim and boxy figure bent down on all fours, with her elbows on the ground and her petite bottom up in the air. Pinot's stumpy backside wagged all together, with his hind legs raised.

A black and white Scandinavian holiday scheme ran across the entire main wall, while the rest of the home remained well lit and furnished in soft neutral tones. The fireplace heated the freshly dried orange garland, giving off a spicy citrus scent. The homemade garland hung from two nails that also secured ivory cable-knit stockings on both sides of the mantel face. White candlesticks, pinecones, and organic bundles of balsam boughs crowded the top surface before the mirror. In the left corner of the room, a medium-sized real Noble Fir stood in a black geometric tree stand. Half a dozen book-shaped gifts sat on a black merino-wool tree skirt that was embroidered with a white pine needle and berry design around the edge. Each gift, wrapped in brown kraft paper and secured with natural twine. Two black bags, a few feet tall, leaned against the wall next to the tree and underneath the window that faced downtown Woodsberry.

"How did, when did you do all this?" V questioned.

"I did it after I got back from my trip, definitely not after the, the bank. I luckily froze cherry chip bread too, it's my nonna's recipe and will be amazing for our breakfast. She sent me this beautiful French bakeware in navy color. I miss her French and nautical style. I got the tree from an old art collector; he runs that tree lot over on the corner of first. He gave it to me in exchange for a few bottles of Dry Creek reds. Which I have more than plenty of. Speaking of vino, can I pour you a glass?" Ella proposed.

V nodded her head up and down. Her short red hair swayed. The girls met at the seating area. Ella poured from the previously opened bottle of 2017 *Lancel Creek Vineyard* pinot noir into two stemless wine glasses. V swirled her wine around in her glass, while Ella sat down on her plush swivel accent chair, bringing her legs up and crossing them. Adjusting her comfort, she pulled a velvet red ochre lumbar pillow from her backside and placed it in her lap. Leaning forward, she picked up her wine from the octagon-shaped wood coffee table. Ella took a few sips of her favorite wine, savoring the juicy acidity and silky tannins.

"I'm going to keep saying this. Thank you, for being here for me. For staying the night. I've been, *pretty* alone. It was scary. In the hospital, no one could even visit. Then all the questions and interview requests. My mom wants me to come stay with her right now, but she also doesn't want to risk getting sick. I only have a few weeks left here, anyway. This *is* my home. You know you're like a sister to me, but my actual sister should have been here. Every time that I get a call from a friend or someone wanting to interview me, I get shocked that it isn't her," Ella sighed.

"Well, first miss, I wouldn't rather be anywhere else. Yes, the pandemic is still a raging bull, but this is just tragic and deserves attention from friends and family, not news stations. When the pandemic started, I wanted to quarantine with my family, but they would've driven me nuttier than a *PayDay*. Family isn't always blood, it's the people you bond with. The ones that act as a compass, guiding you to goodness, accepting you, and loving you unconditionally. I'm grateful to have such a kind, creative, and prepossessing woman as a sister. It's a blessing that you're here, that you're alive. But you are right, Lia should have been here when you got home. Did she even send a text?" V inquired.

"Aw, I love you V. I'm thankful to have you too. You're my southern charm. But that's the thing. Lia has said nothing. After that quick trip for the nine-night chant with her and my dad last month, I thought-I'm just sick of the trials with her! But considering that I almost fucking *died*... I'm so sorry for that, I'm just," Ella sobbed.

"No, darlin'. Do not apologize," V cooed back to Ella.

V rose from Ella's mauve sofa to kneel down on the carpet in front of her best friend. She teared up as she placed her hands on Ella's exposed knees from the ripped holes in her skinny, light denim flares. V believed the best thing that she could offer was consoling her in silence. Ella hunched over, braless under a saguaro green boutique kimono top. It had a single thin rope attached that she tied into a bow around her slender waist, exposing a hint of natural cleavage and a tiny belly roll below. The ruffled shoulders and frilly sleeves flowed from her petite, hourglass figure. V could see the bags present under her eyes now. Tears showed the dark puffy circles that Ella tried to cover up. They streamed over the concealer, down her cheeks, onto her prominent collarbones, and past her chest. Earlier in the day, Ella pulled her long brown hair in to a loose fishtail braid, it loosened over the hours. V thought to herself, *how could someone so benevolent endure such an odious happening. How could that same person remain almost ethereal in grief?* She let her friend cry freely as she held onto her, acknowledging her pain, and praying for her recovery.

ooo

Ella and V changed into their matching set of black and red plaid pajamas, a soft flannel long-sleeve top and ruffled flannel shorts that V had monogrammed for them three years prior. V joined Ella back at the coffee table where she was already waiting for her, with fresh drinks that sat on round cork coasters. *The Best of Pentatonix Christmas* album played in the background over a *Bluetooth* speaker.

"So, I made this drink for you, and we have all the supplies for the care packs over there," Ella said.

"You're a doll. This looks divine. Before the work, let's do gifts!" V proposed.

"Aw, yay, yes!" Ella cheered.

V picked up a canvas tote that had a red deer design printed on the front for Ella. Ella pointed to the kraft brown wrapped gift with a silver spoon ornament tied to the top with twine. V retrieved her gifts as well, setting them down before Ella and Pinot.

"*Ooh*, I love this bag. So cute. You know me and my totes," Ella beamed.

"Totes lady, I do. Now open it!" V sang.

Ella closed her eyes tightly, fighting to abolish the stinging memory of opening the pair of stiletto boots in the same spot mere days ago. She took a deep breath in, opened her eyes, and plucked the green tissue paper from the top, pulled out three gifts, and placed them on the carpet next to her. Opening the first, a square box with a red and green strawberry ornament in it. Ella's plump lips crept up her defined face. She held the box close to her chest and mouthed, *thank you*.

"A pop of color on your neutral tree will be cute," V chirped in a southern accent.

"I love it so much. A food ornament is hilarious, but I appreciate that you heard me out on the phone about berries. I hate what that bank robber said, but I can't lose myself because of it. Aww, Pinot is going to go nuts for these homemade apple peanut-butter dog treats! I swear you are the dog whisperer even though you're a cat person. Your new kitten, Uncle Fester, is so adorable," Ella gushed. "What is this, though?"

She peeled matte red wrapping paper off of a box, with a photo on the front of a rose-gold whistle ornament on a chain.

"That is a mindful breathing necklace. It's a little device to assist you in breathing better, well, more effectively when you feel anxiety or stress coming on. I mean, with what happened and all, I think you could benefit from it," V noted.

"I've never seen this before! I'm so excited-I mean, I'm not excited to be stressed out. But to be able to use it immediately when I need, that is a tremendous benefit. Especially, considering it's been a struggle for me already. Thank you *so* much."

"You are most welcome. My, you always top the silver spoon ornament. I don't know how, but they get better every year. My obsession with silver spoons is in full force now…" She held a stack of three toile navy designer notebooks, and a matching designer pen on top, secured together with a dark blue velvet ribbon. Each notebook had gold gilding on the page edge, reflecting brilliantly in the warm glow of the fireplace. "This is too much! I am not using these at the law firm!" V rejoiced as she held up her gifts.

"We have virtually no one else to spend the holidays with. No work parties, no networking, no family gatherings. We're just a pair of cat and dog moms. A little self-indulgence is anything but selfish at a time like this. And I know you've had your eyes on those for a while," Ella said, bubbly and raspy.

"Goodness, I love them. I also love these drinks. My lord, I must get the recipes. What was the last one we had?"

"Of course! I have them all written in my nonna's notebook. You could take photos of the pages. The last one was a Sicilian Mistletoe. It has vodka, Averna amaro, cinnamon syrup, and homemade maraschino cherries. It's my favorite, it's so simple and sexy. To me, it emulates the holidays perfectly. And for this one, I jazzed up a festive little Campfire Cocktail that I found online. It has marshmallow flavored vodka, *Baileys Espresso Crème Liqueur*, almond milk, chocolate sauce, and I torched the marshmallow on top," Ella exclaimed.

V was already taking photos of the cocktail with her smartphone. She tucked her golden sunrise red hair behind her ear, smoothing it to her skinny shoulder. Ella observed her with amusement. V displayed her signature focus face, which involves one side of her peach lips pulled inwards while she squints one green eye. After getting the right shot, she relaxed her pale ivory skin with sandy freckles across her cheeks. Confident that her photo will get plentiful likes from the renowned foodies floating in the internet pool.

"*YUM*, the graham cracker crumble and the touch of chocolate syrup are so light, but delectable. What is it about being by the fire, that is just so cozy and fulfilling? Enjoying the warmth with someone special, while the shared heat washes over you with a sense of wellness. Promise me that our sleepover pacts will never get old, even when we do!" V remarked in an attractive, sharp voice.

"Oh, I promise, we'll be doing this forever. But to be honest, I was a little worried about how I was going to act. When I brought Pinot to the park to go potty. I got this creepy feeling that I was being followed. This sort of cramping in my chest, and a prickly sensation on my neck. I turned around and there was a guy, like, ten feet away, but he ended up walking the other way. Pinot didn't even bark. I was on edge when the building maintenance man was knocking earlier too. I think I'm getting paranoid. People can't recognize me with a mask on, right? So, how could they judge me or know that I am the killer on the news. I don't want to be grim, though. We should be having fun, just as long as we don't get shit faced and text our exes," Ella beamed, releasing an anxious giggle.

"Darlin', I have absolutely no expectations. You're going to feel unsafe because you were in an unsafe situation. It's as fresh as apple pie. I know you are brave, a go-getter, and a doer. But give yourself the space and time. They got the guy that had got away, he's not coming for you. As for the other, he was antagonizing innocent people to their deathbed. You saved yourself with a pair of stiletto boots. You saved Gertie. My point is, you're not a killer, you're a *survivor*. That doesn't mean you're superhuman, though. Cry and cry some more. I'll be here for you. You're a good person, Ella, an exceptionally good person," V maintained.

Ella's thick eyebrows rose and bunched together. A tear escaped from the corner of her hazel eye. "Thank you so much, V. I just need time to believe that."

"You're in luck because time is on our side. But for *you*, not him. Back to getting shit faced. Hangovers and regrets are a drag, so cheers to getting heavily buzzed and having a hydration persuasion later!" V cheered.

She clinked her campfire cocktail against Ella's drink.

The two women sat down on square tufted velvet floor pillows in front of the fireplace. Flickers of light danced off of Pinot's bluish gray flat face and wrinkled skin. He slept noisily on his own miniature round floor pillow between the both of them. They had an array of travel-size products displayed on the hearth before them. The women packed a thick pair of socks, hand sanitizer, a wet wipe pack, two granola bars, a water bottle, mints, a cheerful note, and a disposable rain poncho, into plastic gallon-size zip bags. They took sips of their campfire cocktails in between their activities, in hopes to benefit the local homeless people that sulked the streets down below.

"My mama and I used to do this back in my Texas hometown. Before my dad got his real estate license and the house flippin' business. We weren't so well off when I was a kid. Not exactly countin' cans for change either, though. I think I resonate with people in poverty, just a little more than my colleagues, at least. My, how they can complain, without taking breaks to breathe," V explained in a southern accent.

"I could totally see that. I mean, you work amongst people coming from *Ivy League* schools, and this area is pretty snobbish. It's between the haves and have nots, a combination of old wine money and new pot farms. The homeless problem was awful before, but now with a lot of businesses closed around the square, it's worse. And I don't know how to help that. I guess I shouldn't complain, I won't be living here after the New Year. As much as I go back and forth on this, it would be better to not live downtown after what happened. Thankfully, I get to keep my retail space. But I do not know what I'm going to do about my home," Ella fretted with a sigh.

"I'm sad that you have to leave your unit. You made this one of the most beautiful little spots that I've seen down here. *So*, I was thinking of how I could help you. I can't just do *nothing* after what you've been through. It would be hard to watch you haul your bags on your own and heal somewhere random. Would you consider taking the Bonnes Bay rental home?" V proposed, while squinting one green eye back at Ella.

Ella put the half-filled plastic bag down on the carpet. She pulled her plaid pajama waist band up above her waist and adjusted herself on the cushion. Lengthening her short legs outwards and crinkling her toes in red Sherpa lined slipper socks. She gazed into the fire as she processed the offer.

"How much would it be? My only income right now is royalties and selling a few larger pieces a month, much less than before," Ella finally replied.

"Oh, I'm not asking you to do it as a favor for us. It would be a gift for *you*. No cost. Well, not no cost. I was thinking... Maybe you could provide some art for the place. It's off the market until next summer, naturally. My parents normally live in it for half of the year. Mama wants to redecorate it, but it is a gorgeous place, it's quiet out there, and safe. You'd have more than enough room to work on your collection and decompress. Mini gym, hot tub, private ocean-view. I know what happened to you was traumatizing, but you seemed crestfallen before this. The best part is, you would only be fifteen minutes away from me, versus an hour!" V enthused.

"Oh wow, I'm not even sure what to say! It would just be me, alone though?"

"I-well, there is one person who could stay with you. I know she's been a bad egg lately, but Lia literally works at Bonnes Bay Luxury Senior Living. Ella Russo-Redhouse! You could make a preacher cuss! Just say yes!" V shrieked.

"Jeez! What is my problem? It's a yes! Wow, yes, yes. Oh my god!"

"This will be good for you. Just watch! I'll tell ya, salt water is truly healing."

The roar of excitement in the winter wonderland woke Pinot. Ella and V took the final sips of their cocktails and stretched over the small Frenchie to side-hug.

Tears formed at the corners of Ella's eyes again. "I'll take these in for us," she said and used her plaid sleeve to wipe them away quickly as she stood up. "Sheesh, we should eat something. This is such an unconventional menu. I clearly had drinks on my mind, but I have a winter butternut squash soup on the stove, for us! Ooh, turn it up, please! This is my favorite holiday song!" Ella squealed.

V smirked at Ella's minor intoxication. She turned the music up, and followed behind her best friend, dancing towards the kitchen. Ella placed the sticky cocktail glasses in the sink and put two stone bowls into the microwave.

"Have you ever listened to the lyrics? I think *White Winter Hymnal* is original to *Fleet Foxes*. I love them and it's beautiful, but sort of dark, huh?" V queried.

"Honestly, all holiday songs are a little dark. At least the religious ones are, to me. I love this song the most, though, it's unique. So, speaking of guys."

"Oh lord, you're not thinking of texting the asshole, are you?" V implied.

"Ew, no, no. He's already playing daddy with his new fiancé and her two kids. I was going to say, this guy from my childhood. The one that I told you about, he was my first crush. I swore I was in love, and now I don't even know what the word means. Anyway, he reached out yesterday, on *Instagram*," Ella thrilled.

V raised her thin eyebrows high and pulled her lips to one side, staring openly.

"*Mhm* girl, you better not leave out a single detail tonight."

Ella nodded her head as she ladled a candlelight orange soup from a lapis blue cast iron pot, into two warmed bowls. She topped the squash soup with chopped chives, pumpkin seeds, and a drizzle of grapeseed oil. She then sliced a loaf of rustic French bread, while V poured the remaining pinot noir into new thin stemmed bowl-shaped wine glasses.

"Cheers to us, to Hózhó, to Christmas, and may we have a very merry night ahead of us!" Ella cheered warmly.

ooo

THE JOURNAL

December 15th, 1988

I T IS INTERESTING to me how the most ordinary of places become engrossing, only under extraordinary circumstances. A simple little mart beguiled, because of her, Sofia.

It's cold and dreary out tonight, miserable for most people, but not me. I needed to get out of the house. Space is hard to find in a full family home. I'm still not used to it. Liquor and smokes have been getting me through. I went to the mart earlier for a mild remedy. Parked on the side, and just as I got out, I stepped in the right pothole that splashed water up my jeans. The direction of wind against me, a trickle of rain against my cheek in just the right spot. The musty smell of wet on concrete hit me in just the right way. All of this drove me straight down memory lane. To freshman year, a couple of weeks before Christmas break…

When Sofia was less filled out, but just as beautiful. Just as dumb, but a lot more fun. We snuck out to buy beer from some seniors on the side of the little mart. We didn't *know any better and overpaid for the 6 pack by $5. We sat on milk crates behind the building, facing the open ballpark field we walked across earlier, to get there. She brought her dad's bottle opener; the beer tasted disgusting, but we chugged the bottles down, anyway. I wanted to get wasted and go look at Christmas lights with her. She wanted to go to Steve's party. He had invited her and not me. Steve told her his buddies got the blue stuff to play quarters. It didn't matter because we forgot what we wanted after we became so consumed with laughter between gulps. It was the first time that we had gotten drunk. I was still freezing in my neon windbreaker. But those eyes, Sofia's little planet eyes, had an irrevocably warming effect. A swirling yellowish orange lit up an atmosphere of possibilities for me. She can go from graceful to dorky in 5 seconds flat. I lost it when she got beer up her nose. Her snorting was out of control. It was equal parts loveable and hysterical. She wiped her animal print faux fur sleeves on her face, trying to hide the mess, but the wind and rain were picking up. Sofia was getting more wet and spreading an assortment of running mascara, rainwater, and beer around her pink cheeks. Her wet golden bangs piecey and flat against her forehead. She said I was lucky, because I'm the only one in the world who could ever see her like that. Sofia smashed her empty bottles on the pavement, and I copied her, like rebels without a cause. We ran across the ballpark field that connected to our neighborhood. Dying of laughter, holding hands for stability, and relishing in the wet chaos. Good times.*

Jackie interrupted this moment of my reminiscing. She pulled into the mart parking lot next to the truck. I stood there like a rock, my hands by my side, with the truck keys still in my hand. Jackie gave me a malicious grin and said, "I could grab you a bag for your head. I'd be embarrassed to go inside, too. Or you could just off yourself already."

ooo

MAPLE MAYHEM

December 18th, 2020

"**P**HEW! I AM overjoyed that you and Logan took this offer. It's about damn time you took a vacation, all those hard-working days, for an extended leave of absence with pay. Yes, boy," Charlie chanted.

"Definitely! I'm stoked, two months off. Feels like I hit the jackpot. They've been itching to get rid of me for a while," I laughed off.

"Don't I know, I've had to hear exactly that from Dan for years. If this year has taught us anything, it is that we have got to seize the day. We should celebrate living, every day, not just a few times a year. Kind of catch twenty-two, though. Y'all need to be *extremely* careful. You do not want what I had, by any means. And you need to abide by all the rules about the testing and what not. Michaels was ecstatic to have two young and healthy men to accompany them on this trip. He actually sounds happier about it, than when we were going. If it weren't for the fatigue, brain fog, and recovering, I would have invited you guys instead of replacing us. You and Logan are going to have a blast. Just make sure that you're aware of your surroundings out there. Just be *careful*. Hear me?"

"Absolutely, always. Am I going to get that information from Michaels still, about the letter?" I questioned with desperation.

Charlie's thick salt and peppered eyebrows raised. He scratched at his smooth and shaved chin. His skin, a clear, healthy warm brown.

It is *so* good to see him this way, after all that he has been through.

"That's what I also wanted to touch on. Had a *lot* of time to reflect on our talk. Son, I understand where you are coming from and I feel for you, I do. It can't be easy running every which way with daunting scenarios. But nothing has happened since the card. I don't believe that it *was* a genuine threat. Foggerton is small. Unfortunately, your mother's disappearance was the talk of the town for a while. It is an unsolved mystery, after all. Despite the coincidental circumstances, someone was just being a real, real asshole to you. Excuse my French. Nothing has come about it, and we want it to stay that way. I can't stop Michaels from talking to you about his experience with the murders. But for your mental health, I'd suggest enjoying yourself and not to seek the meaning of that note."

"Right, nothing has come about, best to leave it be," I lied.

"*Right*. Good, good, that's what I was hoping for. Gloria and I just want you boys to have a good time and return home safely," Charlie said, beaming back at me.

My smile faded. I rubbed my quartz tattoo on my wrist. The lines of black ink raised to the same height as my scar. I could feel my face heating and I wanted to mask the reason behind it. I tried to focus on the holiday music playing in the living room.

"*So*. Ms. Stella Russo-Redhouse? This year really is straight out of a scary movie. Truly horrendous, that poor girl. I remember when you two were inseparable at a time. Starting the Jelly Club and all. Y'all just ran around outside like geese and only came inside for supper," Charlie said, letting out a deep chuckle.

"I honestly still can't believe it, it's tragic."

"The positive is that she's alive and we'll continue praying for her. But, uh, Logan had mentioned that you reached out to her, naturally. Since you are going to California, I just wanted to let you know *why* they moved. Her mother, Ava, I brought her in for questioning when your mother disappeared. It wasn't a secret amongst the other parents that Ava despised your mother. She was some kind of jealous. Talk about small-town battle of the house moms here. Claire simply over-achieved all motherly duties. A neighbor saw Ava leaving your house that morning. She had sold your mother a pair of earrings from her business, Row Me Russo, which was uncharacteristic to make a house call. Nothing came of it, but the other moms wouldn't let it go that we questioned her. They hated her after that. I just didn't want to withhold anything else from that day and hope you can put a close to that chapter, finally," Charlie said.

"Wait," I began, interrupted by Logan.

He popped into my doorway with a candy cane sticking out of the side of his mouth.

"Yo! Lights are all up. You guys have to come outside!" he beckoned.

I reached forward and put my hand on Charlie's broad shoulder, parallel to mine.

Eager to leave the room as soon as possible, I changed course.

"Charlie, I appreciate the talk because you're right. I just gotta keep going."

A healthy Mr. Dawson smiled back at me as I followed Logan out.

ooo

Red, green, and clear Christmas lights outlined the white painted exterior. Clear lights drooped down, forming icicle shapes over the black decorative shutters that sandwiched the large picture window. The twinkling lights highlighted powdered snow that planted itself on each louver. Logan programmed the clear light strands over the windows to be continually lit, while the colored bulbs were on a slow flashing system. A few inches of fresh snow blanketed our yard, which made it simple for Logan to push wire stakes into the soft ground. Five small sets on both sides of the stone walkway. The sets had round plastic peppermint decorations secured to them with duct tape. He also lined the pathway with pre-lit red and white candy cane markers. They shone brightly; each at one-foot high.

"Bro, this is fire. But y'all are leaving soon, and who has to take it all down shortly after? Me," Devon complained.

"Yeah, yeah, better late than never. It's not even for us, it's for Dad and Gloria," Logan retorted.

I reached down towards the earth and scooped up a few inches of clean snow. Rotating and pressing my hands together, I formed the perfect snowball, packed without edges. Keeping my eyes on my target, I took aim.

"Uh oh, is that the fire alarm? Better get back to the kitchen, Dev," I teased as I pulled my hand back behind my head and pitched the ball of snow speedily at the center of Devon's apron. It smashed against his chest and crumbled down to the walkway.

"Ah! Aight, okay, okay, y'all watch out," Devon shot an empty threat.

Devon left us grinning behind him on the sidewalk as he jogged back up to the home, crossing his arms and shivering. He wore a Kelly-green polo under an olive cotton canvas bib apron, jeans, and untied tobacco-leather boots. His laces flailed against wet stone and dragged against the smooth white porch steps. Gloria and Charlie came out after he had reentered.

The couple had been born and raised in Monroe County, in a lakeside community just half an hour east from Foggerton. They had walked in snow to the same high school in their day, yet they couldn't tolerate leaving the house if it was below thirty degrees in the present. Dressed from head to toe in winter apparel, resembling walking sleeping bags. I could barely see an inch of their skin, with their matching white puffer coats that were zipped to the top over ugly Christmas sweaters and black slacks. Charlie wore a fuzzy red and white Santa hat, while Gloria had her coat hood secured on her head and pulled down towards her eyes. All of this for just a moment's glimpse.

"Oh, my heavens, Logan! The lights are beautiful, *just marvelous*! A white Christmas with my favorite red and white candy decorations," Gloria elated.

"Well done, son. This looks great. This might have been the craziest year yet, but you boys have put on one of the most wonderful Christmases that we have had together in some time!" Charlie said.

"Agreed love. And I'm sure it will look even *more* lovely in a few hours once it gets dark. Right now, I am freezing and would love a cup of cocoa," Gloria persisted.

"Let's go dear. Dev said he had some kind of moosh boosh thing for us to start," Charlie replied to Gloria.

The both of them scurried up the path. Gone as soon as they arrived. I turned my head to the left and said, "Dude, our house looks sick. You made it look like a retro candy land. Now Mrs. Cranston won't harp on us anymore."

"For sure, thanks for doing the strands on the porch railing. The icicle lights are tight," Logan poked.

"The easiest ones. Sorry bro, I just don't have that artistic eye," I replied with air quotes.

"What you got for dad is outstanding enough. What time is it?"

"Almost two, I'll go bring up dad and gloria's gifts."

"Cool, I'll find the bow to stick on his *Mirror* fitness box. If you could just lean it against the wall next to the tree," Logan replied.

I wiped my shearling moccasin slippers on the mat by the shoe rack, keeping them on through the house for the bare concrete in the basement. I got to the last step of the stairs and felt a tingling sensation on my cheeks; it felt just as cold as it was outside. The chill was protruding even through both my light gray Aran shawl collar cardigan and the red plaid button down underneath it. I twisted my head over my right shoulder, noticing that the chocolate-colored aluminum hopper window that faced the backyard was open at a 90° angle. I couldn't see any snow, but the wind drifted flurries in from the ground above me.

The afternoon sun broke into the basement, through the rectangular window facing the backyard. It revealed an active shower of dust from the wood ceiling and metal beams above. Our washer, dryer, and free-standing utility sink occupied the space in the left corner, diagonal to the basement steps. Fine powdered dirt coated the cardboard boxes, a few snowboards, and Logan's tripods for photography. They lined up against the unpainted brick wall. We have a series of miscellaneous canvas coverings thrown over additional storage that snaked around the back walk area. Christmas presents lined up against the unfinished frame of the stairway. Spiderwebs housed the four corners of the room, silky strands weaved, and intertwined with the rafters above.

"Dude, Logan!" I yelled up the stairs.

A few seconds later, Logan's dimpled smile appeared in the doorway by the hall.

"Yeah, Murph?"

"Did you know this window is open?" I implored.

"My bad, yeah. Can you close it? I turned the heat off to air out the entire house while you guys were grocery shopping earlier," he confirmed.

ooo

"These salmon creamed cheese appetizers are *divine*," Charlie said.

"Thanks dad, I'm glad you like them. This is an amuse-bouche, a palate opener. Try the salmon roe blini with your bubbly!" Devon shouted from the kitchen.

"Don't mind if I do," Charlie said, raising his prominent brows and bobbling his head as he leaned toward the coffee table.

Gloria, Charlie, and Logan sat comfortably on the black sectional sofa that faced the entertainment center, with their backs to Devon in the kitchen. They enjoyed their holiday celebration with laughter and debating which movies are the top Christmas films of all time. I retrieved the champagne bottle from the counter that Devon was offering to Charlie.

"Dude, your brown sugar glazed ham looks crazy good. Are you sure you don't need help with anything?" I offered.

"Nah man, thanks for offering though, *again*. I know you haven't played sheet music in a hot minute. Maybe you could get the mood going? Oh, actually can you bring that plate of cranberry brie bites over too?" he insisted, followed by a wink.

I lifted my thick eyebrows and said nothing. Dropping the tray before Logan's hungry eyes, I weighed my options if I wanted to make a fool of myself or not. I poured champagne for Charlie and Logan. Next, exchanging the champagne bottle for the hot cocoa on the coffee table. I passed it to Gloria at a sluggish pace.

The mallows crowded the surface, sugary liquid spilled from the sides. She's too distracted by the holiday feature film to notice.

My Yamaha upright piano served as a decorative piece instead of a recreational one. Placed against the wall between the entertainment center and the window that faced the front yard. The piano had more dust than human fingers to grace the surface of it, because I only played a few riffs here and there over the years. It didn't quite bring the same joy that it did when I was a child, but I kept it after my dad left almost a decade ago. It reminded me of my kind mom, who would wait for me after school every day by sitting on the leather bench and ready to play. She was always so enthusiastic to ask me what fun things I did or what I had learned. Even though I had nothing exciting to report to her, she always responded, like it was the highlight of *her* day. I couldn't give these keys up. It was the last I had of her, besides a few photos.

I unfastened the black football buttons on my cardigan, took it off, and set it down on the couch, next to Logan.

"Real talk, you playing? Damn, it *is* a good Christmas over here," Logan exclaimed.

"Baby, turn the movie down," Gloria said to Charlie.

"Murph! Okay! We are ready!" Charlie elated.

I smiled and prematurely took a bow for my new little audience.

Shit, I haven't played in a while.

Receiving a glass of champagne that Logan had handed me, I swallowed half the contents and sat down on the bench. I placed the glass on the windowsill to the right of me, at an arm's length away.

I opened the polished ebony fallboard, taking a deep breath in, and stretched my fingers. I sat up straight and played arpeggio. My right hand on the C chord and starting my left hand with C, E, and G. Moving the melody up to D. Back down to C, to F and repeating an open melody. My fingers flowed across the keys, effortlessly broken, but smooth. I imagined my mom sitting next to me, playing a *Silent Night* just like it was 2001 again. My peripheral vision caught the snow falling.

Perfect timing for a Christmas ambiance.

Finishing on a C note graciously, the decrescendo melody hummed as I held both hands down, then lifted off. And went straight into playing *symphony No. 9 in D minor* by *Ludwig van Beethoven*. My fingers played the keys while my mind replayed the memories of my mom explaining the significance of *Beethoven* to me, that this song represents the conquest of worldwide brotherhood against conflict and fear. She always did that in our lessons, sprinkled some kind of deeper meaning in them. A dose of ethics with our joy or pains. I turned around to see if my spectators had fallen asleep.

Charlie, Gloria, and Logan stared at me from the couch. Devon viewed from a standing position behind them. They all had a sort of gleam in their eyes, head cockeyed.

"Oh, um, well, I just thought I'd start with a simple piece first," I said.

"That was magnificent Murph, magical," Gloria whispered.

The four of them clapped for me. A laugh escaped my lips as I peeled back a wholesome smile in response.

"Dude, that was sick. Aight everyone, head on over for prayer because dinner is hot on the table!" Logan exulted.

I licked my lips, turning back to face the piano, and closed the fallboard. I grabbed my glass to finish the rest of it. Movement outside caught my attention just as I tipped my head back for a sip. Someone stood outside, staring at our home. Standing tall and statuesque, behind a soft mask of trickling snow, with their hands placed inside their dark parka pockets. Dark face mask, sunglasses, maybe light skinned. I put my hand up to wave. They backed up and side-stepped behind the leafless maple tree that was planted on the verge between the sidewalk and street. They ominously teased about their presence. A winter parka tail peaked out from one side of the shaggy bark of the thick trunk.

I leaned closer to the window to see who it was, but the snow was coming down harder now. I stared hard, trying not to blink, remaining focused. I banged my forehead on the glass. A loud thud brought everyone's attention back to me. I speedily twisted my head to the right, facing a slew of concerned expressions.

"Dang, Murph, take it easy with the bubbles, huh?" Devon snickered.

"Yeah, my bad," I said.

I huffed an impatient breath out and brought my gaze back to the front yard. The coat was out of sight. I couldn't see any sign of the visitor now.

Did I have a greater-sized audience than I had thought?

ooo

DAMNING DEBRIS

December 20th, 2020

ELLA FIDGETED WITH a pen between her middle finger and thumb. Wondering what it would be like to be Lia, so carefree and rebellious. To let go and not have to worry, live in the moment, and reap the repercussions later on. She leaned her head back on the lightly cushioned sofa frame. The Frenchie in her lap squirmed and stretched his short legs. He opened his pushed in snout to yawn, exposing a tiny red tongue, while his bat ears remained upright. Ella lovingly read Pinot's bulging blue eyes. She beamed and wondered how nice it would be to just nap off the qualms of the world. Instead, Ella is forced to face her self-defense killing with dignity, while helping others and preparing to move. Her holiday list was overwhelmingly at three pages long, with only five days until Christmas. And her packing list had grown to six pages long with only a few weeks to go.

"What? Don't look at me like that. I was just taking a break," Ella spoke to Pinot.

She scratched the white patch on his chest, he snuffled back at her. Ella picked Pinot up and placed him on the abstract cream and brown carpet. She got up to mirror her dogs' actions and stretched her legs, dressed in olive-green linen overalls. An inch of skin showed between the long-sleeved white crop top and loose-fitting trouser bottoms, as she raised her arms towards the ceiling. Ella strode to the front door to retrieve a thick navy rope dog leash off of a chunky pegged hook from the pine wood entryway wall shelf.

"Come on Pinot!" she yelped to her dog.

Pinot raced from the couch side to Ella's feet. She secured a festive red plaid harness around his body and clipped the leash lobster claw to his harness. Ella pulled out a pair of short and tan *UGG* boots from the bench cubby and slid into them. They used the elevator to get down to her gallery/studio on the first floor. Ella spoke to her dog as if he were a human, explaining that she would take him out for a walk after they heard from Auntie Lia.

"*Hey* sister from the same mister!" Lia answered on the first ring.

"*Hi*, did you get my texts?" Ella questioned impatiently.

"I did, yeah. I just figured it would be better to chat about things in person. But, now that we're talking, I think it would be outstanding to live there with you. If you *really* wanted me to? I thought I pissed you off, though."

"I'm not *pissed*. Confused and hurt, yeah. Why haven't you reached out to me? It's been over a week," Ella pressed.

Lia breathed heavily into the phone. "I felt, I *feel* responsible for the massacre."

"What! What are you talking about? Unless you sent racist psychopaths to rob the bank, I don't understand where this is coming from or why?"

"Well... I can't believe I'm saying this out loud. I wished that you would have something incredibly inconvenient happen to you. But nothing, to this magnitude," Lia whined.

"Seriously Lia? What do you mean," Ella peeved as she hooked Pinot's leash to the eyebolt screw on the register counter and put Lia on speaker mode. She tucked the cell phone into her linen bib pocket against her chest. Ella awaited Lia's explanation and cleared her throat audibly. A young woman walked by with three large shopping bags and peered into the storefront. Ella power-walked to the window to lower the six-foot wide black out shade, to avoid being seen in this frustrated state.

"Okay, I know this sounds so messed up. You just have this *artsy chic, wine country wedding, humble hottie thing*, going on. You boast of success without a posse or any help. Of course, I had green *Jell-O* thoughts. I'm the loser who lives with five college kids and has to work on the edge of the county line. Why? Because I crashed into a freaking apple orchard on Highway 12. And I'm the one who gifted you the boots! This *is* all my fault, I'm humiliated," Lia explained, her voice fast but wavering.

Ella paced the interior of the well-lit room.

"Whoa, whoa, Lia. First, those boots *saved* my life. I wouldn't be here today if it weren't for them. And did you forget that I canceled my wedding? My fiancé cheated on me. Depression in quarantine. I survived a bank massacre. Now, I have to move. I'm not exactly a trophy right now."

"Yeah, I mean *no*, I didn't forget. Those were bitter resentments from the past. I just had a guilty feeling that my negative projection came true!" Lia wept.

Ella laughed, a forced and raspy cackle. She threw her hands up in comic relief.

"Alright Lia, stop. Just stop. I'm not superstitious like you and dad. And I am livid. Because instead of having you here when I got home from the hospital, you've been avoiding me. You can't believe in this crap," Ella pressed harshly.

"Yes, I believe in this stuff. If it wasn't me, it has to be the painting. Ella, listen to me. Things like this, just don't *happen*. I guess in twenty-twenty anything goes, but you're like all over the internet. Smash the freaking painting already!" Lia pleaded.

Ella groaned noisily. She rolled her eyes hard; her patience met its limit. She walked straight to the back wall, where her father's gifted painting hung. She closed her eyes and reached out ahead of her. Opening her eyes and scowling, she lifted the frame off its hook, holding it at an arm's length. She admired the intricate details, the turquoise, ochre, white, black, and steely hues. They formed a Mother Earth motif, a rainbow, sacred mountains, and prayer feathers.

Turning to face Pinot, who was now fast asleep across the room, Ella assured herself that he was a safe distance away from her.

"Are you there? You can't deny that something caused this!" Lia squeaked.

Flinching as she lifted the frame a little above shoulder height, Ella pushed her thumbs forward to align the back of the frame to run parallel with the floor. She released her grip and surveyed the fall.

CRACK!

The Navajo sand painting smashed against the dark hardwood floor; glass shattered inside of the frame. Ella let out a deep sigh of relief once she heard cheering on the other end of the phone line. She giggled, joyous and silvery from the adrenaline.

"*See*, didn't that feel good? I told you it completes the healing when you destroy it. Tsk, throwing off your own balance by leaving it as a display piece," Lia shouted.

"It did a little. But don't blame what happened to me, on yourself. Those men were predators. This is my philosophy. One could look at the grains of sand in an hourglass with desolation, wishing that time would slow, for their last days in a hospice with family. While someone else is wishing for the sand to hurry through one bulb to the other, with high hopes that their son will soon return from Afghanistan. The sand moves without us. Pain is perspective and wishing is wasteful," Ella recited.

"Whatever tomato, potato!"

"That is definitely not the saying, but okay," Ella retorted.

"K, I still believe in superstitions and reading the signs. Anyway, now that the air is cleared, I have to get packing cause we're going to be roomies!"

"Yeah, but no negative vibes at the house, okay? Be proud of who you are, you are beautiful and very talented, it isn't a competition. I love you," Ella replied, calmly.

"I understand. I'm sorry, love you too. Have you heard from mom? She'll be back soon, but I want to make sure everything will be *Gucci* for dinner."

"No, she's probably swamped. V and I are going to go decorate her house. I'm making her dinner and putting it in her freezer. It's a shame that mom is eating alone. She has stressed me out about not wanting to get sick, yet she's the one who's flying around... You two are exhausting. And I already know that you want tofurkey and sparkling water," Ella delivered.

"You are on top of it! We are a pain in the derrière, but you love us! She's probably just hella busy. I'll let you go, and I'll see you soon!"

"Sounds good, Ti amo."

"Ciao, amore," Lia said before hanging up.

ooo

DÉJÀ BOO

December 22ⁿᵈ, 2020

MY HEART IS racing, palms sweaty. I never know how to lead the conversation, and so many things get lost between two twisted pairs of copper wire.

Please don't pick up, please don't pick up.

"Hello?" Ella answered.

"Hey Stella, oh, Ella, it's Oisín," I stammered.

"Hi, you. You're silly, I have caller ID. I'm happy you called, I thought you might not."

"No, *no*. I've just been packing, and we've been doing early Christmas stuff here. It's great to hear your voice, after all this time. Sounds like you lost the Upstate New York nasal tone, no more *faww-gerton*. But still raspy and pretty."

"Aw thank you, but you don't sound nasally. Just deep and manly," Ella praised.

Why is such a simple compliment making my stomach soar?

"Ah, thanks. Um, so, that's dope about you moving to the beach. I'm really looking forward to seeing Cali *and* you," I said.

"Me too! After what happened, I'm just excited to hit the refresh button. And it's a perfect time that you guys are visiting. Our county is finally in the orange tier. Just don't catch the *Corona* on your way here," Ella said apprehensively.

"No way, well, not *no way*. I still can't believe everything that Charlie went through. We are going to be careful with social-distancing, masks, testing, the whole deal. I feel the same though, like our trip is a reset, sort of. Logan is so stoked to see you again. He was joking about getting the band back together," I laughed off.

I listened to Ella giggling for a moment. Jesus, why am I getting aroused?

"That's cute, I wouldn't mind hearing you play *Alicia Keys* again. Or *Beethoven* would be heavenly. V mentioned that there is a piano at the house, though I'm not sure what shape it is in," Ella hinted.

"Ah, so you still remember our talent show gig. I could do that. If you would do your modern dance thing from the show," I bargained and chuckled.

"Alright, Oisín Murphy, we have a deal. Your trip sounds amazing. I'm excited for you," Ella said.

"Me too, yeah," I responded, short.

I just want her to keep talking. Her voice sounds like a velvety hot chocolate on a snowy winter's day. Inviting, comforting, and sexy. Melting all at once.

"So, what are you guys doing for Christmas?" I asked.

"I have to get groceries for our dinner soon. I'm cooking dinner for V and Lia at my place. We don't celebrate Christmas in the religious sense, but V does. I'm also preparing a meal to put in my mom's freezer for when she gets home. And then

I have to set up for *Zoom*, so we can say hey to our nonna in Bergamo, Italy. We'll do a short video-call to our dad and other grandparents, as well."

"Oh nice! Sounds cool, but also like you've got your hands full. So, wait, where are your mom and dad?" I asked.

"Sorry, I thought I told you, my dad moved to Navajo Nation when we were little. And my mom, she's actually *there*. I mean, in Foggerton. I know it's pretty desolate in good ole Foggerton in the winter. But with business closed, it's worse, the product is sitting there. My mom is shipping the spring collection home and then moving the rest into storage until, who knows when. She had to be there for the two-week quarantine rule, I guess. But will be back in a few days," Ella replied.

"Oh, cool, yeah. Kind of embarrassing. I forgot that she still had her business downtown. I guess that shows how little I've invested in jewelry. Um, okay, well, I'll let you go. Maybe we can video chat when I get to Florida?" I insisted eagerly.

"That sounds perfect, I hope you have a great night," Ella said warmly.

"Have a good nigh-I mean enjoy your day, bye Ella," I stammered.

"Buh bye, Oisín," Ella replied. I could hear her giggling before she hung up.

Sitting at my desk, I set my phone down and propped my elbows up on the surface. I ran my fingers through my medium-length hair and exhaled. With my head in my hands, I pored over my cell phone.

Should have called her sooner...

"What's got you all smiley, Murph?" Logan grinned from the doorway.

I jerked my head back and put my hands up.

"Uh, oh, just got off the phone with Ella. She actually just sent a photo."

Wow, I have no words.

I leaned in my chair towards Logan to let him judge the selfie. Ella was smiling sweetly with a large and naked mouth. No pouting, no duck lips, or tongue out. Just a genuine smile as she stared deeply into the camera lens with pretty eyes, hazelnut, gold, and green. Staring straight into the viewer's soul. Her face, square with a glowing complexion, and a straight and narrow nose. Long, mocha-glazed straightened hair ran past her shoulders, to a length beyond the dimensions of the photo. The selfie also revealed that she wore a black fuzzy V-neck sweater, her cleavage was prominent.

Innocent enough, but sexy as...

"*Dayum*, that's little Stella? *Hmm*, okay, you forget that hype I put on your self-confidence because she out of your damn league," Logan teased with one eyebrow raised.

"Shit, yeah she is, huh?" I said in defeat, tugging at my unruly and long beard.

"Nah man, shut up, you look like if *Jake Gyllenhaal* had sex with *Jake Gyllenhaal* and then one of the *Jake Gyllenhaal's* had a baby," Logan heckled.

He laughed so hard to himself that he put one hand on his flexing stomach muscles and the other on my broad shoulder.

"What does that even *mean*?"

Not amused by the comparison. I still chuckled at Logan's contagious laugh.

"Hey, I'm not ashamed to say the man is a good-looking dude. Yo, you want to hear this joke I have for when we get to Florida? So, a priest walks in a bar, followed by a big ass alligator-" Logan started, but I put my hand up.

"No, I don't," I said, shaking my head, but still laughing.

"You sure you don't want to come with us? I have a feeling that Dev is about to wife Vanessa up, always snatching my ladies when he comes back," Logan said. He tilted his head back and rolled his large brown eyes.

"No thanks man, you guys have fun. I'm just going to pick up a garbage plate for dinner and finish organizing. Remember, we're leaving tomorrow," I replied.

"Duh, dude, how could I forget? Later!" Logan shouted and exited my room.

ooo

Halfway through reaching for the game controller, I hesitated and instead pulled my phone back out to look at Ella's photo. I'm going to lighten my load of clothes packed and get some fresh shirts in Florida. I have to up my game, though I don't think I stand a chance. It's worth trying. Because she makes me *feel* something, even from the brief communication. A youthful flattery. It makes me think back to the days where we would climb the wooden playground, sneak out to the woods after dinner to run around, swim in the bay, and practice music for the Jelly Club at Logan's. Prank calling people, monkey bar contests, playing flashlight tag at night in the woods. To trick or treating and trading all my *Milky Way* chocolates for her *AirHeads* and *Fun Dip* candy. Things changed the year before the Russo-Redhouse family moved away. I saw Ella differently. I acted differently around her. *We all did.* More aware, sort of protective, but interested. Now here she is, a breathtaking grown woman with a career in California. But tragically, also at the center of heroic but horrifying headlines. I should probably practice our song, because at this moment, the title is all too relatable now.

The sun is long gone by seven in the evening. I closed the shades and turned the Christmas tree lights on. I searched the internet for the sheet music to *Fallin'* on my cell phone. Such a solid song with soul. Although I'm grasping that we had no clue what the lyrics meant as kids. I felt a flutter in my stomach, thinking of Ella again. I opened the fallboard and straightened my back, placing my right hand where it needed to be for the first three-note chord.

BANG! BUZZING HUMM!

Lights out.

"What the hell?" I barked.

Light from my cell phone emitted a glow over the corner of the living room. I turned and pulled back the curtain shade to see if our neighbors had power. We have no streetlights on our road. But all the neighbors had their regular interior lighting and exterior holiday lights lit.

"Cool," I said, scoffing.

Meow.

A scuffling and short cat cry forced me to lurch my head back. I held up my cell phone and turned the flashlight mode on.

Was that in the hallway or basement?

I took a deep breath in and contemplated calling Logan before investigating. He would just explain to me I need to man up and check the circuit breaker in the basement.

Could that have been Stew, the stoop cat, finally?

"Stew, kitty, kitty," I muttered as I pat my jean pant leg.

Silence.

I breathed out quietly. My eyesight adjusted to the outlines of the black lounge chair and long sectional couch, to the dining furniture and empty kitchen. Our neighbor's holiday lights flashed red, to white, and back to red. It glowed through the kitchen window that faced the side of their home, forming a line of light down the main hallway. I hadn't noticed exactly *how* bright their lights were before; it's never been this dark in here.

"It's cool. I'm cool," I mumbled to myself.

I quietly moved from the piano to the entertainment center.

MEOW!

Oh shit. Human or cat? Am I hearing things?

I hurriedly walked on the balls of my feet to my bedroom, the first door on the right. Nothing weird in my L-shaped living space. I scanned my light over my desk and pulled the drawer open to find my favorite river knife. My father gave it to me when I was in high school, and I've kept it ever since. It wasn't in its usual spot. I flashed my light towards the hallway as I backed up to get my baseball bat under the bed.

Creak.

Oh, hell no.

I grabbed the bat and bolted towards my bedroom door frame. Swiftly exchanging the bat to my right hand and phone to my left. Stoic, I tried to determine my next move. Attempting to listen for further movement in the house, but the hammering from my heartbeat in my ears was deafening.

Is this the point where I call police? Or am I overreacting?

I bolted outside of the door frame and into the hall, looking left, looking right. The blinking red light in the silent hallway made the hairs on the back of my neck stand. With my back to the wall, I stepped towards the right, making my way past the primary bedroom on the other side, past the guest bedroom, past the garage door and shared bathroom. The basement door was wide open, I proceeded down the steps.

I'm working with three balls in the air. One, not trying to make a sound. Two, listening for noise. Three, racking my brain if the damn door was open or shut earlier.

I've never been good at juggling.

A cold sweat broke out on my temple, sending an icy drip of paranoia to its death, splattering on the old wooden step next to my foot.

It's cold again, like the other day.

The hair on my arms rose to the occasion, as I continued to hold a batting position with my phone secured to the butt of the bat. With a heavy step, I lowered to the last plank of stair. It let out an obnoxious creaking noise, making me boil over. I crept around the corner and flashed my light up to the open window.

The most terrifying version of déjà vu.

A wintry night air rode at the back of a howling clamor through the exposure in the basement wall. I pushed the window hard, closing it and locking it. My heart was throbbing in my ears still. I struggled to listen for *anything*. Mind clouded.

A foul odor invaded my nostrils. Burning my brain when I attempted, poorly, to sniffle up the running snot. The smell was so strong that it instilled a bitter taste in the back of my mouth, making me want to hurl.

I flashed my phone towards the back of the basement where the breaker box lived. I worked faster now; I can't stand it down here any longer. Pulling open the gray-blue panel, I moved the switch all the way to its 'off' position, back to 'on'. I heard a few beeps and click noises from upstairs. I'm assuming that it is the smoke detectors and appliances resetting. Just as the lights came on, my heart rate came down.

The taste of dread dissolved, but the unwholesome rotten cheesy eggs aroma remained.

I rounded the corner to head back upstairs when I saw *him*. Orange and white fur peaked out from the side of the washer, underneath the utility sink.

"*No*, buddy, Stew. Did you come through the window?" I whimpered.

I ran to his side, throwing down the bat and bending before him. His hair was damp, cold, and matted down.

"Buddy?" I wavered.

He faced the back wall with his back to me. I gently pulled at his belly to bring him out. A wetness forced my hand back. The sight of a deep red liquid dripping from my fingertips like honey sent me rocking backwards. I scooted further towards the base of the stairs. Terror sucked my breath away.

"Stew, *noo. God no,*" I cried, choking back tears.

Fixated on the deceased cat. *Our* cat, murdered. The view held me captive and misty-eyed until it didn't. Something shiny reflected from the overhead lighting.

I got back on my feet to inspect. It's my river knife, from my dad. Someone placed it beside Stew's poor body. My hands shook as I retrieved my knife and threw it into the white utility sink. Steadying my breath, I turned the faucet on. I painfully surveyed Stew's blood washing away from my hand, the stream of it diluted in the sink, from a rusty deep crimson to a soft pink, disappearing into the drain. I grabbed a thirteen-gallon trash bag from the surface of the dryer. And carefully pulled Stew's lifeless body into the bag, gently placed my knife inside with him and tied it. The smell petrified me, seasoned with the saltiness from my running tears and snot.

No human could have fit through the window, perhaps a small child. This is my knife, but I could never hurt a soul, neither could the guys. I'm trying to be logical, but this isn't possible. None of this makes sense. And poor Stew, this beloved cat suffered at the hands of someone. Because of me?

It became an out-of-body experience, watching myself covering my mouth and nose, to lugging the plastic bag upstairs. Without regard to any outside matter or intrusive thoughts. My emotions possessed my body, the overwhelming grief for Stew replaced previous fear...

"I'm so sorry, Stew. I'm so sorry," I repeated, between fretful snivels as I lowered the shiny black bag to the bottom of our garbage can, outside.

ooo

THE JOURNAL

December 24th, 1988

MERRY XMAS EVE to me.

I've been able to pull up my grades by doing the work for the both of us instead of just trading. I'm sitting at a pathetic 2.8, C average. It's better than the scoring that I brought upon myself earlier in the school year. Rejoice all unholy ones. It is finally winter break and tonight was radical. It reminded me of simpler times with my mother and father. When I was gifted toys, dominoes, and advent calendars with pictures behind the boxes. That only lasted so long. Father gifted me ravishment and gifted mother with a bullet to her head. That's what they said. A bullet from father's gun penetrated her skull. No soot in her lungs. They concluded it was a murder-suicide. My offering was a smoldering and fiery end for him, paid with his own cash, so we're even.

Colombo Xmas tree is massive and drowning in silver tinsel and oversized foil decorations. By the looks of it, you'd think that a hundred kids live here. But no.

All the wrapped boxes, festive bags, and colorful baskets are all just for Sofia and Gianna. It's no surprise what lives inside the packages. The girls circled every single item in the Argos catalog. Mr. Colombo flipped through the TV guide like it was a novel, sipping his egg nog between pages. Mrs. Colombo made us hot cocoas; Gianna was already scarfing down a chocolate basket dessert with berry cream. She's going to be a spaz soon. Still, she's pretty tolerable now. I only got each person one gift, two for Sof, they opted to open mine tonight as their Xmas eve gifts. I stole Gianna a new video game for her master system. The game is strategic to keep her at bay and she totally freaked for it.

Sofia gushed over the leather skirt that I bought for her from Woolworths. She liked it more than mother's Akoya pearl necklace. That gift made her blush. She rejected it with pursed lips and forced a smile. I'm not offended. She's told me a bazillion times that her cheer bear friends are all about 'the ropes of faux' right now, that she wants to look hot, not like a librarian. As if anyone will ever make that mistake. Why women care about pearls so much is beyond me, it's an organic gem bred from death. Mrs. Colombo informed me that pearls are actually "bad omen" as gifts. That they bring the wearer misfortune unless the receiver counters the act with a dime or payment. Cool. If I knew that was a superstition that people believed in, I would have tied the strand with a red ribbon and hung it up in Jackie's locker. I could have broken the locker mirror too, just for extra gits and shiggles.

Funny enough, Mrs. Colombo has no problem holding onto Sofia's gifted necklace for safe keeping. I know she knows what they are worth. She put them on display in her vanity cabinet. Whatever, I don't give a rat's ass about them. They've been driving me crazy, actually. Every dream, there they are. It's as if mother is screaming from the grave at me to get rid of her necklace. Nope!

Even if Mrs. Colombo pawns them, it isn't a loss. I've got dough coming my way. She loved the lace tablecloth that I picked out, it's all the rage now, double brownie points for me. Good riddance to the shitty old-fashioned floral display that reminds me of mother's choice of décor.

After the girls ripped through their presents, Mr. Colombo handed me a wrapped replica clock of Mr. Rossi's sculpture at Eat O'clock for me. It isn't multiple feet wide or sculpted by a famous artist, but I dig it because it's gnarly that Sofia told them what I like. She thought of me. I accepted it without a trivial show to Mrs. Colombo.

I've become quite the actor; Shakespeare would clap like a mother... See, a clock is a gift that also brings bad luck. I fantasize about time, it's everything around us. We exchange our time for valuables, for sex, for family, for friends. But a clock is a bad luck symbol that time is running out. To gift that to someone is to imply exactly that. Scrumptiously sinister, something that I know Mrs. Colombo knows nothing about. For one, she gifted her husband a watch for Christmas, and she loves the shit out of him. It left me to laugh off that one alone. Win some, lose some.

Winning... is acing a series of improvised impressions of having new dog allergies. So now, Fido stays outside sometimes. They let him sleep in the heated garage at night on his dog bed.

Visited John earlier too, brought him some of Mrs. Colombo's ginger fruit cake and spritz cookies. I bought him the new R.E.M. cassette. I didn't steal it. I don't pinch on gifts for the dude. We got into an argument, though. He still thinks I'm "suckling off the teet of soon-to-be-betrayal." He's just jealous and rightfully so because I've got it made right now. He lectured we are too shitty to join the pristine for long. I had to disagree. I explained to him we can do so much more than that, we can soar far above them in the right conditions.

For the first time, I concluded my dispute with a proverb; it charred my lips but served my argument well. (Even a broken clock is right twice a day.)

Things are looking up for me, for us, he'll see. And besides, I'm getting claustro-phobic here, looking forward to jamming out with him at the cabin. John will quit his bitching once we get there. Just one more night of crippling jingle bell a ring a ding, donkey dongs, sugar high, nutcrackers, and spice.

ooo

BREAKING RESOLUTIONS

January 6th, 2021

P OP MUSIC BLARED over the electric car speakers. V nodded her head and swayed her shoulders as she steered the wheel left and then turned it to the right, trailing the winding road at a furious speed, until she reached a stop sign.

"You are kind of scary when you drive," Ella nervously laughed.

"Oh, sorry darlin' I don't get to do this back in Woodsberry. Especially with the autopilot mode. You should see me without a passenger, slower than a Sunday afternoon," V replied with a wink.

"Right, okay, I'm assuming that means *not* slow in V talk?"

V shot Ella another quick wink in response, her green eyes twinkled. She peeled out from the abandoned fork. They continued along the road where sky-high eucalyptus trees formed a tunnel over the road. Ella stared up through the sky roof, admiring the blue backdrop just past the long, slender, oval-shaped leaves. She could smell the minty, camphor-like scent. It sent her stomach spiraling in every direction. Her mind cleared, and she felt a building sense of gratitude.

Bonnes Bay, a picturesque and old-fashioned town along California State Route One. Ella and V drove past a few quirky art shops, a deli and ice cream shoppe named Ocean Scoops, a bakery called Cake Chest, and a single gas station. All of which have long since lined the one-road town of Bonnes. V's family vacation home lives on the eastern side of Bonnes harbor, an aged base for fishing boats, locals, and visitors alike. It faces the Pacific Ocean, where the official State Marine Mammals steer themselves. The gray whales seemingly move weightlessly through frigid waters, in a vertical direction with their fin and lower bodies. Unlike the majestic beasts, tourists have migrated to the area in the more recent years. Travelers visit from afar during the summer months to stand at Hell's Point, hoping to catch a glimpse of the whales. Only to be disappointed, because the migration season to watch gray whales, is January.

"Welcome to 1604 Silverstein Drive!" V gushed.

She shook her short ponytail, red hair swaying from side to side, mirroring her shoulder movement. V turned right and parked in the two-car driveway off the secluded, dead-end road. Ella politely smiled. Her eyes remained plain, staring ahead at the dark garage door. She considered that this living-situation might be a further reach from society than she first expected.

The pair stepped out of the car into fifty-degree weather accompanied by ocean air. Ella wore blue jean short shorts, a beige high-neck tank top under a long brown plaid and wool jacket. A coconut-colored beanie with a fuzzy pom-pom stretched over Ella's head and silky, straight hair. She took in the exterior, observing the tall Italian cypress trees bordering the front and sides of the home. Displaying a very twenty-twenty aesthetic with a six-foot distance between each tree. Ella revered them as both lovely and haunting. Tall, dark peppercorn fencing ran behind the trees along both sides of the house. From the top of the hill, she could see that they leveled the fence to the sandy beach below, resembling stair steps. Her brows relaxed as she admired the privacy of the copper and cedar-clad home. Appreciating that it also wasn't loud in appearance, blending well with the natural shades of its surroundings. Built well, anchored to the hillside by a galvanized steel frame, and protected with ample privacy barriers. She listened to the waves crashing below as the wind kissed her cheeks, leaving a touch of salt.

"Miss Ella. *Yoo-hoo*, are you coming?" V sang.

Ella rushed to meet her at the front door. Her checkered slip-on shoes made no noise on the driveway to the stone path that cut through a small grassy front yard. She pulled her coconut beanie off and stepped in the doorway after V.

Her eyes widened.

"Yippee! I get to give you one of my one-star tours!"

"What? Why one?" Ella probed, grinning.

"Mhm, because I don't give tours. I just stage, list, and lock the key at the front."

Ella giggled and shook her head.

"First, *wow, wow, wow*. I mean, from the outside, you'd never know. This place is decked out, like literally, on a hill, in front of the ocean. What would you even need to say?" Ella elated.

"*Right*, miss, that's what I'm saying. So, the two other homes on this road are unoccupied at the moment. The one neighbor that I know, she's a single mom, real nice. I phoned her the other day to ask if her and her son were back. She said they are quarantining in Sausalito. She may come around, but I highly doubt it. So, you three are going to have the entire block to yourselves. You look around, while I get your surprise from the refrigerator. I'll meet you upstairs!"

Clip, clop, clip, clop.

The noise from V's chunky vegan leather boots made Ella freeze before entering. Blinking rapidly, she held onto the doorway casing. She pulled her breathing necklace out from under her top. She took a deep breath in through her nose, filling her belly with air. She gently exhaled through the device for a full eight seconds to aide the oncoming panic.

"Oh shit. Darlin', I'm sorry I didn't think," V apologized.

V took her boots off where she stood and walked them over to the front door. She placed them in one of the shoe cubbies built into the wall, under the staircase.

"No, no, V, really I'm fine. Sorry to hold up the show," Ella said hurriedly.

Squinting, V closed her mouth and pulled one side of her peach lips towards her ear as she cocked her head.

"You know what, you'll be able to keep these babies in good shape, if you ask your guests to wear slippers or flats on them instead. That's what this wall cubby is for. It's the least any of us can do for you, Miss Ella."

Without waiting for a response, V flashed a contagious smile at Ella and bounced back towards the kitchen in her socks.

A reassured Ella put her necklace back inside of her top. She tucked her shoes into the wall next to V's boots. Taking another deep breath in, she walked through the coastal-chic entryway. Beneath her feet, a light and dark quarter-sawn sycamore flooring. Above her head was a massive bronze lantern-shaped chandelier with four electric candelabra's. Seduced by the luminescence, Ella continued towards the open living area. She passed a bathroom, the garage entrance, and the staircase to her right. There was a vertical wood and metal wine rack enclosed by a glass case to her left. The white walls remained moderately naked, except for sporadic oversized mirrors with identical distressed mocha brown wood frames. She calculated the amount of work that was in store for her. A myriad of natural light shone through the windows that faced the ocean. Her stomach fluttered at the thought of watching an ocean sunset every night from the living space. Floor-to-ceiling sliding doors centered the wall with beige gauze shades drawn up to the ceiling above them. The open kitchen facing the living room reminded her of her previous home, except on a *much* grander scale.

She continued to observe the area, noticing a flawless baby grand in the left corner of the living room. It stood a little over five feet with a rich tiger mahogany veneer, highlighting a reddish-brown finish. She twirled around to gawk at the kitchen, which ran the long way parallel to the beach. V was fixing something up at the counter, but Ella couldn't tell exactly what from where she was standing. She admired the blooming white orchid flowers on the marble island. Ella twirled back around and grazed her fingertips over the stark white couch sheet. Another couch cloaked in white sat parallel to the front wall, a sofa armchair on the side of it. A four-by-four Navajo white tufted ottoman centered the room, in front of the large couch, with a wood inlet tray in the middle, serving as a coffee table. V had placed sailing books, a passionate purple orchid duo, and a stack of wood with brass anchor coasters on the tray. A porcelain lined ventless fireplace positioned against the right wall, filled with driftwood logs and copper crushed glass. Next to that, there was a wide brown leather lounge chair and paired ottoman in front of it.

Now at the glass doors, Ella observed the narrow deck that runs the width of the house. Her eyes lit up when she saw the gray stone jacuzzi spa to the right. Two terracotta planters with beach succulents sat on each side of the spa steps. Long, straight aluminum stairs centered the deck that dropped to waterfront access. She could make out a person about a quarter mile away, walking along the edge of the water. They kept their head down, dressed in all black. Ella thought to herself that they must have a rough day to have walked down this far. She learned of the eight-mile walk north to the state park beach. Less than one mile south of the home, were dunes that stretch for miles.

"Voila lady! I made you this yesterday and wanted to make it look all purdy. Hey, did you even look at the second story?" V chirped.

"You should have shown me photos. This place is... bliss."

"Oh, I sent you the address. I assumed you would look it up right away."

"I didn't-oh *wow*, that is a gorgeous pro range with double ovens and red knobs. And the marbled backsplash, just sensational. This is like a kitchen for a professional chef! Sorry, it's stupendous. Are you sure I can legitimately live here?" Ella shrieked.

"I'm so happy that you like it, don't be silly. So, I made you these choco-late-dipped strawberries because I know you love them. But Ella, try to eat some proper food, too. Here's my lunch charcuterie. I gathered all the components from Ocean Scoops. The meats and cheeses are local picks, prosciutto, genoa salami, brie with raw honeycomb on top and an aged goat's milk cheese. Then we have dried apricots, olives, marcona almonds, raspberries, and sea salt dark chocolate. Here are some water crackers and pear slices for a base. *And* I got your favorite, 2017 *Lancel Creek Vineyard* pinot noir to toast with. You've got me hooked on this whole 'forest floor meets succulent red berries' life. So, hello to the new year and new beginnings!" V cheered loudly.

She clinked her glass with Ella's before taking a sip.

"Distinctly heavenly," V proposed.

"You're seriously the best. I knew you would fall in love with this. But oh my god V, this is such a gorgeous spread. I can't believe you did all this. You'll have to let me know care instructions for these white marble countertops. The gray micro veins running through them are art on its own. I promise I will paint a few mind-blowing, custom pieces for your walls! I was actually going to do a dry January but, this definitely deserved your cheers," Ella said fast and raspy.

"Oh yeah, piece of pie. I have an entire binder for ya. Did you see the table yet? I thought you might appreciate it. Come, come! This is a repurposed ship wheel under the glass, made by a local artist. How cool is that?" V proposed, shaking her head with one side of her lip pulled upwards. "Hey maybe I can link you two up, huh?"

"It's more than cool. I love it. Everything about this home is an ocean lover's oasis. Ooh, about that, I was going to ask you... Would you mind if Oisín and his friend, Logan visited here. Maybe stay a night or two, they're traveling but taking rapid tests and extremely careful," Ella prompted.

She made a flat line with her lips, exposing her teeth.

"Someone is blushing... Of course, you can. You do not need to ask me if you can have house guests in your own home."

"I can't. This is not real. It's so wild to me," Ella responded, laughing.

"It's real, you're a comical creature. I wonder if your sister will have the same reaction, since she works out here, now."

"She's going to flip, there's no way she could be *that* used to the Naso Coast to overlook this extravagance. My texts keep failing to her by the way. I was trying to see how Pinot is. And I wanted to follow up with the craziness on the news, something about the United States Capitol. I think that there was a riot, inside the actual building, which would be horrifying, but I could have read it wrong. Is no service the con to this castle?"

"I think I got a notification about that too; my heart would break for this country if it's real. But, no on the con! The best service is upstairs, especially on the deck, outside of *your* gorgeous room. Come on lady, let's go. And you must elaborate on this little rendezvous that you have planned. Is the Logan fella cute?" V queried.

ooo

SAILING
SPECULATIONS

January 10th, 2021

TWELVE BALLERINAS STOOD around an enormous circle. It resembled a clock with taped Roman numerals to the floor, where each ballerina stood on, respectively. The women glowed under individual spotlights, while the surrounding areas remained inconspicuous. The women were expressionless, although I could make out that they had an attractive skin of various tones and shades, sand, sienna, umber, carob, bronze, porcelain, brown, ivory, beige, golden, ebony, and olive. Each ballerina raised their arms toward the dark sky above us. Dressed in black long-sleeve scoop-neck leotards, dusky seamed tights, and burgundy mesh wrap skirts with some kind of weave detail on the waistband.

Synchronized, they rotated their leg at the hip, turning out their satin black point shoe and knee outwards, away from the front of their bodies. They lifted and extended their legs to the side, pointing them at the middle of the taped clock design, where I sat cross-legged in a daze.

The ballerinas danced, flowing elegantly, balanced, and symmetrically. They were immaculately light on their feet, jumping from one foot to the other. Leaping and landing with strength and grace. Their muscular physiques were alluring. Although I watched them with curiosity, they kept their deep stare ahead of them, in whatever position they took on. The women never once acknowledged me.

I glowered at the starless sky. That had no end in sight. I could see a teeny white orb far away; it gradually grew in size as it got closer. The round white object coursed straight towards me. I scooted to the side to avoid it, forcing it to strike the solid black laminate flooring below me. It rebounded into the air directly after contact, back down to the floor again, and repeating the action with shorter airtime between each bounce. The final landing of the gem influenced the clock design to produce noise, though it wasn't a real functioning timepiece.

Tick, tick, tick. TOCK.

All the ballerinas halted at the sound of the *TOCK*.

Each ballerina faced me, with their feet turned outward, one foot sitting directly in front of the other, the tip of their pointe shoes extending past each heel. They had their arms raised above their heads and leaned faintly onward. Expressions transitioned dramatically to scowling at me, their eyes welled up, and they breathed profoundly.

"Do you remember the twelfth of December? Remember? Remember?" The elegant dancers screamed in question.

No sound escaped my lips. Instead, I picked up the gem from the black floor. The ballerinas began screaming harrowing cries. I dropped the pearl and protected my ears from the piercing calls. The somber sky released a thunderous clapping. It rained hundreds and thousands of white pearls down on all thirteen of us. The flooring directly below languidly melted; gravity pulled me down with it. The dancers lost their balance on the shifting floor. Their bodies loosened out of fifth position. And they wobbled backwards, falling onto their backsides. Now, with all of us affected by the liquefying laminate, I spotted them sliding towards me. The tip of their pointe shoes transformed into razor-sharp knives. Broad, long blades with straight edges. Only a few feet away from me now. I closed my eyes to await a bloody death.

ooo

"Dude, wake up, *wake* up," Logan whispered. He shook my arm.

The sensation of falling quickly replaced with jerking forward. I peeled my eyes open; Logan was hushing me with his finger to his mouth.

"Chill Murph, chill. You're going to wake up Michaels and Debbie. Damn, that tres leches dessert twisted my stomach, bro," Logan said deep but softly.

"Shit, sorry. I-aw damn it Logan, it's too cramped for the Godfarter to be aboard the *Hunter Thirty-Three*," I mumbled back at him.

The gross smell sent me into a gagging fit, reminiscent of the disturbing cat discovery. From the main cabin, I threw the quilt off my body, rolled off the blue single sleeper sofa and tip-toed across the hardwood flooring to the toilet compartment near the primary cabin. I closed the door gently behind me. The cleaner air in the reduced room eased the anxiety building. It wasn't enough to soften the anger that was triggered. Scrutinizing my reflection in the mirror, I frowned back at the dripping sweat from the unmodified growth of beard evenly distributed on my face. My thick brown eyebrows brought down low and close together. Blood vessels near the surface of my segmental heterochromia eye became enlarged and dilated. A result of not being able to sleep on this rocking vessel anchored at White Boulder Cove.

I can't escape this shit, even when out at sea.

Limited water on a yacht sailboat. Means limited showers. Turning on the multi-functional faucet-shower head, I splashed my face with warm water for a few minutes, attempting to wash away the saltiness from my burned lips and eyes. I glanced back at the fogged-up mirror and read.

Lies

It was written on the condensation, beyond that, a dark figure stood where I was standing. I backed up into the wall with wrath and clutched my face. Looking back at the mirror, I could see that it was just fog on glass and released a deep breath out.

My plain white tee-shirt was soaking wet, revealing half an inch of body hair through it, from my neck to my abdomen. I lifted the wet shirt off my body and placed it on the miniscule counter space. Pink sunburnt skin outlined my farmer's tan. My defined abdominals and v-cut muscles remained soft white to pink. I picked up the aloe gel on the floor and applied it to my brawny arms to lessen the sting. I quietly made it back to port side, where Logan was no longer.

ooo

I awoke again, this time because Michaels announced to Debbie that he was going to check the *Raymarine.*

We sailed around the southern Florida coast on a beauty of a yacht sailboat, the *Hunter 33.* It is a midsize cruiser, that is definitely one of the best for performance without lacking on luxurious interiors and space for the four of us. It has a teak wood interior that Michaels put a cherry finish on to keep it stylish. We've had plentiful seating, spaces to sleep, and have enjoyed the entertainment-ready cockpit. The aft primary room has a spacious double berth and abundant storage for Michaels and Debbie, while the forward cabin offers enough privacy for Logan.

It has a U-shaped galley with snow quartz *Corian* countertops, a two-burner range, an icebox, and a deep sink. I sleep in the salon where I pull apart the drop-down table. I have no complaints.

"Good morning Murphy! Sleep well?" Michaels quizzed, cheerfully.

"Oh yeah, pretty solid," I lied. I got up and put the table back together.

"We have some pastries in the galley if you want to chow down on those."

I nodded and opened the plastic container to retrieve a blueberry muffin and set it aside. I changed into pelican gray board shorts and a clean white tee-shirt before joining Michaels on deck.

A patchy, light haze cloyed the morning air, with only a few miles of visibility out. I lowered the fold down swim platform at the stern to sit on. Enjoying my muffin as I reflected on the past few weeks, my carved calves dipped in the water. It's already seventy-five degrees out, soon to be hotter. I scrutinized a rocky shoreline chock full of travelers, crowding in large groups, walking around in shorts and tee-shirts, collecting beach treasure. They explored an area close to where our stern ties are secured to metal spokes in a large boulder.

No wonder Charlie and Gloria *had* to pass on this trip. It was a necessity that we replaced them. Michaels needed a four-person crew, but the world is not quite back to ordinary. We are just desperate to make it so.

Water ripples escaped me with each kick of my foot in the turquoise coastal waters below. My body rocked gently in accord with the *Hunter 33*, over the littoral zone. I put my wireless headphones in and played *Silence* by *Marshmello (feat. Khalid)*, on repeat. I received a text message notification just as soon as I thought of Ella.

Ella: Hey, how's sailing? How is the vacation!

Me: It's good! Michaels and his wife are pretty humorous. They spend a lot of time fishing. Logan is taking a lot of great shots for his portfolio. I'm trying not to burn too much lol ☼ Kind of ironic though. I went from quarantine on my computer and spending time in our home-gym, to end up mildly alone out here. Music has been a savior. Not trying to complain, I'm blessed. How's your art coming along?

Ella: Aw, you know, I can relate. It should elate me I'm in this massive and beautiful home, mostly alone. But I have a good line for that... *Trust the solitude. Sometimes it can bring you back to you.* The art is challenging. I'm managing multiple projects. Lots of walks on the beach with Pinot in between and these incredible lattes from Ocean Scoops in between. We should video-call soon! ☺

ooo

Solitude, I finally have it. I prayed that the dazzling marbled surface of the ocean would put a calm to my meddling thoughts. To experience metanoia, a transformative change of heart. *To put the past at bay.* But this mystery is driving me deeper into irrationality. The fatiguing part is masking it. I can't stop thinking about what Charlie said about William Campbell during dinner in October. Because it doesn't add up. I'm a dock worker without a college degree and it perplexes me how I could be the only one fighting for my mom, with this vague information that is severely off.

If you take the time to place a freshly dead body in a clock position to point to Roman numerals, then why would you stop at nine? You wouldn't. Like this note suggests, there are more...

Twelve pearls of mine.

Charlie told me, 'William admitted he was ridding the world of beautiful women who rejected him. There isn't much information on him because he was silent after conviction. He was a loner, in and outside of prison. He described himself as an organized Mission killer. They have specific demographic targets. They plan well and can live normally amongst us, while doing so. They can murder with weapons at a close range but will not prolong torture. Quickly and efficiently, with little to go off of. But then there are Hedonistic killers. They sometimes leave DNA behind, semen from rape or skin under the victims nails from a struggle. There are Power/Control killers, they might dispose of collected souvenirs and profit from it. CCTV can identify them at pawn shops. They also might brag about assault to friends and family. There are Visionary killers, and they experience psychosis. This could make them vulnerable, especially if they shout to the world that a doll or the man in the sky told them to kill. In my experienced opinion, one of the most dangerous serial killers falls under the Mission-oriented category. Like, the Pearl Point Murderer.'

If you're a meticulous and mission-driven murderer, then why call an end to your journey at nine, let alone with a call on the telephone? What is the point of the letter, then? Or the card?

Seek hell, south of home.

So, I remain close to the water. Where I'm most lethal. I know my way around these boats, the docks, the deadly curves of an ocean wave. Ready and waiting.

ooo

DRIFTWOOD DAYDREAMS

January 13ᵗʰ, 2021

ELLA SET UP a craft table with jars, soup cans, and plastic to-go containers filled with paintbrushes and pencils. Accompanied by primers, turpentine, additional mediums, a box filled with professional oil paints, and two wood artist palettes. A clear tarp protected the concrete floor, where Ella transformed a portion of the garage into an art studio. She left a few empty spots for Lia's motorcycle, boxes, and Pinot's fluffy donut-shaped bed.

The bluish gray French bulldog chewed on a rawhide dog bone in the driveway. To get the creative juices flowing, Ella played Beethoven on her portable speaker. She stood back from her canvas on the wood easel. She took a sip of her chai tea, two sugars, and a splash of almond milk. Holding the cup up to her plump lips, she squinted at her work. She set her teacup down on the craft table and picked out a ripe strawberry from a milky-green glass bowl with scalloped edges. Sighing heavily, Ella threw the strawberry top towards the open garbage can. It landed inside.

A movement outside of the garage caught her eye. Leaving the garage that wreaked of chemicals, she inhaled a breath of fresh air. She stood in the driveway where Pinot continued gnawing on his bone. Ella eyed the pale cream foredune just ahead of her that developed from the roadside. Curious, she observed the chartreuse and sage-green beach grass swaying side to side in the miniature gusts of air. Lifting the heels of her checkered slip-on shoes, she stretched her neck as far as she could. Conscious that she wouldn't be able to view the top of the sand dune from her five-foot-three stance, Ella leveled back down. She shrugged her shoulders and bit her lip, staring ahead.

A white and gray seagull with a sharp yellow beak emerged from the sandy mount, letting out a series of piercing screeches, it dove towards Ella.

"*Ahh*! Go away!" Ella screamed.

The large gull missed her by mere inches. Ella threw her hands up over her head and ducked. It flew past her and up over her new home.

"Jeez Pinot, no barks *now*? You haven't seen *Hitchcock's The Birds*, and it really shows," Ella huffed. "Actually, what are we even doing here? We have a world-class ocean view in the back yard. Let's go, Mr. P!" Ella yelped to her dog.

ooo

Ella worked early each day, when the particularly wet and cold fog presented itself. Thinning paint, making brush strokes, and producing intriguing shapes and colors on canvas, until afternoon when the fog rolled out and the sands warmed on the beach. She would call it quits when the sun came out and she spent the rest of the day reading and watching the sunset with Pinot. Although it is a public beach, it is free from any beachgoers. Ella felt it resembled a luxurious resort because of the sand dunes barricading access to the beach nearest to her home.

Each day, she grew a little stronger. A lifestyle that Ella could only carry out under her unusual circumstances. She strived closer to order, harmony, and beauty. Eager to develop a sense of balance. Her looks shifted as well. Ella's naturally brown hair developed micro-fine sun kissed lights. Her creamy beige skin transitioned to a light tan.

"Isn't that better? We are *so* small compared to it all. It feels magnificent," Ella spoke to Pinot.

They listened to waves lapping, seagulls screeching in the distance, and the sounds of *Mauve*, dreamy down tempo music. Ella poured the last of the filtered water from her canteen into Pinot's silicone collapsible dog bowl before she sat back down in her blue striped and natural Teak wood beach chair. Bringing one knee up to her chest, she placed her bare foot on the chair's edge. The air was dry and cool against her smooth legs and face. Straightening her back, she pulled her heather gray hoodie down over the jean waist gap behind her. Ella pulled her hoodie sweater sleeves over her knuckles and picked at some dried paint from her distressed bottom hem on her light blue short shorts. Staring seaward, she admired the Tiffany blue water as it rolled in over the shimmering champagne sands and then receded back into the cobalt blue ocean. Beyond that, the cotton candy sky had scattered wisps of marigold outlining thin pale pink clouds.

A thumping noise echoed across the beach from the direction of their home behind them. Ella whipped her head around, the messy brunette bun on top of her head bobbled. Pinot began barking with pauses between. Ella repeated her command word in a clear, upbeat, and raspy voice, "Calm Pinot, calm."

Each text message to her sister failed when she attempted to figure out if Lia was home and if she was okay.

"Ugh, this is going to be frustrating with no service. Pinot, what if I get mugged down here? You're the only valuable I have, and you're priceless. Over my dead body," Ella spoke to her pup.

Ella rose to gather her belongings. She opted to leave her striped beach chair, confident that no one would steal it. She secured the rope leash to Pinot's collar while focusing her attention on her towering, two-story, double-decked home. Ella could barely make out anything beyond the tall glass windows and sliding doors. The sun reflected brilliantly off of them.

On Ella's way back to the house, she noticed a new four-foot piece of driftwood on the earth's sandy carpet. She was curious and approached it. Pinot sniffed at the line of seashells that sat on top of it.

"Huh, this is cute. Let's leave a shell and take one."

From her bag, she pulled out a half sand dollar she had found earlier in the day; it reflected peck marks from seagulls. Replacing the white scallop seashell on the log, Ella placed her sand dollar down in its spot.

"That's how you make friends, Pinot," Ella chirped.

His flat face with bulging blue eyes peeped up at her plainly. His short muzzle said otherwise by grunting in excitement.

"Yes, I know, we're going to go get some num-num," Ella reassured her pup.

As they continued the short walk to their home, Ella peered left, down the beach. She thought that maybe the single mother and teenage son had come out here to enjoy their quarantine after all. The boy must have started the shell collection and displayed them on the driftwood.

Struggling to climb up the sandbank with Pinot in one arm and a heavy tote bag in the other, Ella wobbled unsteadily. She got to the paved road and placed

Pinot on the ground. She pulled out her brown leather *Birkenstock* sandals from her tote to slide into.

"Lia?" Ella yelled out.

She huffed at the sight of her lonely white SUV in the driveway, without its high-performance speed motorcycle associate.

Ella entered her new home without having to use her keys. She shut and locked the door behind her. Afterwards, she kicked her slides into a lower shoe cubby.

She shouted out again, "*Lia*?"

Lia popped out from the kitchen wall and faced Ella in the foyer.

"What's up!" Lia peeped.

Both Ella and Pinot jumped back at the same time.

"*Ugh*! Don't do that, Jesus, you scared us," Ella scolded.

"Sorry, sorry! Kind of surprised that Pinot didn't bark, huh?"

"I'm pretty sure his cute bat ears are just for looks. He might have sensory overload," Ella explained.

"Maggie dropped me off. I didn't mean to scare you. I actually called you a few times, but it went straight to voicemail."

"Oy vey. Seems like V wasn't kidding about reception. If that's the worst thing out here though, we've got it good."

"We are hella lucky biatch. I literally feel like I landed the jackpot. To be this close to my work, to Maggie, mending my relationship with *you*. It's awesome. By the way, the noise that you heard was probably my surprise for you!" Lia gushed.

"Ooh! But you know my birthday isn't for weeks!"

"Yas girl, but it isn't for your birthday. It's like an I'm sorry, I love you, I owe you kind-of-thing. Hey, when I was changing the bulb on the eight-light island chandelier in the kitchen, I noticed the wall clock died at noon. Or midnight, whatever. The battery is missing, though. Did you take it out? I couldn't find any in the drawers."

"No, that definitely had to have been V. She's like the most professional boss babe that I know, but also the greatest air head. I'll get some more from Ocean Scoops."

Lia shrugged and nodded before proceeding up the steps. Pinot hesitated on the bottom step, whimpering loudly.

"Aw, Mr. P, you can do it," Ella encouraged.

"Is he struggling still?" Lia stopped to ask.

"No, he climbs up fine, well hops. It's the coming down part that I think scares him, they're also steep and slippery, so it's hard on his hips. We can just carry him down for now."

Ella groaned and stepped back down a few stairs. She wiped her bare feet on a towel by the door, then sprinted to the kitchen to distract Pinot with a helping of his dry dog food. She proceeded back to the stairs and followed behind her sister.

"Have you seen the neighbors at all?"

"No, why?"

"Oh, no reason. Well, I just thought maybe the teenage boy had been on the beach, I found some pretty shells and new driftwood."

"You mean to tell me..."

"What, what Lia?"

"That I can't do my nude beach yoga out there anymore?"

"*Lia!*"

"Dont be so salty, you haven't even noticed in the past week. Of course, I will not continue. Not trying to have his mother call the cops for indecent exposure. Anyway, close your eyes."

"You're not about to get naked in *my* room, are you?" Ella parodied as she placed her hands over her eyes.

Lia pulled back one steely light blue curtain from the glass and wood French doors, securing it with a magnetic white tieback. She repeated the same action with the curtain on the other side.

"Okay, are you ready?" Lia insisted.

"Yes!" Ella shouted. She stomped her naked feet on the obsidian oak rigid vinyl flooring, performing a slapping drum roll.

"Okay, SURPRISE!" Lia yelled as she opened the right door, leading Ella out onto the modern California deck.

Ella peeled her eyelids open and gasped. She absorbed every detail from the transformed oasis. The iron framed lantern sconces illuminated the California poppies, planted in new large round wood planters at each corner of the modern metal railing. The herbaceous perennials sprouted out from the sandy, well-drained soil in each planter, resembling little cups of gold on a bed of cilantro-greenery. Ella remained speechless as she examined the new seating in the middle of the deck, an outdoor rattan sectional five-seat set. Eggshell cushions positioned on chocolate resin wicker furniture; two ottomans, a three-person sofa, and a glass table attached in the middle. Someone assembled a black table-top fireplace on a rectangular bronze coffee table, where fiery flames performed a sexy salsa dance over lava rocks. The black posts with cable railing refused to obscure the view. A setting sun revealed an intoxicating layer of warmth, stacked from honey on top, dripping down into a thick jammy marmalade, to a layer of cerise berries and an indigo sea below.

"How did you do all this? Are those half wine barrels as functioning planters?"

"Yass girl! Aren't they cool? Me, Maggie, and our co-worker, Mike, did it while you were on the beach," Lia said.

"*Yikes*, I didn't realize that Pinot and I were out there that long. This is insane though, it's so charming and clean," Ella overjoyed.

"I mean, it's kind of to my benefit as well. It's our little sanctuary. It's the least I could do. After you invited me to stay out here with you. I wanted to show up for you, for us. And of course, I talked to V about this beforehand, more so to check that I could put the old teak chairs in the garage and if this deck could manage the weight. She's ecstatic and excited to see it," Lia explained.

"Wait, how did you pay for all of this?"

"That's the other surprise, I got a raise!" Lia sang.

"Oh my gosh, Lia! Wow, congratulations!"

"Thank you! I'm so happy that I could cry. Maggie is going to come pick me up soon, we're going to have dinner at her place and then I'll be back tomorrow after work. If that's okay. Will you be okay alone?"

"Yeah, of course. You go have fun and celebrate; you deserve it. I'm so happy for you. I guess you're rubbing off on me because I have to say, we are pretty damn *lucky*. *Ahem*, does this mean you two are official?" Ella implored softly, with one brow raised.

Lia's smile could light up all of Death Valley on a winter's night.

"Yesterday, she asked me to be her girlfriend at Ocean Scoops, as if we were fifteen back in high school. It was the cutest thing ever. And... I said yes to the best!" Lia, delighted. She expressed joy by snorting and cackling, her most natural laughter.

Ella giggled at the sight of her sister's jollity.

"Well then, I guess you'll be the one penciling *me* in from now on. Don't forget I want to do that closet party with you and V before Oisín and Logan get here."

"Of course! Girl, I will not abandon you just because I'm in an actual relationship now. But also, I know you're busy hustling with your collection. Maggie will be here soon. But what is the piece in the garage that you're working on?" Lia explored.

"It's okay Lia, I am super happy for you. I guess great minds think alike because I wanted to surprise *you,* too. I'm doing your portrait, from the photo of you doing the red handprint across your mouth. I understand it better. We are part Indigenous, and I'm proud of that, but I've been blind to our culture. And what the bank robber said to me, it haunts me. *I saw your kind along the pipelines. Now* I know what he meant. My therapist suggested I express myself through my artwork to heal, alongside my professional canvasses. If it comes out well enough, you get the original and I'm going to sell prints at the gallery. So that I can contribute profits to this amazing organization for missing and murdered Indigenous women," Ella said, exhilarated.

"Damn, girl, you've got one gigantic heart. I'm honored that you're doing that for me, my first pro portrait by my sissy. *And* you're getting involved with such an important organization. I know you won't heal overnight, but you are the strongest person I know. For real. This just proves that. But do not let the bastard haunt you. Yeah, it's easier said than done, but when those demons arise, if you see him or hear those words again, take a breath. Then repeat to yourself, *you can't haunt me.*"

Lia leaned down to put her arms around her sister's petite frame, Ella squeezed her tightly back. Lia's phone vibrated, lighting up through the front pocket of her heavy-duty clear PVC backpack.

"Oh, that's Maggie. Alright girl, you have a great and relaxing night. I'll see you tomorrow," Lia said.

"I really can't thank you both enough. And I can't wait to meet her. *And* congratulations, again. Ti amo," Ella said excitedly.

"I'll tell her. Ciao, amore!" Lia chirped brightly on her way out of Ella's room.

ooo

"Hi," Ella answered a video call in a low-pitch voice.

She held her phone up to her fresh face.

"Hey Ella, it's cool to see you," Oisín said, grinning back as he smoothed his brown hair over.

"*Ooh*, look at those *Oisín* eyes," Ella said confidently.

Oisín chuckled and said, "Oh yeah, the segmental heterochromia, I always forget until someone says something."

"It's not a defect Oisín, they're mesmerizing."

"Speaking of, uh, you look really nice and comfy."

"Oh yeah, this is *super* cozy, I just got out of the shower. V has these white cotton waffle robes in each room, it's like being wrapped in a cloud. Is that a tattoo I spy?"

"Oh, yeah, it is. It's a clear quartz tattoo, like a crystal. I got it for my mom when I turned nineteen, when, when they declared her dead. Claire means clear or bright, so I went with a quartz. The artist incorporated the lines with my scar, from, you know, the day I fell in the ice. Do you have any?" Oisín inquired.

"How could I ever forget that? That is incredibly expressive, Oisín. I love it. But no, none for me. I've never really had the urge. You're going to die when you see Lia's arms. She actually had me do a few pieces for her sleeves. They look pretty great. If I may say so myself. How's the trip going?" Ella asked warmly.

"It's going really well. Logan and I are having fun dodging people at ports, lot of maskholes out. We met one of Michael's cop buddies. He made us a bomb steak and potatoes dinner on his houseboat. This guy, his name is Seamus Finnegan O'Malley, that's about as Irish as they get. But we call him Finn for short. Him and Michaels have been giving Logan a run for his money with the anecdotes. We played cards and talked about the worst boating fails we've seen. It was a good time."

"Aw, that sounds like fun. I'm so jealous. It seems like law enforcement has surrounded you, your whole life. Those guys *and* girls definitely have their own special humor. And it's like free security," Ella replied sweetly, and laughed.

"Yeah, Logan and I have been pretty lucky in that aspect. I'm always entertained by Charlie's friends with their jargon and their food... always plentiful. I sort of suck at cooking though. I used to do it with my mom and dad a lot, as a kid. Kind of lost the mojo, I guess. I saw some of your food photos on Instagram. They look dope!"

"Aw thank you. It is mostly V's goodies. I devise the cocktails, but it's been a challenge having an appetite since the bank. I love cooking though! It is so satisfying to have music going, with a glass of fine wine, while you marry fresh ingredients. My nonna sent me her little recipe notebook a few years ago. I use it a lot. Or was using it a lot, *before*, you know. I miss cooking and I know things will be prime when I get back to it."

"I understand. That sounds a lot more romantic than my failed attempts at cooking. Burned toast, undercooked chicken, and overcooked veggies, rough. Have you done anything fun since moving in?"

"Ah, I'll have to make you a special dish then. Hmm, I'm more inspired than ever by how peaceful and naturally spectacular it is here, so my work is coming easy. Aside from that, I love the books that V has here. I had to put mine in storage, there's just too many. V designed each room here to have a full bookcase and the titles reflect the theme of the room. Mostly all nautical or drama fiction. But my room is the primary suite. It has a pretty feminine design and there's a lot of poetry in the case. I found a book that was released a few weeks ago. I'm obsessed. Oh, I can show you room actually," Ella said as she switched the camera view on the video call.

She waved her phone over the luminously lit interior. Showing the white shiplap walls and ceiling, the dark flooring, and two white Victorian chairs with a pale steely blue trim. Between the Victorian seating was a dark brown end table with a white wood lamp base and cream lampshade on it. In front of that, Ella laid out a shaggy white donut-shaped dog bed, where Pinot slept noisily in. The seating area ran parallel to the long tufted steely blue ottoman bench at the end of her king-sized bed. Two all-white night tables with glass tops were on both sides of the bed. A large white duvet cover and pillowcases that matched the room's theme of steely light blue and white. Crystals dangled from a bronze three-light mini chandelier. It hung centered from the sloped ceiling before the French doors. Ella moved the phone to show the front of the room where a full-length mirror leaned against the wall next to a walk-in closet. Her bedroom door was to the right of a walk-in bathroom. Ella brought the phone back to the Victorian seating, where a low but wide bookcase ran flush with the wall beside it.

"Do you like it? I could show you the bathroom, there's a standing claw tub, which I love. But it's a little messy in there with my skincare products," Ella said. She switched the camera view back to selfie mode.

"I highly doubt that it's a mess... That is definitely a feminine room, but it's a sick layout, really cool design," Oisín said, deep and sleepy as his head dipped forward.

"*Ah*, I'm so sorry. I'm putting you to sleep," Ella giggled.

"No, oh, no. I haven't been sleeping the best on this trip. It's just catching up to me, that's all. We're on Finn's houseboat with Debbie and Michaels until we fly out. We cut sailing short, but he has this place decked out. That is dope that you get to rent a fully furnished home, though. You like reading a lot?"

"I love it! Last year, reading was pretty much my savior. But even before that, I got hooked on the, *Our Shared Shelf Book Club.* But this is the poetry collection that I'm reading now. I mentioned it earlier. The structure is to imply an anarchic take on traditional poetry. To experience angst *with* the writer. Centered on impermanence and imperfection. But it's magical and healing for me, in a way. V is a genius to include these little touches in here," Ella said, holding up a poetry book with an enormous ocean wave on the front.

"I liked the lines you sent before. Feel free to send more, it's cool to see what you're into. Still a book nerd and a fellow thalassophile. Hey, I also remember you being the sick skater chick leading our Jelly Club back in the day, too," Oisín said, and chuckled deeply.

"*Yes*! The camo capris and baby tees. I just wanted to fit in with you guys so bad that I forced myself to skate. Then we would compare our scrapes. Oh my god, remember when you and I confronted Andrew Ross in the woods. Because he kept calling logan and me racial slurs? He was like the size of both of us combined. We thought that the concept of jumping someone was to pounce on them and then that was it. He threw us off his back and we went flying into a pile of leaves. It scared us shitless, but he's the one who ran away crying," Ella said fast and animatedly between raspy giggles.

Ella and Oisín laughed together, harmonious, and natural.

"Oh man, yeah, good times. You were definitely a tomboy for a minute. But we were more impressed with how intuitive you were. Ah, is that your pupper? I'm so excited to meet him. He looks like such a cool little guy."

"Yes! He's so excited to meet you too! Aren't you Mr. P? He's still getting used to it out here and pretty tuckered out," Ella said.

"Well, I should hit the hay too. But I'm counting the days down until we get there. I'm excited to celebrate your birthday and to quarantine all together. I hope you have a good rest of your night."

"I'm so excited too. Thanks, *Oisín*, goodnight," Ella said, husky and low.

"Sweet dreams, Ella," Oisín replied, besotted.

Ella hopped off the bed and plugged her phone into a USB cord on her nightstand. Pinot stirred, snuffling loudly. He rolled over from lying on his side to an upright position on the dark floor. His eyes bulging and alert. He trotted toward the French doors, barking rapidly and repeatedly.

"Oy vey Pinot, do you need to go out? You can't play with the big cats. A mountain lion would eat you."

Ella pulled back the linen curtain and flipped the switch for the back lights. She opened the door and closed it behind her. Pinot continued barking from inside.

"See Pinot? Nothing. Calm, Pinot, calm," Ella commanded.

Ella listened to the rhythmic ocean waves crashing below. She walked to the end of the deck and leaned over the modern cable railing to observe the beach near her home. Her heart stopped when she recognized a dark figure standing in the sand near the aluminum stairs, staring up at her. A face that reminded her of the bank robber that wore a black ski mask, white skin exposed through the mouth and eye holes.

Ella inhaled sharply and closed her eyes, although she still felt the ardent gaze of a watcher. She took a deep breath in, filling her lungs with oxygen. As she exhaled, Ella repeated in a stern voice to herself, "You're not real. You can't haunt me, you're not real!"

Opening her eyes, she no longer saw the ghastly vision.

She was alone, or so she thought.

ooo

THE JOURNAL

January 15th, 1989

I CAN'T BELIEVE THAT I went to church for Sofia today. She dragged me along with her family. She insists I make new habits for the new year. She also thinks that I shouldn't be spending time with John. What a crock of shit. Everyone seems to know what's best for me, but absolutely no one even asks what I want or how I am. Not that I would answer them honestly. Sofia wants me to be "forgiving" — I know well that these random influences are because I found out Jackie is the one who wrote, "Pee yew! Sofia's pet monkey stinks like eggs!" IN GROSS LIPSTICK, on the inside of the wood wall by the restrooms at the ballpark.

David and Mike must have broken into my locker, because when we returned to school from winter break, they welcomed me with a dozen rotten eggs in my locker. They are the pathetic monkeys, Jackie's heinous pets.

There's something about the smell in a church, dingy and pungent. It makes me want to ralph. The eggs stunk like shit and so did sitting on a pew with strangers in no air circulation. Grody dude. I take two showers a day. The smell that Jackie is referring to is her upper lip.

There was one amusing part of the morning. I counted the number of times that dragons are mentioned in the Book of Revelations. Thirteen, my favorite. I never noticed this before. Although, most times, father forced me to listen to him read, I zoned out or fell asleep. It must be a sign. Thirteen is my favorite number and I love dragons. I'm reminded now that it took thirteen years until father assessed I was old enough to beat on. Insisting that I wake up and stop being such a weakling. Satan is farcical like that. Throwing the one three at me, like he's teasing a disease. Watching and waiting for me. I don't play for the above or below, just the here and the now.

Because both have deceived me so.

Now, when the clock strikes thirteen, I retreat to my mind fortress. Where I imagine dragons, their fiery breath consumes the entire town of Venoice, burning everything holy and unholy to the ground. That's the thing about dragons... They don't discriminate. And the unholy lead the holy sometimes. When and where will these people learn?

Anyway, I went with the Colombo family to church without protest. Because it's adorable how Sofia wants to change me, while I desperately want to change her.

After the service, Sofia's father asked us to stay in for the day, for family time. We didn't partake in the board games. Instead, Sofia just laid out on the living room floor flipping through her Blue Jeans magazine. She's such a betty. Her button nose looks upturned when you look at her from the side. Her dark roots are peaking out from the bleached blonde. Keeping it short and sassy. I listened to (Don't Fear) The Reaper and Sinful Love on my new Walkman over and over, pretending to read my book, but really staring at her deadly fine ass while I vegged out.

John gifted me this book a few weeks ago, A Clockwork Orange. He got it from a homeboy that he was selling some meds to. John's dad has to be the dumbest pharmacist in the state. How does he never notice the missing meds? John's buddy lives somewhere on the border of Pennsylvania and New York. He runs a personal library out of his basement for the rebels at his school. Nerds. I still want to see it. Sounds bitchin'. Homeboy told John that other teens come from afar just to checkout books from his collection of banished or banned X-rated literature for free. I may have to make a trip up there; I've been dying to go to New York. And those guys sound like my people.

My review of A Clockwork Orange:

I like the title more than I like anything past it. That's a lie. I love/hate it; it stirred me alright. It's wicked in the right moments. But the premise is one hell hole of mistakes—for the main character, not the writing. Alex is totally mad. I shook the book in my hands so many times, that people walking by me at the beach asked what novel could make someone that angry. Me being in my head-to-toe black parka with a black fur hood, said I was practicing for a deadly Shakespeare play. Without a doubt, they thought I was some goth and left me alone.

Back to the book. I wanted something more raw and realistically warped. The senseless acts of violence and gang shit are going to get you behind bars. Duh. The ending is bogus. The writer might not be writing from the heart unless he's taken one before. A heart. There is no stopping once you get a taste for blood. Feed the fire with nibbles less conspiring until you can devise a plan to hunt for your main course. But no one can survive off a single dinner... for their entire life. The craving comes back. Or so I've been told. So, the main character, Alex, in the most organic of circumstances, would not have lost the taste for terror in the end. Gnarly read, I give it 3 stars. I'll check out the movie, maybe it's different.

One thing I can't wait for is learning how to ice fish! John is going to teach me next week. Walking out on ice to fish, pretty rad. I bought some safety tools like a spud bar, ice pick, and a rope. These things might come in handy for other fun recreational uses. Jackie, maybe?

John said we have to take snowmobiles to get to the abandoned beach after we enter the state park and head east through trails in the woods and closed campgrounds. Where rumored ghosts act as gatekeepers to keep you from enjoying the tranquility just past them. Then you come out to the shore where there's an old, abandoned building, a playground falling apart, and a deserted beach. He says it is the perfect spot for someone to go missing. I retorted back to him, "Don't threaten me with a good time." Hardly believable, but I'm trying to not be a weakling. So we went, naturally.

John wanted to set up a little shooting range for practice. I told him no. It's not because I'm a baby about my father using a bullet on mother, but it's because guns are the easy way out of everything in life. Knives on the other hand, that takes strength. He said that I have aichmomania, which is an obsession with sharp, pointy things. Whatever. He's obsessed with his dick, so. He quit his bitching once I set my duffel bag full of knives down on the old picnic table by the beach. Suddenly, he's a knife expert too. Inspecting my pieces, feeling the weight, grip of handles, looking over the fixed blades. He ripped the old 'closed' notice off of the wood bathroom building and began slicing through it.

Lake Erie has nothing on this eerie abandoned beach in northwestern Pennsylvania. I've been finding myself by the water more often and it's a bitchin' kind of life from here. This place will become my becoming. It is a peaceful place to kill.

Dinner, that is.

ooo

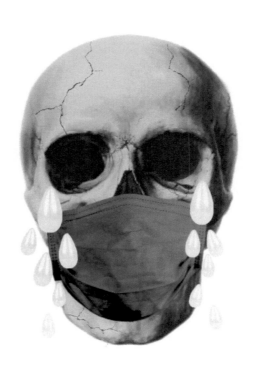

KNOTTY RED

January 23rd, 2021

M I A bad person? I'm fuming and he's dead, but I'm not necessarily angry that he's dead. But I didn't even touch him. I should call the police. I can't move, or maybe I don't want to move. Wait, if I'm okay with this, could I possibly be a psychopath? Psychopaths are born, sociopaths are made. If my father had something to do with my mom's disappearance, then he would most definitely be the Pearl Point Murderer. Which could mean that I have killer genes...

Maybe my mom found out what my dad was. That finding could have led her to become the last girl, the ultimate woman, on the clock. Or could my mom have been running from something? Did she fake her death to protect herself or me? Is he trying to find her after having received the life insurance? I've seen no signs of abuse. They loved each other, truly and deeply. She would never leave me, willingly. Is it unrelated to the pearly staged murders entirely? But someone killed all those women, teenagers really, and they don't seem to have received the true justice they deserve either, even with William rotting in his grave.

ooo

Rewind to earlier in the afternoon...

Logan is in the galley preparing a fruit bowl for the cookout. I should at least shuck the corn. I can't make sense of these gibberish writings, anyway. I paused in the corridor. My heart stopped and dropped to my stomach.

"Wh, where, where did you get that?" I stuttered.

"Hey man. What, this? I was just borrowing it. Is about time that you joined us. Michaels, Debbie, and Finn are at the grill. You ready?" Logan insisted.

"But *where* did you find it?"

"What's your deal? I found it in your pack. What I gotta ask for permission now?" Logan asked sarcastically.

"No, um, no. It's just, I thought I threw it away, a while ago," I said deeply.

Logan set the pineapple down on the cutting board over the sink. He closed his mouth and scanned me from top to bottom. Chewing the inside of his cheek. Still holding the river knife my dad gave me, he lifted his arm and pointed it towards me. The overhead light reflected off the blade and blinded me for a second.

"Now, *why* would you throw away your favorite knife, in the entire universe?" Logan probed.

A series of explanations sped through my mind, a tornado of bullshit.

"Uh, yeah, it was, my favorite. Until I noticed, it had a shitty dull blade. Just chuck it okay," I stammered.

"Huh, *okay*, Murph. Will do... Are you going to help me bring these out?"

I turned from him to exhale and headed to my cabin.

"Yeah, yeah, in a minute," I muttered.

Following me, Logan ripped the letter sticking partially out from my back pocket.

"Dude, no. Give it back."

"Nah, man, what's eating you today? Is it a *love* letter?" Logan teased as he held the folded sheet of paper behind his back.

"No, it's-hold on," I said, hesitating.

We continued into the back cabin, and I shut the door behind us.

"Alright, I give in. It's a letter from the Pearl Point Murderer."

Logan jerked his head back; he wrinkled his nose and raised his full upper lip.

"For real, dude?" Logan groaned.

I sat down on the plaid bunk, awaiting the disgust to expand across the rest of his face. He pulled the paper out from behind his back, unfolded it, and read.

"Murph... What, the, hell, is this?" Logan questioned.

"Like I just said. It's a case that Michaels was on back in the day. Well, I wanted to ask him about it a while ago. But with some research, I found it online before we got out here and printed it. I don't expect you to understand," I answered him.

Logan hiked up his classic black chino shorts and sat down on the bed next to me. He unbuttoned the top button to his white polo and then rubbed his neck. He glanced at the window next to me. Observing the old sailboat next to Finn's houseboat. Where an old man stood on the bow of his boat peculiarly. The sun was setting behind him. His shape was more of a silhouette, but I could make out his long white beard and bleach bald head. The old man stared straight back at Logan, tipped his head down and then raised his right hand to wave a mini confederate flag.

"Bro," Logan said, deep and furious.

"What the hell?" I yelled. I stood up from the side of Logan.

Sliding the window shut, I threw my middle finger up at the old man and ripped the blinds down.

"Fuck that guy!" I said heatedly.

"Yo, I'm sick of this shit. Seems like it's gotten worse after election *if* that is even possible," Logan retorted.

"I know, I know. It's damn disgusting," I said.

"That guy is a dick and will die alone, though. Back to this," Logan said, placing the letter down on the space between us.

A fury was building up inside of me. I sat back down to redirect my energy.

"Alright, this is going to sound… *all sorts* of crazy. I wanted to decode the letter and talk to Michaels about it. Because on my birthday, I received an envelope with a red clock seal, inside was a menacing square card, about my mom. Here, look," I said.

I leaned forward to pull out my wallet from my back jean pocket and slipped the thick white square note into his open palm. He read the note that *still* makes my skin crawl.

Twelve pearls of mine.

Mommy floats in time.

Seek hell, south of home.

Where the key lies in the stone.

Afterwards, Logan raised his eyebrows, glaring ahead at the glossy wood door. He tugged at his gold square-shaped stud with round diamonds.

I should have told him sooner.

"This is what you and my dad have been having private conversations about, huh?" Logan asked in a low, deep voice.

"Yeah, yes. I should've said something sooner. I had to protect you guys and figure it out on my own, you know," I blurted out.

"Protect us from what? Murph, come on, you can't be serious. You're one of the most calm and sensible people I know. You're the first person to debunk and give a serious tone to otherwise ludicrous situations. This explains them nightmares. You ain't sleeping right, you're edgy."

"Dude, it's all right here. *Lies in the stone* and *lies deep vengeance.* Creepy and distinct diction. Whoever sent this card to me, has to be the same person who wrote the letter to Sapphire News. And it shows that there weren't just nine victims. The guy who was executed was a *liar.* You know what this looks like..." I suggested.

"Sorry bro, it looks like traumatic stress. Looks like my best friend, my brother, *lied* to me. You missed hiking, paddle boarding, and my sunset shots for the Gold Coast Sapphire Traveler Guide. Bro, we are on vacation! Yeah, it sucks to be social-distancing and wearing masks. But this is *your* first vacation in a long time. We were going to be in Thailand, after ten years of planning and then shit hit the fan. I honestly thought that it relieved you when it was canceled. But when you jumped on this, at a month's notice. Man, I was ecstatic... But *no,* you agreed to this offer, because of this ridiculous note!" Logan snapped.

"That's my bad about missing out on all that, and I apologize. But it isn't because I'm harboring on this. I actually did all I could do and got nowhere with these writings. It's because I'm a freaking lobster. I'm not trying to show up in Cali like an Irish peeled potato. Could we rewind all of this and go meet up with every-one for dinner? Maybe talk about it later."

"We are talking about it now, and I see you trying to change the subject. Did you even debunk the possibility that it could've been a couple of kids? Nah, but you're going to hear me out on this, okay? I sound old as hell, but these days, teens are *disturbed* as hell. They're on the internet, every waking moment and obsessed with all this dark shit. We had *Blockbuster*, wood parks, and ran around outside in whack ass jewel-toned clothes. Some angst high school kids are probably cooped up in their basement, as most people are during this time. But instead of being productive, they decide to stir the hot pot, and get some rage out on someone else. Maybe they researched mysteries of Foggerton Bay and who should come up? No one can explain what you said you saw and how you fell into the ice. I mean, I believe you bro. But no one can also explain how your mom disappeared into thin air before Christmas. These kids probably got your home address from a simple people search and boom, you're their next savage Satan project, ya feel me?" Logan elaborated confidently.

"I just want justice for her! I did my best to wait for her, to wait for something to come up about her. I know it seems crazy to only act on it eighteen years later, but I want justice and she deserves that. What else do I have?"

"Yo, what you have? You have a family who has been there for you through thick and thin. And our friends ain't going anywhere, sports will pick back up in no time. I lost my mom too. You were there for all of us during her cancer and now I'm trying to be here for you. It isn't weak or unmanly to talk about your feelings and thoughts, it's *empowering*. All this self-care and self-love advertising everywhere, but bro mental health is just as important for men as it is for women. And what you have before you is sunshine, water, and beaches for days. We're not in New York, no busting your ass on black ice, no scraping snow off our car window, or blasting the heat. You are with friends and family, *now*. I think you're not doing justice to yourself by re-living the past... Look, we've got a little over a week left until Cali and then our fine as hell friend is waiting to reunite with us. I got a feeling she's got eyes for your old Irish ass. Murph, you gotta talk it out. Really no excuse when there are virtual therapists now. You have more than enough money to afford that," Logan lectured.

Why is he never wrong?

"I got caught up in dreaming, I guess. Probably went a little too far. You're right though. I have everything I've ever wanted right before me. It's this time of year, that I end up missing her most. And this note didn't help. I know you miss your mom, too. Sometimes, I wish my dad had found his Gloria right after as well. Maybe things would be different," I said solemnly.

We sat there in peace, listening to the water slosh against the exterior of the houseboat.

"Not trying to be harsh, just being real. I wish you would stop punishing yourself. As a Christian, I believe that she's in a better place. Willing you to live your life to the fullest. Remember that compass she gave you, the one that we all wanted on your birthday. What were her words to you, something about the path to righteousness."

"Right, that *was* my favorite compass, which went missing the day that she did... I know what she engraved on it. I'm trying my best," I replied.

"Alright, yo, when you get that inkling that something is wrong, beat that mother trucker down and bury it. Like the *Sopranos*. It's the only damn advice you get when you refuse to talk to a pro. If you will not do that, try your best to put this out of your head. For Ella's sake, she doesn't deserve this. Not after everything that she's been through, too. And when she's welcoming us with open arms to hosting our quarantine out there."

"Truth, I need to get my head right. I know, I can't mess it up."

"See, *bro*, I knew y'all was hitting it off. Damn, for half a second, I thought I had a shot," Logan exclaimed.

He sarcastically served me with a side eye and tugged at the short black hairs on his chin.

"Ha-ha. Why look elsewhere? Isn't it fun sharing Vanessa with Devon?"

"Ahh, brothers got jokes now, huh? Hurry your ass up."

"Alright, I'm going to shower quick, and I'll meet you guys up there. And uh, thank you, *again*."

"Ay, I'm just paying you back for all the years you did the same," Logan said.

He got up and placed the card on top of the letter. Walked over to the window and pulled the blind cord down. He cranked the window back open. Fresh, salty air blew in.

"Want to do the honors?" Logan insisted, pushing the paper towards me.

"Yeah, alright."

I accepted the literature back into my hand. The texture of it gave me chills. I stuck my arm outside of the window and tossed the letter and card. They floated down with the Florida wind blowing them towards the slip next to ours. I turned around to avoid watching them drown in the marina waters.

"Good?" Logan asked, upbeat and hopeful.

"Yeah, I'm good," I replied with an open smile.

ooo

I wiped my hand across the fogged-up mirror above the sink. Frowning at my wet, patchy pink and lightly tanned skin. Healing, but still sensitive to the touch. Staring back at my reflection, I attempt to see my mother in my facial features. To see any lasting resemblance to her in my eyes. My dad's eyes are a rusty beer brown, while hers are a light glacier blue. The segmental heterochromia perfectly combines the two. As hard as I try, I can't seem to identify any trace of her any longer. The older I get; the more I see of him, in structure, at least. Aidan James Murphy, the most prominent feature my dad has, is his straight, sharp, pointy nose. He's an inch shorter than I am, with a similar rectangular body shape, broad shoulders, muscular arms, and thighs. Dark brown hair, almost black, in a disconnected tapered haircut. Thick black brows and always sporting a five o'clock shadow. Wildly crooked bottom teeth that barely showed behind his thin lips, unless he smiled. That's what I remember at least. It has been almost a decade since he left Foggerton, so I don't know what he looks like now. Sometimes, I wish I did.

I dried off and changed into a basic white tee-shirt, navy blue chino shorts, and clean classic white slip-on shoes. As I pulled on a thick knit fisher sweater, I could hear yelling outside. I lifted the blinds to the back cabin window again. I could see the old man on the boat next to us waving his hand, holding up a soaking wet piece of paper. I scoffed at him.

Not this guy again. I'm already late.

Signaled by his hollering, I walked out onto the back deck to see what was going on. The sun had set, but our large steel sconces lit up his port side well.

"What? What do *you* want?" I asked firmly.

"Ya damn black pal is littering up and down this marina. Little snowflakes, think you can come here after your riots and then just dump all over our homes? Y'all don't belong, now git! Git back to the assholes y'all crawled out from!" he said in a crackling and high-pitched voice. A spew of spit escaped his thin lips with each angry word. The old man clung to his black suspenders, with his left hand, over his dirty white tank top that connected to khaki slacks. He stared back at me, scowling deeply, with twitching eyes.

"Little motherfucker," I said, deep and low.

I pulled off my ivory sweater and threw it on the wood deck. I grabbed my face mask from my pocket and secured it on. Then sprinted through our houseboat, ran up the stairs and jumped to the main aluminum dock. I dropped to the stern of his old sailboat.

Darkness.

ooo

I can't avoid reporting this guy's death like I had with poor Stew.

I dialed the police, grimacing down at his limp body.

"911, what's your emergency?" the emergency dispatcher answered.

"Hi, um, there's been a death, eh, a heart attack, I think. An old man had a heart attack on the boat next to our boathouse," I said, rushed, stuttering.

"Sir, what is your location?" the dispatcher questioned.

"Sorry, yes. I'm at the Boathouse Marina at Sapphire Glass Beach, at the live-aboard wet slips," I repeated clearly.

"Sir, did you check his pulse? Is he breathing?" the dispatcher quizzed.

"No, he's not breathing. He is dead. I heard him screaming. And when I went to go talk to him, he just stopped and grasped his chest and had a heart attack. There was nothing I could do. He's on an old sailboat called, The Knotty Red," I repeated calmly.

ooo

THE JOURNAL

January 24ᵗʰ, 1989

WE GAINED A new president four days ago.

John and I celebrated tremendously in the cabin for it!

However, "Now is the winter of our discontent."

Sofia has been getting brunch with me less and less, she's also been distant. I'm one of Mr. Rossi's best customers, though. He sees me on the regular, so I can't disappoint him. I guess she hasn't been THAT distant. We live together. But I miss the thrill of using other people's money to treat us out. She would always doll up for it, for me, or maybe just to be seen by the football jock straps. I'm trying to keep afloat, too. Sofia has increased my project load. I refuse to fail out of high school. I wonder if I would have been the valedictorian if it weren't for Sofia needing me. Shit, not every little thing is about Sofia, though.

We lost a great today, to the electric chair.

It's hard to describe what it's like to watch idols rise, just to fall. Simple traffic violations to being spotted, palpable out and about. So overly self-assured and irresponsible. Did he not study Ramirez? I was 14 when I learned of his work AND his mistakes. An exaggerated reaction to self in public led to being caught after a car chase. Never react. Never react. Never react. Like my mother, she had it right. Keep your head down and stay in the game.

In all the time of being grounded, alone, or in detention. I discovered a grand thing or two. Isolation gets the gears turning, lights the fire, connects the wires. I learned from lining up dominoes to pass the time, the best little friends, dressed in black and white. Teachings of patience and careful executions of steps. If a SINGLE bone is out of place, you will lose the race. Everything you've worked for could come crashing down, because of one simple bone...

But I don't want to fall, not from this high.

ooo

WADING WATCHER

February 1ˢᵗ, 2021

"HI MAMMA," ELLA answered.

"Stella Marie Russo-Redhouse! Emilia told me you invited Oisín Murphy here, this happened, sì?" Ava requested in an Italian accent.

"Well, I…"

"Maledizione Stella! Cosa ti avevo detto! Male, male, male!"

"Ugh *mamma*! English, please. I'm turning thirty-one, I'm too old for this. I have to be able to live my life for myself. I did everything as you asked when I was a kid when we moved. I ignored his instant messages, didn't call him, or anything. Because of *you*. I, I didn't even ask or understand why. And he was still hurting. What if it were you that went missing?"

"He tells you that because he's coming to California to inspect us. No, no, no. You say you are over this, but you do not know what this is. I tried to protect you ragazze, but you're right. You're grown, okay... Your father and I love each other very much, un sacco. Okay, sì? But do you remember our family trip to Myrtle Beach?"

"*Of course,* I remember. What does this have to do with dad or the trip?"

"Your father made a mossa on Claire, he make an advancement and he... He made her uncomfortable. He doesn't do well with the drink; you girls know this. But she wasn't avoiding me all those times. I judge too quickly and misunderstand. She was avoiding awkwardness because of your father. When he tells me this, I immediately went to her. Al momento. I brought her offerings, jewelry e panettone to make apologies for his behavior. What do I always tell you ragazze, *a caval donato non si guarda in bocca.*"

"I-I'm so sorry. I'm not looking at fault. I didn't know that's what you went over there for. Honestly, I regret learning all of this. Mamma, it's inspiring that you moved here from Bergamo to pursue your dreams with Row Me Russo, but life isn't all business. Don't you think you two deserve another chance at love?"

"Sì, we do still love each other, but love is respect and I respect his choice to be there for now. That's your cultura too, Stella. If he comes back to California, then sì, I will. But our Aditsan did nothing. And I have nothing to do with Murphy famiglia. The husband, Aidan, maybe he find out by the talk of town. But it was awful to be, how you say, condannata, per niente. I don't wish any child to be without a mother, but I am not the last person to see her. She said she had a date soon. I don't know if with her husband or another man? I tell them everything I know but we still had to move, non era buono. Niente di più," Ava said sternly.

Both mother and daughter sighed loudly at both ends of the call.

"I could never imagine that dad was even *thinking* of cheating on you. After this exhausting pandemic is over, I think we need to have a family meeting. But mom,

Oisín isn't like that. He's not coming here to question you. He was my absolute best friend, and I should have been there for him. Him and Logan are just visiting for a while. And you're always telling me, *la vita è breve*, huh?"

Ava laughed lightheartedly, tickled by Ella's response.

"Ah, sì, now you listen to me? I say this, life is short, to mean about you meeting a fresh man and get married. But you are my bella Stella. I cannot make you do this or that. I want you to be happy e sano, bene?" Ava said softly.

"Yes, that's wonderful, mamma. I want to be healthy too. I feel like I'm on the road to recovery... *again*. I know you care about me, mama. But trust me on this, Oisín isn't coming here to put you on trial. But I'm kind of disturbed. What if Mr. Murphy thought Claire cheated, like, for real? Maybe he was angry and less forgiving about that, as you were with dad?" Ella asked, her voice strained and low pitch.

"Only the stars know, il mio amore. I'm sorry for raising my voice Stella, I don't want to fight. And you know your friend better than me. I should be able to get uh, vaccino soon, to see you and new home. Things will be better."

"You're going to love it. I saw the photos that Lia sent you, but they totally don't do it justice. I hope you have a good rest of your night, mamma, ti amo," Ella replied.

"Ti amo anch'io, Stella, buona notte."

It was a frosty and clear moonlit night. Waves lapped in the distance. A soft wind forced the short flames to flicker. Ella slipped her feet into chestnut shearling slippers and lifted her legs to rest them on top of the ottoman. Securing a fringed golden oak waffle throw across her chest, she leaned back into the cushioned patio furniture. She pet Pinot's dozing head, whereas Ella raised hers to admire the blinking stars above. Trying to count each luminous ball of gas. Imagining that each one witnessed mankind without judgement, without thought. Watchers of the world. Twinkling their existence back to us.

Ella questioned her creator, "Do you know what happened to Claire?"

Unanswered, she snoozed into the evening with her snoring Frenchie. Completely unaware. A pair of human eyes fixed directly on her lightly sun-kissed skin, relaxed pink lips, and prominent cheekbones. The sinister eyes narrowed in on Ella's chest, watching it rise and fall with each breath. They longed to feel Ella's warm skin. Hungered for her bright red blood. Lusted for her death. Wading, waiting, for the right moment.

ooo

THE JOURNAL

February 13th, 1989

G OD DAMN IT!
David poured my milk carton over my peas today. He said, "orphans are lucky to eat, you shouldn't waste food." Which was counterproductive. He's such a Dirty Harry wannabe dickhead. I had just done his literary project too, Sofia begged me to do it and bargained that if I did, she would pay for our meal at Rossi's Eat O'clock. It's not about the money, it's about the company. I have a feeling she'll bail now, anyway.

Back to the ungrateful ass. When he didn't get the reaction he wanted, he took my tray and poured it over my hair. Milk and peas. Dripping from my hair to my jean jacket. Jackie and Whitney tried hard to get everyone else to laugh. But guess what? More people are sympathetic about someone's mom being murdered and then their father dying in a house fire, than not. It surprised me, too.

I imagined cutting David's fingers off and stuffing them into an old-fashioned glass milk jug to leave on his mother's front step.

John was livid. He got up and punched David's giant nose; it was heroic, but totally unnecessary. Sofia left the cafeteria as the chaos erupted. When she walks, it's as if she's floating through the room, never touching the ground below. Her ass-hugging blue jeans, brown clogs and pink top tucked into her Dittos. Her blonde hair bounced as she walked by. I got a strong whiff of her White Shoulders perfume, that she always wears. She wouldn't even look at me. I waited for any kind of condolence or aide to the embarrassment that I just endured...

Nothing.

She never orchestrates these acts, but she also never stops them...

Sofia is a pro at manipulating the manipulator, always basking in the loveliest shades of denial. Yet, I can't help myself. She needs me and eventually she will want me, too. I'm gifting her two dozen red roses tomorrow. One for each hour of the day, and one for each hour of the night. She is the rose to my thorn, intoxicating. There is no pleasure, without a little pain. How I will only suffer for thee.

Because the cheer bears and jock straps act as gatekeepers to pass and fail us. When all they can really offer to this world is date rape. They're in their own league, a prettied-up brand of psychotic. Suicide-inducing murderers. The geeks forget the real meaning of an education, self-worth, and growth because of them. The scale of innocence tips as the self-loathing sets in. Maybe father was right, Matthew 7:6. No more throwing my treasure to swine... No more forgiveness for Sofia's friends.

I'm the mother-fucking alpha dragon. I'M THE DRAGON. They'll see.

ooo

CHAMPAGNE MIRRORS

February 2ⁿᵈ, 2021

"**A**LEXA, PLAY HEAD Above Water by Avril Lavigne," Ella spoke to the speaker on the white-tiled bathroom counter.

She closed her eyes when the beginning piano melody played. Ella inhaled the fragrance of the dried sweet jasmine buds, rose petals, dried pink grapefruit slices, and bergamot cedarwood oil that kissed the surface of the milk bath. Sinking into the depth of the large white standing tub, with brass eagle talon claw feet, and a matching brass gooseneck faucet and fittings. Her softened hair remained floating at the top. Opaque white water shifted slightly, following her movement, creating a wanderlust of steamy fog and florals above her curvy and petite body. The warmth of the water caressed every inch of her body. A forte of courage strung her soul back together, piece by piece, as she continued to hold her breath. She lifted her hands out of the bath and placed them on each side of the tub, rising out of the water. She admired the irony of the lyrics to the song that gave her strength when she needed it most.

A dream from the night before left her feeling physically exhausted. The adventurous night started off with her standing in a tree, the location unrecognizable. Something compelled her to step off the highest branch of an evergreen tree. Her white-spotted brown wings superseded the fear of falling, as they spread out and guided her into flight. She transformed into a Northern Saw-whet owl, soaring in the darkest of dusk, through dense forests. Seeking food with impeccable vision, seeing what the human eye can't. The dream neared the end with her exiting the forest and taking flight over a vast ocean. She found Oisín sleeping, miles from the shore, on the deck of a small wooden sailboat. Giving up her desire to hunt for fish and mice, she felt a profound demand to lookout over him, to protect him from a predator, skulking beyond. When she saw a greater darkness of movement beneath his small boat, she let out a penetrating, shrill call to wake him up.

Once awake, Ella's body felt achy, her mind confused, blaming the strange night flight on lingering bits of stress, living in a new home, and the anticipation to see her old best friend.

Ella stared ahead at the black and white seagulls print behind glass in a white frame, hanging on the shiplap wrapped wall. She picked up her masala chai tea in a periwinkle stone mug from the bamboo bath caddy and took a few slow sips. The ritual of black tea and fragrances were dedicating to her uplifted and enhanced mood, awakening her from a sleepy disposition. The rich scent of jasmine, a natural aphrodisiac, struck her. She bit her bottom lip as she thought of Oisín. She picked up her phone to look at the most recent text message. Noting the time, nine after six in the morning, she opted to send one of her favorite lines, as he requested. She plucked up the poetry paperback from the propped-up book holder on the bath caddy. And flipped to a page with a dog ear. Ella began to text Oisín on her smartphone.

Ella: Good morning☺ I hope you guys have a great last day in the sunshine state. I thought you might like this... *Time. Every flow in a moment is crucially valuable. But know, there's always time to change direction. Your path current is not set, it is malleable.*

Oisín: Hey, you're up early ☼ Now that's dope, def applicable. Thx! Yeah, last day. We're going shopping for a new fit. Don't want to show up in shambles, especially on your b-day! Excited to see ya. Got anymore? We have lot of travel time ahead of us!

Ella: Aw, how fun. LOL shambles from experiencing FL. How's this... *I wonder if the sea, Looks to the moon too, and thinks of me.* Have a great day!☺

ooo

"Hey, hey miss au naturel. You look radiant!" V complimented brightly.

Ella was leaning against the kitchen counter in distressed light blue jean short shorts, an oversized gray hoodie, and checkered slip-on shoes. She laughed light and raspy after she threw a strawberry top in the disposal drain.

"Oh thanks. I kind of look like this every day, though," Ella replied.

"Nuh uh. Well, yeah, the dirty old, oversized hoodie and paint-splattered shorts," V said, before taking a sip from her sunset ombre stainless steel water bottle.

Ella's upturned mouth went crooked into a smile, in amusement.

"No shame, that's your uniform. I'm talking about your skin, and you let your hair dry natural. It's your aura. You're lighting up like a firefly on a July night."

Ella's exaggerated sigh led to a soft giggling.

"You're the best V. I had an amazing morning. Woke up early, did an on-demand cycling class on your fancy indoor bike, took a hydrating bath, made a toothsome avocado toast on local rustic bread, and then worked on your art. I also finished an additional project for missing and murdered Indigenous women. Pinot has been hanging out in his new bed by the fireplace, mostly," Ella sang.

"Uh huh, busy woman. I suspect this glow might also have to do with a certain man, who's name rhymes with *machine*," V poked with a wink.

"*Maybe*... But I'm excited for them both, I swear! I really am excited to see Logan, to talk about his work. I had absolutely no idea how successful he was with his photography career. He's going to just love it here. There are endless places to get great shots," Ella said excitedly.

"*Alright*. Might I also add to my neglectful comment that I am darn excited to see your work for the house! Daddy has been asking me about it every day. I said we mustn't disturb your process. So, where's Lia?"

"Your dad is adorable. I think you both will love the work, or I hope so! I incorporated the cool color palette that you sent me," Ella said. She rolled her sharp shoulder forward in a hinting manner.

"Yay!" V cheered, exposing pearly white teeth.

"Oh, and you might not want to say daddy around Lia, she's going to make fun of you, and it will drive me nuts. She should be here soon, not sure why she's late."

"I won't say it, if she doesn't call me a soulless ginger again, so immature."

"Oy vey, you two. She was being a brat because she had the biggest crush on you. Who wouldn't? But you kept offering to set her up with your co-worker, who's a *guy*. That doesn't excuse her behavior. But you haven't seen each other in forever. Hopefully, she's a tad more collected for the sake of helping me," Ella divulged, sighing.

V inspected the yellow gold rings on her fingers, without a response. Ella opened a kitchen drawer and pulled out a silicone stretch lid, she secured it over the bowl of fruit, and placed it on a shelf in the refrigerator.

"Oh, dear lord, I forgot the goods! Be right back," V said on her way towards the front foyer.

Ella retrieved her sleepy pup from his comfortable plush nesting bed. She brought him upstairs with her to avoid him whimpering and farting at the bottom steps for ten minutes. Reaching her room, she put him in his bed by her bookcase and grabbed her utility knife to open boxes. She heard a creaking noise coming from the guest restroom. Ella froze and held her breath, trying to identify if what she heard was real or not.

"Got damn, these are the nicest towels ever!" Lia screeched.

Ella released her breath and shrugged her shoulders forward.

"*Lia*! What did I tell you about sneaking up on me?" Ella fumed.

Lia held up her bare hands, now standing before Ella, wearing a black short-sleeve crop top exposing her toned abs, with gray plaid skinny ankle pants, and black platform oxford shoes.

"Thought you would've heard me, *sorry*."

"I didn't. If you could say, *I'm home,* or something like that next time, I would appreciate it."

"Okay, sheesh. I rode my bike and came through the garage that isn't exactly *sneaking up*. I'll go put my shoes in my room before V has a meltdown over me, too."

"No, no stay. This house is massive. It's hard to hear what's going on in the front from here. Sorry, I'm just, you know, still?"

"Hey, what did I tell you?"

"I'm not *sorry*," Ella chimed.

"Cool. Now let's get this show on the road. I'm excited to see you out of those rags already. Also, sorry that I'm late. Tammy has been such a wicked bitch at work. She's been giving me shit for dating Maggie, which is none of her business. Maggie isn't even my supervisor anymore! We're directors of our own departments," Lia whined. She leaned her head back and whipped it forward. Her shiny black hair with vibrant turquoise highlights, swayed above her strong shoulders.

"Yikes, can't you do something about that? Like report her to her superior or to human resources?"

"No, she's the daughter of an owner. That's why they stuck her spoiled ass on the front desk. Tammy pops her gum at everyone, ignoring protocol, thinking she's a manager. She sucks. But your girl, Gertie, is doing well. She's way healthier and happier now. That was hella sweet of you to help with her long-term care insurance to transfer her. Woodsberry Senior Living isn't even our competition, they're so far down on the list in the county. There's heavy neglect and shit going on there. I schedule Gertie's classes, it's so sad she doesn't have family. She asked if you'd come and do a paint nite," Lia explored, moving both her eyebrows up and down quickly. Ella laughed at the notion.

"I'll visit with her next week, and I would love to do that. It's like having a nonna here. I love her. I'll consult with the fabulous Bonnes Bay Luxury Senior Living Activities Director."

Lia grinned back at her older sister and skipped to the back patio doors, in platforms. She moved the furniture around on the deck. The sun was going down at a glacial speed this afternoon. A perfect limelight shining warmth on the back of their home, as if the earth were coinciding with the private show. The air mostly tamed, purred a pleasant breeze.

"Hi Miss Emilia!" V bubbled. She entered Ella's room with a wood tray.

"Oh, *hey* V, you're looking spectacular. I love that romper. Where did you get it?" Lia praised enthusiastically.

"Thanks, a little boutique in Texas. You look nice too, very sassy and styled."

"Yum, what is all this?" Ella chimed in.

Lia turned the outdoor coffee table around outside and V set the tray down on it.

"We can't have a closet fashion party without refreshments and snacks! We have an assortment of hard cheeses, popcorn, nuts, and I ordered these incredible galaxy macarons with little edible stars. They're your favorite flavor, *Milky Way,* like the chocolate bars! This champagne is for us, Ella. And for Miss Lia... I got this new mocktail mix drink. I wanted to be sensitive about your not drinking anymore, but it's exquisite. Herbaceous, floral, and bitter, with club soda. I know you don't need a substitution, but this company designed this non-alcoholic spirit with nootropics, adaptogens, and botanicals. So, you'll get the euphoric mood boost, without the hangover," V explained, handing the glass to Lia, who was lounging on the outdoor sofa.

"Wow, you did that, just for me?" Lia questioned.

She graciously accepted the ginger hued non-alcoholic beverage with an orange peel in it.

"Yes ma'am. I just opened it, but the rest of the bottle is in your refrigerator."

Ella beamed, grinning from ear to ear. It comforted her to see the obvious white flag being waved.

"I made us yummy winter bowls for dinner! They have quinoa, cara cara oranges, Brussels, honeynut squash, feta, and onion. With a citrus vinaigrette," Ella effused.

"Holy shit, you two are a foodie's wet dream! Sheesh, on to the wardrobe. I already know what outfit I'm going to give the bad buzzer to," Lia said, snorting.

Lia and V exchanged light smiles and laughed.

"*Ha-ha*, I know you guys are sick of seeing me in these. I have been working my butt off on the art pieces. But I'm also wearing these because, if you haven't noticed, my wardrobe is in storage."

"Wait, are you serious? Why?" V asked.

"What's in all the boxes, then?" Lia interjected.

"Well, I wanted to hit the reset on all aspects of my life. As you ladies know, I lost myself in the relationship with asshole. I'm sure you remember that he constantly had to comment about my clothes. He said they were *too loud*. I ended up as a wallflower, just blending in with my house. Muted and quiet. I want to feel alive and express myself again, get excited about my representation, exhibit an art on my body. I refuse to let the bank robber take that away from me, too. I don't want to be scared to wear stilettos, to dress sexy, or to have blood-colored apparel. The bank was almost a blessing in disguise. It made me want to *fight* for my life. So, I signed up for this fashion subscription, I took a quiz, and a stylist picked out pieces to create outfits based on my answers. I ordered enough to start a new wardrobe. That's why I couldn't wear makeup though. The articles that we don't like, can go back! Just imagine me all glammy for the chic pieces," Ella exclaimed.

"That's hella cool, I like this! Birthday girl gonna look so fly!" Lia shouted.

"Love it, sugar! You deserve to look nice and to feel empowered to do so! Shall we do thumbs up for hang it up and thumbs down for the clothes that need to go back in the box?" V proposed.

"Yes, exactly! Thank you, ladies, for being here for me. For being with me, after everything. You both are golden mirrors, reflecting what I need to hear and see, when I can't always process it on my own. If that makes sense," Ella admitted, graciously.

"Of course, it makes sense! We know you go at your own pace, but *sometimes* people need others, and we love you," V assured, nodding with Lia.

Pinot poked his head out from behind the linen curtain. He blinked with the sun shining against his bulging blue eyes.

"Pinot, come! Join us," V insisted. She pulled a homemade apple peanut butter treat from her pink floral pants romper pocket. He gobbled it down quickly and laid down on the deck between V and Lia. He spread his hind legs out behind him, resembling a frog.

"Okay, I'll go change quick!" Ella said. She took a sip of her champagne and set the glass back down on the tray. She disappeared behind the steely blue curtains.

Lia exhaled noisily as she lifted her legs to sit cross-legged on the sofa.

"V, I'm sorry for being such a biatch before. Thanks for getting this mixer drink for me. I can already feel the effects, and it tastes great," Lia said.

"Aw miss, consider it water under the bride," V confirmed.

"Great! So, let's get some tunes going for this runway! Alexa, play *Oui ou non* by *Angèle*," Lia spoke to the speaker on the table.

Lia and V swayed their shoulders and bopped their heads in rhythm to the beats of the French pop song. Ella popped out from behind the curtain in a light-weight gauzy sapphire maxi dress with white floral embroidery, a plunging v-neckline, and a drawstring waist. She twirled bare-footed and rolled her arms upwards to expose the perfect fit of the dolman sleeves. All thumbs up. Her natural lip balm grin expressed a matched approval. Lia and V shared the outdoor throw blanket, swaying to the music in between sips of their drinks and tossing popcorn at each other. Ella strutted out in a series of outfits. She danced and struck poses before changing out of them quickly. An easy weekend outfit of the lightest blue jean flares with a white off the shoulder cropped bubble top and bow slide sandals. To sexy high-waisted black skinny jeans that hugged every curve, paired with a scarlet silk wrap-front blouse and strappy black heels. An oversized linen white button-up shirt, with a sky blue embroidered bralette and white ripped skinny crops. Flying through the last outfits; an earthy red backless sweater mini dress, a light turquoise knit jumpsuit with a matching cardigan, a pink denim baby doll dress, and a classic sandy paper-bag trouser with a white corset tank top. The girls got drunk off dancing, an ocean sunset, ethereal spring fashion, and an abundance of laughter. Pinot joined in on the fun, running around the deck, providing a rising bark.

Ella walked out in a final cozy set, a matching rosemary textured knit sweater and wide-leg lounge pants. She threw herself over the ottoman in front of Lia and huffed.

"Think I'm settled for life. Those stylists did me a solid. The pajamas and lounge clothes are perfect too. I don't have to send anything back!" Ella chirped, raspy.

"Girl, you were totally a stripper in a past life. That's the quickest I have ever seen someone change. And I used to date one," Lia laughed.

"That was certainly a show you put on. I have to agree with Lia. I haven't seen you this happy in-I'm just so excited that you look like yourself again. It is getting *chilly* though and I am so ready for your winter bowl," V said, her breath visible.

All three women and the short blue gray Frenchie rushed inside. Ella put the tray with dirty dishes on her Victorian chair and closed the back French doors behind her. A loud thud stopped everyone from further movement.

"What was that?" Ella asked rapidly.

"I don't know. It sounded like it came from downstairs," Lia replied.

Ella grabbed her utility knife off the top of the bookcase and pushed the lever to release the blade.

"Well wait, shouldn't we just call the police?" V insisted.

"I hardly doubt that there is an intruder, it's probably the house," Lia countered.

"I don't want to wait for a sheriff to come out here. I already researched the average time it takes for emergency services to respond to this area," Ella said.

"Lord, I had a feeling this was too out of the way. You're right Lia, the house makes noises sometimes. It's probably nothing. And Ella, a knife? I would invest in a gun, if you're worried, but you have to take classes and respond tactical, calmly," V whispered.

"Oh, my lord, Ella, put the knife away. That can't hurt anyone. Can you hush Pinot? Let's just go look. The doors are locked, it's fine. Take a deep breath," Lia said bravely.

"V I love you, but this isn't Texas, it's like damn near impossible getting a gun license in California right now. And the last thing that I want around me, is a gun. Calm, Pinot, calm," Ella muttered forcibly.

She retracted the blade and set the utility knife back on the bookcase. She grasped her chest for her necklace.

V closed Pinot in Ella's room and followed the two sisters, who were tiptoeing down the dimly lit staircase. Lia led the way, and once at the bottom step she shouted, "Hello, asshole!"

"*Lia*! What the hell?" Ella scowled. She shoved past her.

Lia was laughing now, holding her stomach. V shook her head at Lia and joined Ella's search in the kitchen. She then walked past to check the back door to the deck.

"Get a grip guys, it's just the dishwasher," Lia said, her voice sonorous and full.

Lia, desperate to gain their confidence, left the room to check the front door and garage.

"*OKAY*! This is what the noise was," Lia shouted.

Ella and V followed her command and joined her in the garage.

"I don't know how this could happen, maybe from the dryer against the wall?" Lia asked. Looking down at broken glass.

"Oh shoot! Yeah, it could have leaned forward from the vibration. I'll get the broom," V said rushed, in a slight southern accent.

Ella remained quiet as she reached forward to pick a piece of glass up.

"Don't! It's bad luck to touch the glass from a broken mirror, seven years. You don't need anymore of that. Honestly, dude, get out of here, you're barefoot. Let V and I get this. Here I have my leather gloves," Lia asserted deeply.

"And I've got the broom! Lord, Ella, get in the house," V said.

"Okay, okay. Bossy babes. Thank you for doing this. I guess I'll go set up dinner and the projector," Ella squeaked from the doorway.

"Turn the fireplace on, too, please!" Lia shouted.

A shiver crept up Ella's spine, raising the micro body hairs along her back and up to her neck. She pondered how both Lia and V could believe that everything was fine. That they would suggest gravity was the sole cause of a three-foot square mirror crashing to the ground from a leaning position. They heard a thud or thumping noise, not glass shattering. Ella inhaled deeply to exhale through her breathing necklace. She smelled a sweet, confectionary like scent. It reminded her of the blue raspberry saltwater taffy that she had just purchased for the bedrooms. A whirl of suspicions swam in her mind. Ella pondered if someone was attempting to get revenge for the bank robber that she slayed. Yet, she didn't want to retreat to paranoia, the fear, and sleepless nights. Nor did she want people walking on eggshells around her. She needed ordinariness, so she trusted her sister's confidence and put her instincts to bed.

"We took care of all the glass, it's outside in the trash. None of it got even remotely close to Pinot's bed, but I'm going to get him a new one. I'll use the shop vac in there before the *partay* tomorrow," Lia explained.

"Thank you, Lia. Sorry, I got a little overwhelmed and agitated. So, um, do you want to watch the new *Wonder Woman* or *A Little Chaos* first?" Ella asked as she licked a drop of Meyer lemon vinaigrette off her thumb.

"Definitely *Wonder Woman*! You should be her for Halloween this year. You seriously look like Gal. Well, a very miniature version of her, but still. V went up to change. I'm gonna go change too and I'll bring Pinot down. Be right back," Lia said.

Lia left the room. Her clunky platforms echoed with each stomp up the stairs.

"Thanks, but Halloween is like forever away," Ella said under her breath.

Ella finished dressing and garnishing the winter bowls for dinner. She turned the fireplace on, laid out tufted floor pillows, placed chunky wool throw blankets on the floor and set up the digital movie projector.

Ella finished wiping the marble island top and glanced upwards. She gasped harshly and rapidly backed up against the extra-thick, pure copper farmhouse sink. Her shoulders slouched forward as she wrapped her arms around her petite waist, facing the empty living room. An unnerving tall, dark figure stood statuesque with their legs shoulder-width apart, just on the other side of the floor-to-ceiling glass sliders. Cloaked in a maddening, thick, off-white fog, they faced the interior of the home. Ella imagined she was viewing an impossibly long banana yellow rope near the figure, as well. She was convinced that this was the worst of her hallucinations and continued clinging to her body tightly and squeezed her eyes shut.

She whispered to herself, "You're not here, you're dead, you can't haunt me."

ooo

THE JOURNAL

March 13th, 1989

THIS MORNING, SOFIA found Fido by the cans as she was going to leave. Someone poisoned Fido, but the Colombo's think he ate something bad from the trash. If only I had the DeLorean time machine to take me back to see her face.

Sofia was reciting how she found him all day. This is how it went: She called Fido over because she thought he was sleeping. Sofia said, "When I saw the blood and his tongue sticking out, I was so scared, I was pearlized with fear." It sounded like she was impersonating a Boston accent.

I know she didn't actually know the correct word. It's paralyzed, baby, but who's going to correct the bodacious babe in the room. Scaring her by popping out from behind the bathroom door has nothing on this.

Mr. Colombo made up a fancy dinner, starting with grilled oysters and shrimp cocktail cups. It was an effort to cheer up the girls and celebrate the liftoff of the NASA

Discovery Shuttle today. I'm all game for this kind of dining. I studied Sofia as she slurped her first oyster. What I would do to have been that lucky little mollusk meat. Licked, sucked, and slurped on. Yes, she can eat oyster good alright. I kept it to myself that it's an aphrodisiac. It certainly was turning me on, right there at the dinner table.

Her dad attempted to tease the girls by saying that they might find a pearl in their oyster if they were lucky. He was poking playfully at Sofia's mistake earlier in the day. She didn't get it. Anyway, I corrected HIM that the oysters we eat, don't actually contain pearls. I explained to the table that oysters must be alive in order to be eaten and that they have a small heart and internal organs. I told them they can tell themselves that an oyster's evasive nervous system doesn't deliver the same pain response that you and I experience. But that, it is just a fancy form of denial.

Mr. Colombo didn't threaten me for the editing of his joke, instead he offered me some bubbly to pair with the tasty loogie in lemon juice. Probably shouldn't have pushed it by adding the fact that oysters also change genders multiple times in their lifetime. That made Mrs. Colombo uncomfortable. Dinner was not short of amusement, but I had to control my mouth. I guess I'm just high on Sofia's story about her dead dog. And LUCKY me, the little doggy horror show is keeping her from her going to spring break at Sapphire Glass Beach, Florida with Jackie this week.

I thought a lot about mother today; I wish I hadn't. It sort of feels like things are coming full circle. I can't comprehend that at the moment though, going to go console the little lamb for the night.

A dragon and the lamb.

ooo

ENCHANTING ENCOUNTER

February 3rd, 2021

"**I**S THAT SIXTEEN oh four?" I asked.

"Has to be. She said it's the last house on the right. It's the only last house, unless you want to continue driving through that big ass mountain of sand," Logan teased.

"Ah, dude, I should have slept on the plane. Oh um, try not to talk about the bank to Ella," I requested drowsily.

"I'm sure they're not savages and have coffee. And dude, that's a no-brainer. Perk up boo, we in Cali! Yo, who do you think owns the sick luxury electric car!" Logan beseeched.

I smirked at him, as he parked us at the end of the road; a log rail barrier stood between the road and a massive dune. Logan and I exited our metallic gray sports SUV and stretched, attempting to poke the serene soft blue sky.

We endured five and a half hours of fly time wearing face masks on a red eye, from Fort-Lauderdale airport to the San Francisco Airport. Once we landed, we spent half of an hour driving the steep and busy streets of the city in search of the clinic that our insurance covered for our rapid antigen tests. It took an additional hour from start to finish with results. It took us exactly an hour and a half to drive here from San Francisco. And it was the California ride we had long been looking forward to. As the sun rose and heated the bay area, the fog dissipated miraculously. Just in time for spectacular views, as we drove on the world-famous, international orange, Golden Gate Bridge. The traffic was more clustered than we were used to. We approached a tunnel that had a rainbow painted on the arch just before we entered. Once on the other side, we joked about how we finally found the pot of gold. Exploring one of the richest counties in the United States, Marin County boasted of natural beauty, Michelin-star restaurants, yacht harbors, and tall redwoods. Through Sausalito, massive homes stacked up and down the hills, with million-dollar water views at all angles. Transitioning further north from San Rafael to Novato, the size of the towns decreased, but the gas prices didn't. The land was vast and wide for free-roaming cows, dairy farms, and apple orchards.

So, I have moderate jet lag.

Sharp and soaring Italian cypress trees concealed Ella's home, resembling sharp and compact knives erecting from the earth. It's hard to tell exactly how large the house is from the road. I scanned over the parked vehicles in the wide but short driveway. A candy red and steel stylish *Sportster* motorbike, a paper white compact SUV, and a teal haze mid-sized luxury sedan. I felt an itchy sensation on my wrist, my quartz tattoo raised. It must be the climate change. I pulled my blue flannel shirt sleeve over it, as I glanced down at the tiny succulents filling gaps between the pavement and rolled grass.

"Well, hello stranger," Ella said, smiling sweetly with her mouth open.

She stood barefoot in her doorway, wearing a flowy satin baby blue dress that wrapped in the front, with long puffy sleeves and a deep v-neckline.

"Oh, oh *wow*. Ella! Happy Birthday!" I rejoiced.

We both laughed, hesitated, and ran towards each other. She clung to me as I lifted her off the ground. I twirled her around once; she felt light. And I felt like I had ingested a full package of *Pop Rocks* and a can of pop. The spinning released an intoxicating perfume of woods, sweet jasmine, and a touch of vanilla.

"Hey, hey, hey!" Logan said, confident and loud.

"*Logan*!" Ella said raspy and cut off towards the end.

"Now that's a damn birthday getup! Get over here!" Logan shouted.

I lowered Ella down and she ran to Logan's side, on the single road. He put down our suitcases and duffle bags to hug her. Aware that I was still chuckling, I closed my mouth, but remained smiling.

"Holy shit, it's Oisín Murphy," said a sonorous voice from behind me.

"Emilia! Hey *wow*, look at you, all grown up!" I shouted as she strutted towards me, with Pinot by her side. The short dog barked excitedly, wagging his backside.

Lia somehow resembled the child's version of her I remembered. Although she's much taller now with an athletic build. She still has a few freckles and a button nose.

"It's Lia now and you look like a freaking lumberjack!" Lia said boldly.

"*Damn,* all y'all Russo girls be changing names!" Logan chuckled as he approached Lia, they hugged briefly while patting each others backs playfully.

I bent down to pet Pinot. Instantly melted, he gazed up at me with his puppy dog eyes and playful mouth. He looks like he's actually smiling. I stood back up to witness Ella staring at me with amusement. Her beautiful raspberry painted mouth glistened.

"V, come out here, they're here!" Ella shouted.

I went to the road to collect our luggage and brought it to the driveway, when a lean and porcelain, pretty redhead appeared in the doorway. She wore a striped cream and navy fisher sweater and tight dark blue jeans.

"Hey y'all! I'm V. And you are? *Wow,*" V remarked.

"I'm what?" Logan said, looking down at her with a skeptical smile.

"You are *some* kind of beautiful," V said bluntly. Her eyes flashed at Logan.

We all belted out in an unmatched parade of laughter.

"I never had a woman call me *that* before, but okay, I'll take it," Logan chuckled.

"*Ahem,* I think I'm pretty hot," Lia said sarcastically.

"Guys, this is V. V, this is Logan and Oisín," Ella giggled, wide-eyed.

"Oh, dear lord. Sorry for the word vomit. Uh, come, come inside!" V said, shaking her gawkiness off and leading the way.

Ella noticed that I was staring at her. She rubbed her fuchsia lips together and licked them before smiling again. She motioned her hand towards the front entryway after V led Logan, Lia, and Pinot inside.

ooo

I awoke in a mostly coral room. Each wall had subtle murals of white seashells. Lying on a full mattress over a maple wood plank, a bed suspended by nautical ropes from the four corners. I pulled the white quilt off my body and swung my legs outside of the bedding; it didn't swing frantically as I expected it would. That was the best sleep I've had in months, maybe even a year, on a swinging bed in a foreign space.

Go figure. And no murderers, no blood, no pearls.

I picked my phone up from the dark navy dresser, between our beds, and disconnected the charging cord. I felt winded when I read the time.

Holy shit, I slept half of Ella's birthday away.

Twelve missed calls from an unknown number. But not one of them woke me up.

What's the point of having a spam blocker if it never works?

I picked up a piece of light blue saltwater taffy from a vibrant orange strom bowl on the dresser. It tasted like raspberry, not bad. Logan's sport duffle bag was open, with a spread of clothes on the identical swinging bed in the room. I need to spruce up as well. In the shared restroom outside of our room, I trimmed and tidied my facial hair. Shaping it into a short, boxed beard style, keeping the length at half an inch, with a sharp and clean neckline above my prominent Adam's apple. Followed by a five-minute shower, brushing my teeth, spritzing cologne on my neck, swiping deodorant on the pits, and smoothing my medium brown comb over with styling cream. I changed into my new navy dress shirt with dark jeans and saddle brown low-top leather sneakers. I retrieved Ella's gifts from my suitcase and stuffed my phone in my back pocket.

ooo

Once in the kitchen, I could see Ella across the living room. She sat on a deep leather lounge chair in front of the lit electric fireplace, reading a book. From every standing position in this kitchen and open concept living room, you get a remarkable ocean view. The only moderate color on the first floor belonged to the navy kitchen cupboards, matching navy trim on upper glass cabinets that spanned the wall and navy drawers with brass handles. As well as a blue thirty-foot *Safavieh* runner rug that ran behind the marble-top island on the Sycamore flooring. Even with grayish white stratus of cloud coverage, the blanket of textured cobalt blue ocean effervesced, drawing me in.

I joined Logan and V next to the espresso machine. Logan nodded and passed a stone mug filled with coffee to me. He continued his conversation with V. I held up Ella's gift to them. V pointed towards the ship wheel table, as the presents location.

"This house is dope, like for real, it's litty. But like I said, how are you going to have a vacation home with no television? *Lakers* are playing Denver tomorrow. What about the kids who play *CoD* or?" Logan grilled.

"The *kids*?" V shot Logan a wink. "I designed it for a specific clientele. Like travelers who want to get away from their technological run lives. Some people also enjoy sitting in a nice hot tub, to watch an ocean sunset. Or readers, artists, musicians, and people who've experienced hardship, for example," V said in a hushed voice.

"Right, my bad. It is one of the most beautiful and relaxing homes I've been to. You did a solid job. The ship wheel table is trick," Logan complimented confidently.

"Thanks captain, if you're fixin' to have a duck fit during your stay, we have a film projector here, for indoor and outdoors. And if you get real antsy, I've got *Call of Duty World War Two* on *PlayStation* four at my place," V offered.

Logan jerked his head back. His round brown eyes bubbled back at V and his full lips pulled up at the sides, creating the infamous dimples.

I've never seen him not have a smart response back.

Lia came out of the pantry with her hands full, holding hot dog buns, chocolate bars, peanut butter cups, graham crackers, marshmallows, and a bundle of extendable roasting sticks.

"Here, let me help you with that. You could stab yourself," I chuckled as I grabbed the sharp sticks from Lia's side. I set them on the white marble countertop, next to the rest of the party supplies.

"Thanks champ. You've got a little something there," Lia said, nodding at me.

Logan moved around me to rip a sales tag that was attached to the back of my jeans. V took the tag from Logan and put into the trash under the sink.

"Oh, shit," I griped.

"We got you," Logan replied.

"Miss Ella, don't look for a minute, *please*!" V shouted.

"OH boy, okay! And hi Oisín! I hope you slept well!" Ella shouted back to us. She put her book down and raised her hands to cover her eyes.

V rushed in and out of the large walk-in pantry. She came back out three times with a series of birthday décor. White LED string lights revolved around transparent and circular balloons with white balloon weights at the bottom of the LED string. A pre-assembled ten-foot gold and silver balloon arch with green garland and white flowers. Paper crackers with foil gold stars on them, birthday candles, floral paper plates and napkins.

PSST!

Logan extended a step stool towards me to hang the balloon arch from removable hooks attached to the wood beams above us. I glanced back at Ella. She was waiting patiently. I moved the step stool again and hung up the remaining length of the arch. Lia and V finished making cocktails for us, while Logan placed the LED lit balloons sporadically around the massive living room. I put the stepstool back in the garage.

Pinot laid down on a round, plush dog bed beside Ella. The small-sized dog remained chill, even with all the hushed commotion. He seemed to react to the world in his time, an admirable creature. Ella looks otherworldly, sitting by the fire in a cream cable front cardigan over her baby blue dress. Her loose half updo, released long wisps of hair that framed her face and fell down to her sharp collar bone.

We gathered back by the kitchen table, behind the couch. V handed a paper star popper to each of us. I stood next to Logan, V on the other side of him, with Lia on the right side of her. V demanded our attention as she held out her fingers, holding up three, then two, and one.

"SURPRISE!" we all yelled, simultaneously cracking open our poppers.

Snap, snap, snap, snap.

White, gold, and silver foil starred confetti soared across the crisp white couch in Ella's direction.

"OH! Oh, my goodness! Thank you, guys, this is so sweet. I said you didn't have to do anything," Ella said, sweet and raspy.

V retrieved a bright red cake from the refrigerator with gold foil on the smoothed naked frosting. Silver birthday cake candle sparklers sprouted out from the cherry hued frosting on top, surrounded by pink peonies, white roses, and greenery.

"Wow, wow, wow! It's so beautiful! Did you get this at Cake Chest, here in Bonnes Bay?" Ella yelped.

"Yeah, it's from me, Lia, and your mama. Three layers of red velvet cake with vanilla bean frosting," V chirped back.

"I love it! Anything cocoa has my heart, and this is my favorite bakery ever. They truly are a treasure of treats! It's dangerous living so close to it. I'll video call mom later. She's still fearful of getting together just yet," Ella said, looking at me, but speaking to V.

"Happy birthday to a true Aquarius!" Lia said. She wrapped her arms around Ella.

"Thank you so much! I really was fine with just hotdogs. As long as you guys don't sing or remind me of my age!" Ella yelped. She joined Lia and V in the kitchen.

"No singing from us! Devon is the one with vocals, anyway," Logan laughed off.

"Hey as long as you feel celebrated, Ella! Wait, check out the tiger in the corner. I could play a birthday tune on the baby grand if you want," I offered.

"Alexa, play *Cake by the Ocean* by *DNCE*," Lia spoke to V's *Speaqua*, rapidly. Nu-disco funk played in the background. Lia smirked and began moving to the rhythm of the song, in her long, black knit dress. Logan scoffed at Lia's demeanor, and we joined the women in the kitchen. V handed us each a double old fashion glass with pink salt on the rim, pale pink contents, with star-topped stir sticks. V then prepared a special drink for Lia, while Ella looked perplexed, searching for a knife for the cake.

"Where have all the knives gone? Well, we can do drinks first. These have silver tequila, Cointreau, champagne, pink lemonade, lemon juice, and Himalayan sea salt. It is the one thing that I requested from V," Ella explained.

V frantically searched the utensil drawers, cabinets, and pantry. She finally pulled out an eight-inch chef's knife out of a mixing bowl from a glass door upper cabinet.

"Found it!" V celebrated. She sliced the birthday cake apart, meticulously. She swayed in white wide-leg dress pants and a white satin blouse. Licking the tip of the sharp blade as she concluded the task. Logan appeared to be tickled.

Kind of creepy, but okay.

"Miss Ella, you know your drinks," V said as she held her pink cocktail up.

"I'm strictly an IPA guy, but this is dope V, good job," Logan replied to V.

"And I'm mostly a whiskey and beer kind of guy, but this *is* damn good," I added.

Ella held her glass up, chest high, and raised her eyebrows. I can't believe how she looks the same, but not at all.

"Speech, speech, speech!" Lia and V chanted.

"I know the sun is going down and we're all hungry. Thanks V and Lia, for setting up the portable fire pit and tiki torches down there. Thank you, Oisín and Logan, for being cautious with pandemic protocol, it is so appreciated. I just... *this is wild*. Last year, I was low-key miserable spending my thirtieth at a crowded retreat with stuffy businesspeople, art collectors, and buyers. After a fresh breakup, dirty old men conned me left and right. It was debasing. The event surrounded me with everyone that I needed, but no one that I loved. One horrendous pandemic and massively bloody bank massacre later, and here I am. In one of the most enchanting homes, that I've *ever* seen. With my best friends, family, and *you*, Oisín.

You've all gifted me with your generous time, unfiltered kindness, and precious hope. For that, I'm the luckiest girl in the world. I love you guys," Ella delivered.

Damn.

"My, Ella, I know I speak on behalf of all of us when I say, we are *so* grateful that you were born, and that you're here today, *alive*. Cheers to the star of the hour and every second after," V cheered.

"*Woo*, I am dehydrated after that," Lia wavered, wiping a tear from her cheek. She clinked her glass with Ella's. Lia seems like a softie under the façade.

"Yo, that was well-said Ella. Thanks for having us boo, it feels like no time has passed," Logan shouted, clinking glasses with Ella's. He wrapped his long, muscular arms around her. She disappeared into his rustic orange cashmere quarter zip-up.

"Yeah, Ella, thank you for having us. You deserve to be happy, on your birthday and every second after," I added, in a deep voice.

I raised my glass to hers. Instead, she set hers down and hugged me.

"I am happy, Oisín. This shirt looks nice. It really makes your *Oisín* eyes pop," Ella said softly, gazing into my blue and brown eyes.

Logan took a few candid shots of us on his *Canon EOS 5D Mark IV*. He calls it his *fun* camera. We turned to smile for a few. Ella didn't open her mouth for the photo, even though she had beautifully white and straight teeth.

"Gifts!" Lia shouted, interrupting our photo opportunity.

"Y'all start! And Logan, could you help me fill the cooler?" V insisted.

Logan secured his camera in a soft bag on the couch and jogged to V's side, in his black slim-fit tailored trousers.

"I told you guys not to get me anything!" Ella retorted.

"Yeah, right, like we wouldn't get you something. Open mine first!" Lia insisted. I sat down next to Lia on the couch with my cocktail and slice of cake. Ella positioned herself back on the dark leather lounge chair by the fire.

She pulled tissue out of the bag and held up a white blouse with black, white, blue, and yellow ribbons on the arm and a skinny leather belt secured around the waist.

"Lia! This is stunning! Did you make this?" Ella questioned.

"Yeah girl, grazie! It's not just for like powwow regalia or events. I thought it could help you feel more... in tune with Diné."

"You are beyond talented, ti amo! Dad is going to flip when he sees me in it."

"What does Diné mean?" Logan quizzed from the kitchen.

"Some say *the people*. Diné, meaning the up and down, going from no surface to a surface being on Mother Earth. Our dad is of the Salt Water Clan by our grandma and our grandpa is English. We are *pretty* mixed. Not sure if you remember our mom, but she met him in Arizona when she was studying beadwork for her business, Row Me Russo," Lia explained to our group.

"Now our mom provides beads for some women and girls in dad's community. She features the finished products in her retail space for their profit and exposure. Actually, we all sort of share that passion now. Lia's fashion pursuit and my abstract paintings will follow that philanthropic approach," Ella clarified.

"She doesn't produce pearl jewelry, does she?" I inquired, lowly.

Logan clicked his tongue at me. I turned to face him; his eyes bugged outwards as he kept a tight mouth. He sat down on the other side of Lia. And V cuddled up on the white sofa chair on the other side of him.

"Who, mom? No, she's like a modern-day Impiraressa, she does intricate bead work. She won't even wear pearls," Lia enlightened.

We continued to watch Ella open her gifts with enthusiasm. Her mother sent her a *Gucci* sweater. V gifted an overnight stay and excursion at a vineyard and an artist series bottle of olive oil. And Logan gave her a framed photograph of a sunset at the skatepark that we used to hangout at every weekend. She opened my gifts last, the card first.

"Aww, Oisín. This is the sweetest card. Wow, and a hundred-dollar gift card to *Copperfield's Books*? Thank you!" Ella shrieked.

"Thought you'd want some of your own books while you are living here," I said.

She grinned and put her small hand to her chest, grazing her glistening skin.

"Smooth move, *Casanova*," Lia said sarcastically.

Ella opened the jewelry box and held up earrings, gold hoops with dangling white beaded strands that held teeny metal red and green strawberries at the ends.

"Oh, my god! Oisín, I love these! Are these tiny strawberries?" Ella gushed.

"Exactly. I know you guys have your family business and could probably have any jewelry that you've ever wanted. But there was this kind, old woman at the boathouse marina, she does made-to-order jewelry. No two pairs are ever the same. Every time we video called; you were eating strawberries. I think they are a perfect symbol of you, sweet, but *mostly* unique. Because strawberries aren't real berries and they're part of the rose family," I explained.

"My. Are you sweeter than an apiary in July," V bubbled.

"Word, Murph. You're alright in my book," Lia said. She exchanged the first genuine smile with me, for the first time since we arrived.

Ella came to me sitting on the sofa. She lowered into a squatting position in her baby blue dress and short cable front cardigan. She put her hands on my thighs and smiled up at me. I could see her cleavage too well. I shifted my eyes back to hers. Ella's eyes changed from a deep chocolate brown to forest green with gold flecks.

This is what it feels like to want someone since puberty.

Ella raised herself and lunged forward to hug me. She pressed her face against mine and spoke into my ear.

"They're perfect. You are the best, *Oisín*," Ella said my name like it was a piece of Beethoven's music, a sexy lullaby. The way she emphasized the *oh*, resembling a soft moan to the hushed *sheen*, like it's a secret that only we know.

"Well, I'm ready for some wieners! By that, I mean my smoked plant-based frankfurters bitches," Lia said bluntly. She nudged my ribs with her elbow.

Saved by the Lia Liberty Bell.

ooo

Ella and V went down to the beach with outdoor blankets and fold-up chairs. While Logan and I packed all the food and beverages into bags. Lia stayed back to play with Pinot on the floor and catch up with Logan.

"Miss Ella, why did you not show me a photo of Logan? Fine as frog hair split four ways. That was real embarrassing earlier. Talk about a hottie haven in there," V said, staring into the fire.

"I actually found it really entertaining. I have never seen you flirt that way, V. This is such a mess, huh? I mean, I don't even remember the last time that I got laid. Oh no, not that I was thinking of Oisín, though. He is my childhood best friend. That would be weird, right?" Ella insisted, seeking opinion.

"Wrong, I'll do your childhood best friend, Logan is smokin'! Not even just that, he's like *real* put together, polite, hilarious, driven. The unicorn kind," V joked.

"Sure, he's cute, but kind of like a brother to me. Like one that I haven't seen in a long time," Ella replied.

"Uh huh and you feel like Oisín is a brother *too*?" V poked, winking at Ella.

Ella rubbed her fuchsia pink lips together. She turned to eye Oisín and Logan in the distance, walking down the flight of aluminum stairs with coolers.

"Oh darlin', it ain't wrong. You seem happy. If we and *he* could do that. That isn't dirty business, it's a part of the peace, balance, beauty, and harmony that you want. Now, don't ask me how to go about that exactly. Good luck, sleeping in a house full of *hot, hot,* Nashville chicken. You bet your sweet bottom; I'll be back first thing to get my coffee. Cause' that up there, you can't get that at *Starbucks*," V preached.

Ella cracked up, giggling low pitched and raspy. V laughed just as hard.

"What are y'all laughing about?" Logan questioned.

He sat down in the empty chair next to V.

"Coffee," V sang.

"Cool, coffee is my specialty," Logan said.

V hummed back at him, "*Mhm.*"

"Who made that cool driftwood fort?" Lia asked. She put Pinot down on an outdoor bean bag next to Ella.

"The kid down the road. He's been collecting and leaving shells in there, it's really cute," Ella said cheerfully.

"What kid?" V insisted.

"Sorry, the guy, the teenager that you said lived down the road?" Ella replied.

"His mom said they wouldn't be back until Spring," V said.

"Well, I didn't see *him* yet. I saw their SUV pull into their garage the other day. I haven't seen anyone on the beach since we moved in."

"Yo! Y'all want to hear a joke? An Irishman and his Irish buddy were walking down the street. They passed by a bar," Logan joked.

Both Logan and V erupted into laughter. I chuckled and helped him with the fire. Lia handed Ella a roasting stick for her hotdog. Her inquisitive frown transitioned into a tender smile.

Under an awning of stars and next to a moon-splashed ocean. We roasted hot dogs and marshmallows. Drank beer and bubbly water. We listened to waves crash onto themselves and Pinot snore noisily. It tasted surreal, sea salty, and sentimentally sweet. Like a dessert that you crave your entire life, it's indescribable, lingering on the tip of your tongue. This brilliant beachy evening came as that dessert, a perfect chemistry of balanced laughter, hearty stories exchanged, and sweet brief glances across the fire.

ooo

THE JOURNAL

April 29ᵗʰ, 1989

I LISTENED IN ON Sofia and Jackie's call this morning. All they could talk about is Sofia wanting to lose her v-card to Mike in his new off-roader with chrome accents. Jackie kept bragging about how David gave her a pearl necklace behind the bleachers. He basically whacked off his tiny wiener on her. The entire football team has been talking about it all week. $20 says she's pregnant before the school year ends.

These dirty, disgusting halls I will never return to. Grinding sounds from pencil sharpeners and girls bitching about this and that. It drives me up the wall. The only time the institution is tolerable is at nighttime. When John and I break in occasionally to search lockers for lunch money and for the hell of it. Unlucky for us, it's usually just floppy disks, rainbow trapper keepers, books and folders smothered in shit chicken scratch doodles and who loves who notes.

PROM!

I ordered a limo for a few of us, meaning me, John, and his hot date, Linda. I splurged on a fancy bottle of champagne to pop beforehand. Rich people's shit. The Colombo's love that. In fact, they love everything that I bring to the table lately, except for John. They think he's a wastoid. They're just snobs. If they paid attention, they would see that he's actually highly intelligent. And he isn't poor, his dad is a pharmacist, drugs are money, duh.

John is wearing a white tuxedo with a tail and a ruffled shirt underneath. Sofia's going in a long pink satin, off-the-shoulder dress with ruffles and a bow on the back. Teasing the shit out of her hair with a can of Aqua Net. She should be prom queen, but Bitchney Whitney is going to take it. No doubt. John and I have a seamless and quick plan to burn Mike's new off-road vehicle during prom tonight. Man, did he put all his money into it, large tires with deep, open treads, and a flexible suspension. A simple misplacement of the cigarette lighter, while everyone's dancing the night away to "When I'm With You", while the real Sheriff has to report to the parking lot. That's the plot anyway and with luck, the girls will be down for my movie night idea in the basement, instead of going to the sexcapades after-party.

John and I found a wounded seagull on our beach trip last weekend. It bore a great resemblance to like my mother's mini-China figures. Frozen on the ground, as if it were in flight. My mother had tiny porcelain figurines lined up on a small wood shelf in our kitchen. I never understood the significance of a flock of three. I took one of the three seagulls to throw off her balance. She never even noticed, and then father hid her. Seagulls are sky rats, not even remotely comparable to the genius raven. Back to the wounded seagull, I got the longer size of the wishbone, so my wish better come true tonight!

ooo

"I to the world am like a drop of water.
That in the ocean seeks another drop,
Who, falling there to find his fellow forth,
Unseen, inquisitive, confounds himself."

— William Shakespeare

GOT WOOD

February 13th, 2021

"V, COULD YOU put on Ooh Ahh by Grits?" Logan asked.

She played the music on her phone and connected it to the stereo system through Bluetooth. V turned around, smiling at us, nodding our heads in the backseat. She winked at Logan before turning back around; he smiled once she was facing forward. He's been pretty quiet on the drive; this has to be a first. We all sang in harmony, the song took us right back to 2002, bittersweet nostalgia. The girls rolled down their windows. It rained the night before; the air tasted chalky, metallic, but refreshing.

We picked up saltwater taffy, snacks, and beer from the highly acclaimed all-in-one, Ocean Scoops. They have espresso, ice cream, incredible local meats, and cheeses. I can tell that Ella has been struggling to eat full meals. Relatable, even as a child, I had a hard time eating after my mom disappeared. I learned that Ella loves the same spicy chips as me. I bought us three bags.

After Ocean Scoops, we headed north. Ella drove our all-terrain rental on winding California country roads from the Naso Coast to the Dry Vine Valley Exit. We were back to zigzagging through country roads. The scenic routes were a trip on their own. Golden hills in the distance raised and lowered to green valleys, like an organic roller coaster, seducing both the modern and traditional man's soul. Simple earthy elements promoted a sense of tranquility, compared to the intense tropical deco and pastels that Sapphire Glass Beach, Florida blasted us with. Acres of gnarly naked grapevines twisted and turned in rows within vineyards. We passed by babbling brooks, a river, and heaps of wineries with wine-tasting rooms. The exterior of the top producers of wines, ranged from quaint and quirky with corn hole boards and Adirondack chairs to massive, elegant buildings surrounded by manicured lawns, gardens, and bocce ball courts.

"Hey, I know it's not like harvest or whatever, but I didn't think this area would be so, tourist-free," I said.

"The wineries are only offering pickups for wine club orders, for now. My friend owns this winery, his name is Phillip by the way. I've just been *dying* to come here with Ella. Normally, it would cost a pretty penny, but this took very little convincing," V explained, in a slight southern accent.

"Sweet, yeah it's cool to have friends in the right places, or are y'all dating?" Logan asked. Ella shifted her eyes from the road to visor mirror for a split second. A smile flickered across her face like a shooting star. We both chuckled.

"No, *strictly* friends. Miss Ella, sorry, take this right!" V shouted.

Ella swung the SUV on a sharp right and drove us up an unpaved road. The entrance sign read, *Quercia e Vino Ranch, Wine-Tasting & Glamping.*

About a quarter mile drive in, we arrived at our destination on a flat part of land, mid-hill. A skinny, short man with pale skin stood at the designated parking spot by the landscaped outdoor living area. He waved wildly in a salmon sweater and khaki pants. He wore a face mask to meet us as we parked. He introduced himself as Phillip, the owner of Oak and Wine Ranch.

He hugged V for a full five seconds and elbow bumped with Logan and I. But he just stared at Ella, who hung back by our vehicle to adjust her tight high-waisted dark flare jeans. Ella stretched her arms up to the tall oak tree, her burgundy flowy blouse lifted as well, exposing her tight abdominals. Phillip explained to us *we were now in God's country, the right country*. Two Christians, one Catholic, and one spiritual person. Yet, his choice of wording still irked us. Mostly because, the night before, we had talked about how vineyard owners used to use an army of enslaved Native American workers on the land during the gold rush, in the mid-nineteenth century. He continued to tell us what we could already assume about the area. That it was a slower pace of life, that there wasn't much traffic, if any. And if we needed to make a phone call, we could access the best service through the woods, at the top of the hill. Phillip informed us that there were a few local vintage stores a mile north and an Oak Grove Grocery store open until six, if we needed anything else for our stay.

The setting completely shifted once we put our bags in our rooms. V and Ella paired together while Logan and I claimed our cottage room. Phillip loosened up.

I would think that Logan has competition, but V likes him. Even with his embarrassing lack of response to her quick wit. I have a feeling that will change soon once he snaps out of his funky shock. Ella rubs her lips together every time that I compliment her. I think it might be too weird that we were once friends. She might still see me as that little kid in Foggerton. I'm an adult and can handle being just friends. But how she looks at me, how she says my name. I can't help thinking about her before I fall asleep. Sleeping and waking, it has been seamless, for once in a long time.

We rejoined Phillip outside of our cottage. He set up a black tablecloth, over a picnic table with benches, on the low deck. Phillip placed a board in the middle of the table, with intricately designed prepared meats, cheeses, fruit, and some jams on top. He made four place settings with plates, water cups and wine glasses. He uncorked two pinot noir wines. And repeated the act with one oaked and one unoaked chardonnay wines. Water carafes and glass Mason jars filled with ferns occupied the remaining area on the table.

"This is some set up, Phillip. We appreciate you for doing all of this on Valentine's day weekend," Logan said, looking down at him.

Phillip placed four menus next to our silverware on thick fabric napkins. He studied Logan's face, which was smiling, showing off a pair of dimples.

"Well, I owed this to V. She sold me my forever home at a *remarkable* price. Now, I would like to find my forever gal, if you know what I mean," Phillip said in a fake, deep voice.

Logan nodded and scratched his smooth cheek. His wavy, line-up, fade combination is flawless, after V had a barber friend make an outdoor house call to us. He sat down on the bench next to me, in an almost identical outfit to mine.

Phillip straightened his back to elongate his figure above us. Logan and I are about the same height and still taller than Phillip, when sitting on the bench. We listened to Phillip as he explained the terroir, the wines, and the wine-making methods to each wine. We learned that the fog at night and hot dry sun during the day is the most ideal condition for pinot noir and chardonnay. It was far more entertaining to watch Ella's facial expressions mocking Phillip each time that he would turn away from us. Phillip continued in a condescending tone, and used his hands often, waving them in the air each time he described his vineyards.

At one point, Ella kicked my brown leather boots with her low-heel burgundy booties. V nudged her in the side with her elbow. We enjoyed the food and wine, but it was exhausting to listen to Phillip's detailed lay of the land. He wrapped up the presentation with additional details of how to drive the *John Deere Gator* down the hill, and insisted we lock the entrance gate after he leaves. Phillip provided V with another lengthy hug and rubbed her back slowly. V flinched awkwardly and laughed.

We all sighed an overdue breath of relief, as he took off in his massive, lifted white truck. An eruption of chortling and matched facial expressions broke out.

"Lord *almighty*. Now for the fun! Why don't we all change and meet back out here in ten. We need to secure the gate and then we can explore," V sang.

There was plenty of charm at this rural resort ranch and I could absolutely see how this could be romantic on a two-person basis. White-painted farm panels sided the cottage exterior, with a matching white fencing around it. Country style lights hung from a tall oak tree to the roof. There were yellow Adirondack chairs between natural wood stumps around a fire pit in front of the cottage. V was filling an old farm sink on the low deck next to the picnic table with ice, glass beer bottles, and filled water carafes. A variety of trees encircled the landscaped living area. They had round plots of dark bark and bright green plants. Phillip left the surrounding areas to rustic charisma. Our forest-like hill overlooked acres of spectacular vineyards.

Phillip kept the inside of the cottage fairly simple, with necessities. Decorated with fresh flowers, incense, a farm-chic galley of storage, appliances, local art, a wine tasting menu on a chalkboard, and a bulletin board of things to do in the area. Logan and I are used to living in tight quarters with each other, and without qualm. But this cottage bedroom is far too small for two athletically built men over six-foot tall. I changed into my thick blue and light brown flannel. Five months ago, I was swimming in it, now it is slightly taut on my muscular upper arms. I changed out of my navy slacks, into fitted dark blue straight leg jeans and laced up my brown chukka boots. The temperature was dropping quickly. I added a navy-blue puffer vest and a gray beanie.

Half an hour later, I met with Ella and V outside of our wine country cottage.

"Hey sugar, why don't you guys start the fire," V proposed.

Ella changed into tight black leggings, short brown hiking boots over tall wool socks. And she threw a burgundy puffer jacket over her long sleeve white Henley shirt. Ella's shirt had the first three buttons undone. She retrieved two beers from the ice tub and popped the caps off with an opener, handing me the second. Her hair was up in a tall and tight ponytail. Her tanned skin glowed under the oak tree lights.

I'm staring again.

"Yeah, *sugar*, we'll be right back," Ella jested. She tipped her open beer towards me and clinked it with mine. The girls got into the Gator, turned the lights on, and disappeared down the hill.

"Logan? Dude, are you done examining the kitchen?" I shouted towards the cottage.

I started the fire, using the cedar bark that Phillip put in the basket for us. Stacked the twigs, sticks, and wood splinters over that, creating a pyramid shape. I used the long-neck utility lighter to burn the dry brush, adding some more tinder and then stacked wood logs in a crisscross pattern.

"Ay! Murph, there's no coffee up in here. Now what am I going to make for V?" Logan pressed. He put his hands on hips and pouted his full lips out.

"Uh, well, I saw V's name on the grapefruit carafe. That dude has got it bad for her to bring fresh squeezed juice," I responded.

"Nah, coffee is life juice. V comes over every morning before work *for* coffee. She even left her thermos there last-oh, *okay*, stop looking at me like that. Murph, yo, stop laughing," Logan chuckled. I let out a deep and joyous guffaw.

"Bro, I can't help myself. She's into you, *not* the coffee. Make a move already. You know what tomorrow is... It's V day, V DAY! Get it?" I said, snickering.

"Damn, ya got jokes. I know, I know, we just talked about this. First girl I been nervous about making a move on. But you know what, you need to make a move too. You and Ella have this undeniable tension, like y'all be staring at each other and communicating some freaky shit, saying nothing. I might not even see V again after we leave, and that would suck. But realistically, it's been a short time and we live across the country. Y'all are some deep intellectual magnets for one another, what's the deal?"

I grinned and handed Logan a beer.

We all layered extra clothing and gathered by the fire for warmth. V and Ella huddled together in a teal double puffy camping quilt. The night was just as, if not better than, Ella's birthday. Laughing, joking, sharing more stories. I haven't had this much time off in my entire life and haven't spent this much quality time with a group of people, not since I was a kid. It was intimate, genuine, and educating. Learning about them, learning about myself. It felt like my heart couldn't get any fuller, busting at the seams with gratitude stuffing. Brain matter overdosing on serotonin. That's the other thing, it's a safe space to abolish gender norms and restraining emotion. Logan and I needed this, too. I discovered my brother when I met my best friend in elementary school. This trip reunited that adventurous friendship.

A variety of folk pop songs with sultry guitar riffs and seductive vocals played in the background from V's *Speaqua*.

"So, how did y'all become the Jelly Club? I heard you guys talking about it the other day. Is it like, a book club or something?" V asked.

The three of us Foggerton childhood friends cracked up.

"Ella wishes it were a book club. Hey buddy, you want to take on that story?" I insisted, patting Logan's back with might.

"Hey, it still can be!" Ella shouted.

She tipped her head back and drank from the IPA that she clung to. Nails painted a marshmallow white. When she tipped her head back forward, she shook her head, swaying her long ponytail and the strawberries that dangled from her gold hoops.

"Our families, Dawson, Murphy, and Russo, we took a shared family vacation to Myrtle Beach. Us three went further down the beach, but Ella told me not to go in a certain spot of water. I went anyway. I saw this thing floating in the water that resembled a cabbage. Naturally, I picked it up. Well, it was a cannonball jellyfish, and it stung my hand when I grabbed it. It didn't sting, really. It was more super itchy and irritating. The manly man that I was, cried and freaked out. I ran up to the beach and screamed that I was going to die. But this man here, cool as a cucumber, told me to hold my hand out. He whipped his dong out and straight up peed on my damn hand. Little Lia ran off, crying. Bro, you scarred her. And Ella here. She was cracking her ass off on that beach. She laughed so hard that she lost her voice," Logan recited animatedly.

V's green eyes fizzed back at Logan, entertained by Logan's story telling.

"So, I called us the Jelly Club after that. We always stuck together and wanted to start a band, but... we only got to play once in front of an audience," Ella trailed off.

"Hey V, so the *Lakers* play the Nuggets tomorrow. I could, uh, make you dinner afterwards if you would like?" Logan proposed.

"Hmm, that is a yes and yes," V answered.

They smiled at each other and sipped their beers.

"Aw man, Phillip left limited logs," I complained.

"*Mhm*, he probably wanted us to turn in early or something," Logan said.

"It's probably because of the wildfires in the past. It's been so dry, this season, that the trees are bribing the dogs!" V explained.

"Yeah, he probably only left this amount, because it rained last night," Ella said.

"Well, I don't want to turn in, *yet*. Do y'all?" Logan asked, watching V.

"We should spend some more time out here, soak it all in!" Ella grinned.

"Uh huh, well I sure as hell am not going out into the woods to get wood," V said.

"Bears, mountain lions, serial killers, oh my," Logan tittered.

"He has double electric fences. We're talking deer and skunks," I answered.

"And a killer couldn't hop over that? It is real cozy being by a fire at home and on the beach, but out in the woods... gets creepy, puckers the bottom," V said drunkenly.

"What? That's so silly," Ella spoke, laughing off.

"You ever seen any horror movie ever? Crazed serial killers all up in the hills. Lurking in the forest, waiting to hack, hack, hack," Logan chimed in with V.

"Ch, ch, ch," V added.

"Oh wow, you two. It's wild that movies and shows profit from people's obsession with killers. I feel like society should be intrigued by the psyche of murderous instructors from Indigenous residential schools. Or logging sites, where Indigenous women and girls are disappearing from. Or with commercial fishing, murdering our oceans. Those things are scary to me," Ella voiced in a serious tone.

Ella illuminates over selfless passions. A star amongst humankind.

"I'm with you on all of that, Ella. It is crazy. Logan and I try our best to be on the money with sustainability back at home, at least," I agreed.

"Yeah, I try to be eco-friendly as much as possible. It's just that, nature rules my heart, so why would I turn my back on it by contributing to its departure?" Ella said warmly.

"For sure. And it is nonsensical how death and gore excite people, yet they can't handle going to a haunted house on Halloween. Anyway, if anyone is in the woods, they're probably illegally hunting," I said before pausing.

"Ahh, what I think Murph is trying to say, is that there aren't any crazy clown killas out in chilly wine country. My bad for starting that, but I ain't going. Not about to be that mythical negro that Hollywood is all about. That shit is old," Logan interjected.

"But I do, hear you, Ella," I said, deep and low.

Ella smiled back at me and leaned forward to knock her beer bottle with mine.

"And Logan, I am with *you* on that! So, one, two, three, not it!" V shouted and put her finger to her nose.

Logan, V, and Ella all had their index fingers placed on the tip of their noses, smirking back at me. I threw my hands up. And put on the utility gloves that Phillip laid out near the fire pit and grabbed the flashlight.

"Alright, I'll be *right* back," I said, grinning.

I know damn well that Logan is about to make a movie reference to my last words. I could hear violent laughter in the distance now. Logan was most likely telling his sidesplitting jokes. Fairly certain that V will enjoy the one about the Oxford student and the Texan.

This was a ridiculous idea; we are all already drunk. If there are any crazy clowns, I'll ask to borrow their axe. Phillip clearly didn't chop that wood himself. Pansy. I walked past incense cedar trees, flashing my light on their straight and wide trunks, showcasing the reddish-brown bark. The tops loomed above me. I enjoyed the melodic tone of crickets, massaging their wings against each other, forming a symphony. I'll just get to the top of the hill, pee, and head back.

A branch snapped, echoing in the distance.

I twisted around on the slope unnaturally. Dropping the flashlight to put my hands out in front of me, I fell to the ground. A sharp twig stabbed the squishy flesh between the middle of my thumb and index finger.

"Damn it!" I said, inhaling sharply.

The insects of the night went silent, abruptly.

I groaned as I stood back up. I could hear my wet, hot blood patter down on the dense earth floor. Squeezing the small puncture wound with my left flannel sleeve.

"Logan? Phillip? Dude, stop playing," I said sternly.

Unamused and unafraid, I stared ahead, waiting for a response.

A figure dressed in a long black parka with a thick fur-trimmed hood moved sluggishly out from behind a thick cedar tree, ten feet away from me. The sound of leaves shuffled under heavy weight. Our shared space in the dark woods went back to silence.

"*Hello*? Are you just going to stand there?" I said forcefully.

The person took one step forward. They raised their hood ever so slightly.

"What-wait? *Mom*? Is that you?" I interrogated, stammering.

The person who resembled my mom lowered their hood back down, turned away, and ran. Breaking free from my paralyzed stance, I chased them. Sprinting horizontally from where I fell. Darting around tall trees and over short stumps, crunching twigs, and smashing down damp leaves.

I squinted and slowed down.

I lost her, but how could I lose her?

I halted and held my breath, but the drumming in my ears, from my heart-beat, drowned out the footsteps that approached.

It was too late.

I felt hot breath against the back of my naked neck.

"*Hello*," someone whispered in a throaty, indistinct voice.

I whipped around. Large black hood, all-black clothing. Tall, bulky, white, vaguely masculine up close. I could smell their breath. It reminded me of the raspberry saltwater taffy candies that I have been devouring at Ella's.

Terror crippled me; it froze every muscle in my body.

POW!

Lights out.

ooo

Back in Bonnes Bay...

"What the actual shit, Tammy? This is *the* Luxury Senior Living of Bonnes Bay. This is *a* special resident, Gertie Schmidt, in memory care no less. And we are in a pandemic, you're not supposed to let just *anybody* in here. I have already told you, make sure that every single visitor confirms their identity first. And *then* make them sign the visitor log. Also, where the hell is your mask? Be professional and, on your shit, if you want to stay here," Lia scolded.

"Ew, Lia, aren't *all* the residents special here? That language isn't very professional. What are you going to do, tell on me to your little lover?" Tammy ridiculed. She mocked Lia's valley girl voice and continued twirling her long blonde hair with the tip of her pen. Popping her gum forcefully back at Lia.

"And change that freaking *Ole Miss* tee-shirt. You need to wear your uniform, like everyone else that works here..." Lia retorted.

"Okay! Don't get *too* hot and bothered, Lia," Tammy said.

She stood up quickly and pulled her classic red tee-shirt off. Tammy stood behind the reception desk in a lacey black bra, extra busty with her toned abs flexing. She bowed her head and bent her knees to curtsy for Lia.

"Wow, you are *so* done here! Just wait or don't wait, you might as well get a head start on gathering your things, you crazy bitch," Lia sneered.

Tammy rolled her eyes and continued popping her gum behind the reception desk, dumbfounded.

Lia knocked on Gertie's door, a three-minute walk from the reception area.

"Hi dear, I'm so happy to see you," Gertie answered.

Gertie wore a dusty pink and white floral night gown with a collar. She motioned for Lia to come into her furnished unit.

"Hi Gertie, I am so sorry to bother you this late. I just wanted to check and make sure that you are okay. I heard you had a visitor here today?" Lia asked.

"Oh, I did? Hmm, well, I'm quite fine, dear. You look nice. I'm looking forward to seeing your pretty sister, to learn to paint like her," Gertie asserted softly.

"Aw Gertie, you are a sweetheart. She's excited about that. Could you possibly tell me about anyone who came by?" Lia asked.

"Hmm, let me think, dear. Oh, they gave me this. She said it was a gift for you. He told me to tell you that," Gertie muttered.

Lia bunched her feathered eyebrows together at Gertie's confusion. She observed the frail woman pulling a white pearl strand necklace out from under her nightgown collar. The pearls glistened in the room light.

"For me? Who did? Was it a guy or was it a girl?" Lia asked purposely.

"You know, come to think of it, I am not sure. They were kind of plain, dear," Gertie said. Her hand shook as she tried to unclasp the necklace. Exhausted, she gave up and put her veiny small hand to her sunken shoulder.

"Oh, that's okay, Gertie, you can keep them on. Did they have short hair, or? Hm, that's strange, those are Akoya pearls, but it looks like someone took them from another necklace. For high-quality pearls with superb luster, they should have knots between each one. It needs to be restrung. I can do that for you next week. It looks like you're missing a few gems, too. I can have my mom, Ava, order those," Lia stated, assuring.

Gertie smiled back at Lia from her wood rocker chair next to her bed.

"Alright, Gertie, I will make sure that you receive no more unexpected visitors. Although, this necklace is leading me to believe that it was just Mrs. Daughtry down the hall. Maybe just don't mention this to Ella. You know how protective she is. You're a part of our family now and we love you." Lia said.

Lia leaned forward to hold Gertie's hand and gave her a brief hug.

"I love you girls, too. I had always wished that I could have children. God didn't make me that way. But he granted my prayers, with you two, like daughters. Never give up on faith, deary," Gertie said.

"Aww, Gertie, you're melting me. We certainly have faith in you. I'll see you on Monday, okay?" Lia replied, still holding Gertie's frail hand.

"Oh dear, you forgot this," Gertie said, motioning to her neck.

"Thanks, that is sweet, but it looks beautiful on you. And hey, it's Mrs. Daughtry's loss, she's not getting it back. You keep it, okay?" Lia reassured.

Gertie nodded. The wrinkles on her snow-white skin multiplied as she pulled the sides of her thin lips towards her little ears. Lia placed the new, pale pink cotton quilt over Gertie's lap that she bought for her.

ooo

THE JOURNAL

June 3rd, 1989

R EADY TO GET this graduation over with and on to Mike's party. He better keep his hands to himself, though. Jackie is pushing Sofia to lose her v-card to Mike. Total bullshit.

I'm ashamed to be graduating with this atrocious score that I put upon myself for this bodacious fox. It better be worth it. She hasn't mentioned California since our fight a while back, and her parents haven't mentioned schools. We're in the clear with that. Backup plan: I wrote a college admissions essay for every eligible east coast school I think her dumb ass could get into. So, we can go together.

Note: *Organize funds and budget for a house on Monday, get some filing done with Mr. Colombo. Figure out credit and see if I could qualify for a mortgage loan.*

Sofia is wearing the white Akoya pearls for the ceremony. It's remarkable how she loves them now, after her mother told her their worth. Shocker. Seeing them on her turns me on like a light switch, though. All the pain that I endured while father made me wear them. It all makes sense now. They led me to her. Whip, push, shove, and blood. Assaulting my innards. So much blood, so much sweat on the kitchen floor. None of it compares to the wearer before. Mother's bones found within the scattered and burned structure of Lucifer's home. We both suffered at his expense. He was no Galileo, but quite precise and intuitive enough for a while. Not enough to succeed... I will be.

I researched in the library, expanding my knowledge on gems and gemstones. It's an old wives' tale to never wear pearls on your wedding day either. This symbolizes sorrowfulness and tears; they will usher in bad luck in the future. Trouble and turmoil between the couple and deterioration in your relationship. Makes sense why my father gifted them and forced mother to wear them for their nuptial day. Double whammy for mother. Inspirational food for thought.

"The world is my oyster I can achieve whatever I want to in life."

ooo

TIDAL DEVOTION

February 15ᵗʰ, 2021

I FOUND ELLA LYING on her bed, petting Pinot. He didn't bark when I knocked on her doorway frame with my knuckle. Instead, he wagged his bottom and snorted opportunely. Ella's room was bright, I admired the details of the steely blue accents and whimsical curved furniture. I unwound the cloudy saltwater taffy wrapper and popped the chewy raspberry goodness into my mouth.

"Hey um, since Lia is at Maggie's and Logan is with V, I was thinking of grabbing sandwiches from Ocean Scoops. Did you want one? I could even get you a cupcake from Cake Chest if you'd like?" I offered.

Ella sat up, crossed her legs in gray jogger sweatpants, and pulled off her worn gray hoodie. She had a white tank top underneath it. I could see that she was braless. Ella ran both her hands down her center part and smoothed her long, wavy, and shiny golden-brown hair with her hands. She brought the thickness forward from both sides, over her chest. I smiled and sat down at the end of her bed, smoothing the white bedding down from my weight. Pinot rose from her side and repositioned himself against my backside, absorbing my warmth.

"Hey, I'm not starving right now. How's your face feeling?" Ella asked glumly.

"Oh, I'm fine. I'm glad I didn't break my nose. Guess I'm a fish out of water. The more important question is, how are *you*?" I inquired.

I hate lying to her.

"I still can't believe you tumbled down the hill and ran into a tree. V, and I still feel bad for making you go up there. I'm alright. I don't know why I expected her to live forever. She was ninety-five. And after the bank... She was just so frail to begin with. I guess the heart attack was inevitable, but she just didn't strike me as being in poor health. She was a fighter, you know. I just wish that I got to say goodbye," Ella whimpered.

"I know, I'm so sorry, Ella. I know this doesn't make it better, but I'm glad Gertie had you and Lia towards the end. What you did for her, that was kind as hell. I made you something earlier, kind of corny, but ya know, given the circumstances. Well, I needed V's help to print it for me. I'll be right back," I stammered.

I returned to her with a tissue-wrapped frame and sat back down next to Pinot.

"It's nothing big, I just," I paused.

She pulled the tissue paper off of the five-by-seven whitewashed wood frame. Her full lips pulled back at the sight. A poem from Ella's favorite collection, placed behind the picture glass. She read.

Tidal Devotion

She dove right into,

Swirls of deep Prussian that grew.

Entangled within the velvet hues.

Swimming against current is not easy to do.

He was the one, tender and true.

Not the strain and pain of heavy-weighted blues.

She let the waves of his praise submerge her.

In sets, then altogether.

They anchored through all types of weather.

A give and take. That could never be better.

"Oh, my gosh, *Oisín*. This is gorgeous and will complete the room. You know what's funny, I was wondering where this book disappeared to. A little birdie told me you have been reading it. And even though it isn't really *your* thing, you made this because it's *mine*?" Ella queried.

"I did, yes," I answered her.

"You really are something," Ella purred.

"Aw no, this is just something small. I hoped it would cheer you up... and I think it's working?"

"It is not small. It means *everything* to me."

"Yeah, well, about that. The passing of poems, back and forth. I can't help thinking back to when we were kids. How we would all draw weird animals and write notes to each other in our Jelly Club book. I, uh, I don't want to push you, or force a narrative that isn't there. But I don't want to leave in five days, without telling you how I feel. I'm not good at this. I've avoided talking about feelings my whole life. Logan has beaten me up for that, rightfully so. You both have given me strength to be, vulnerable. Ella, I really care about you. I admire you. I *want* you. I think about you constantly, even when we are in the same room... Is this, at all how you feel too?" I asked.

Ella's hazel eyes fixed intensely on mine. I gave her a half smile, unsure of how she received this information.

"What took you so long, Oisín Murphy?"

She set the framed poem down on her nightstand.

"Well, I, didn't want to jump into anything or assume," I started.

"Oisín, I feel like I've longed for you my whole life. This isn't too soon, it's exactly right," she said.

Ella swung her legs over the right side of the bed and walked over to me. She squatted down before me, placing her hands on my jeans, just as she did on her birthday. She kept her nails short with marshmallow white nail polish. Her hair long behind her. I could see her dark nipples raised through her tank top. I gazed back into her eyes.

"Sorry," I said uneasily.

She raised up to meet my eyes.

"I'm not. I want to get lost in *there*. Cerulean sea waves that crash against the specks of golden sunset and rusty brown sands. True, *Oisín* eyes," she said confidently, shaking her head.

"And yours, are like shooting gilded stars against a changing dark dusk. Those two go together pretty well, don't you think?" I insisted.

My heart pounded. I swallowed hard. I put my hands on her hipbones. Feeling the warmth of the exposed skin between her top and sweats. Ella sucked in her bottom lip and released it, wet and shiny.

"Ella," I gasped

Her lips met mine, soft, wet, and pillowy. I spread my legs and pulled her in towards me tightly. Eyes closed, we kissed passionately, tongues melting into each other, rhythmic.

Pinot snorted loudly. Ella pulled away. We opened our eyes and chuckled.

"*Okay,* Mr. P., I think you need some fresh air," Ella said, leading Pinot out to the deck and placing him on his donut bed, where he lied down. She came back inside and shut the door.

She put her hands on my shoulders. I picked her up, and she wrapped her legs around my waist. My erection grew. We picked up right where we left off. Licking, kissing, sliding our tongues against each other. Our breath heavy, in sync. I held her weight with my left hand under her ass, squeezing her cheek hard. I slipped my right hand underneath her tank top, sliding my hand against her smooth skin until it met her plump breasts. I cupped and caressed them gently. She pulled her head back from mine. She lowered her thick eyebrows. Her eyelids heavy, gazing into my eyes seductively.

So sexy.

I lowered her down. Ella stood up to pull her tank top off. Her supple breasts were beautiful. She tousled her hair and pulled my charcoal gray Donegal sweater off. I unbuckled my belt, unzipped my blue jeans, standing in navy boxer briefs. She side smiled and licked her lips. She pulled her sweatpants down and kicked them behind her. She wasn't wearing any panties.

I gulped.

She pulled my boxers off and admired my hard dick beneath the short brown pubic hair. She grabbed a condom from her nightstand drawer and slid it on me. It sent a shiver up my spine.

She pushed me onto the bed. I fell back slowly and scooted up to the headboard. Lying down, my head on her pillow, with my legs straight out. She kept her gaze on me, crawling towards me, her breast hanging and jiggling. I was *past* seduced. She spread her legs with her knees and shins pressed to the bed. Straddling me, lowering herself onto the tip of my dick. My breath grew heavy. She felt smooth and tight. I thrusted my hips upward, gradually. Filling her completely with my body. She let out a light moan. Her long brown hair curtained the sides of her petite body. She leaned forward and placed her soft hands on my chest. I put mine on her silky beige thighs, squeezing. She rose and lowered onto me, riding me in harmony with my thrusts. My dick throbbed intensely, sending chills up my spine. I couldn't take my eyes off of her. I grunted heavily, watching her breast bouncing up and down. Beads of sweat glistened on her chest. She went faster and faster, closing her eyes to moan and opening them to fix back on mine. I stimulated her with my thumb. I could feel her pulsating.

"OH, *Oisín*!" she screamed.

I swallowed hard and moved my hand back to squeezing her thighs.

She moaned loudly, letting out a sexy, raspy scream.

"Oh, oh, Ella."

Ella squeezed tightly around my dick; I could feel her pelvic muscles contracting.

The build up was so intense, my rock-hard dick pulsed wildly, sending me into an orgasm following hers. I grunted loudly.

Elle remained on top of my body as I convulsed. My legs and fingertips went numb until I felt light-headed. She raised herself off of me gently and then swathed her divine body in the soft white bed sheet. I extended my left arm out for her to lie down next to me, she nestled her head into the nook between my chest and shoulder.

"*Whoa*," we said at the same time.

ooo

Ella took advantage of this time to craft what she called Love Letter Lasagne. She said it was in honor of Gertie's passing. She explained to me that Gertie reminded her of her own nonna in Bergamo, Italy. Ella adapted her nonna's recipe for Love Letter Lasagne and perfected it to her liking, with updated ingredients, instructions, and a wine pairing. She filled the entire kitchen and living room with the pleasing aroma of onion and garlic simmering.

"Alexa, play *Make Someone Happy* by *June Christy and Bob Cooper*," Ella spoke as she layered lasagna noodles in a ceramic navy ruffled loaf pan. I put a scoop of Pinot's dog food into his stainless-steel dog dish. Ella giggled.

"What?" I asked.

"Sorry, it's just that you haven't stopped smiling since we got down here."

"Well, you haven't either," I chuckled.

Ella plucked a bottle of wine off the tall wood and metal wine rack, uncorked it, and offered a glass of pinot noir to me. Ella placed her free hand in mine and performed a twirl. Bare-footed, wearing a black canvas apron over a white floor-length dress, with a high slit. Mesmerizing, as lovely as she is on the outside, her insides dazzle twice over.

"Here's to you, for cooking this incredible meal. To us for finding each other again. *And* here's to Gertie, may she be watching over you and Lia with smiling eyes."

"Cheers," Ella purred. "The baby might need a little love. Beethoven?"

I played *Moonlight Sonata No. 14 in C-sharp minor* by *Ludwig van Beethoven,* while Ella's fresh, cheesy, and savory lasagna baked. Soon after, we savored the smooth wine with the mouthwatering dish. It made me question every piece of food that I had ever consumed before this. She stimulated my *appetite*. I feasted my eyes on her smooth, golden skin. Aroused and whirling in a sea of Ella's words, her satin hair in my hands, her tender lips on my lips. We whale watched from the jacuzzi spa and sipped on wine into the night. The Pacific Ocean breeze teased us as we made love once more, cloaked in the tantalizing moonlight.

ooo

Love Letter Lasagne©

Un amore che vale la pena aspettare.
Serves: 2 | Time: 1 hour, 20 minutes
Cutting Board, Skillet, Pot, Small Bowl, Loaf Pan

Ingredients:

Salt & pepper, to taste
2 tbsp EVOO
1/2 cup of fresh minced onion
3 cloves of garlic, chopped
4 oz lean ground beef
5 oz sweet Italian sausage
5 oz crushed tomato
3 oz tomato sauce
2 oz tomato paste
2 tbsp water
2 tsp of white sugar
1 tsp of dried basil leaves
1 tsp of dried oregano
1 tsp of Italian seasoning
6 lasagna noodles
1 egg
1 tbsp fresh parsley, chopped
1 cup ricotta cheese
1/4 cup of grated parmesan cheese
8 oz shredded mozzarella cheese

Directions: Preheat oven to 350°F

Boil a pot of water.

Sauce - In a skillet, drizzle EVOO. Over medium heat, sauté garlic and onion for a few minutes. Add sausage and ground beef, cook until well browned. Stir in water, the tomato (crushed, paste, and sauce.) Season with sugar, spices, salt, and pepper. Simmer on low for 15 minutes, stirring occasionally.

Cook - 6 lasagna noodles in a pot of boiling water, about 7 minutes. Drain.

Mix - In a small bowl, egg, parsley, ricotta cheese, parmesan cheese, and pinch of salt.

Assemble - In a bread loaf pan, pour 1 cup of meat sauce across bottom evenly. Place 2 noodles over the sauce. Smooth 1/2 of the cheese mix evenly over noodles. Add half of the meat sauce left onto the cheese mix. Repeat with 2 more noodles, then cheese mix, then meat sauce. Top with remaining 2 noodles, add the last of the meat sauce. Sprinkle mozzarella across the top, evenly.

Bake - Spray foil with cooking spray, to prevent sticking to cheese. Place the foil over the loaf pan and bake in a preheated oven for 30 minutes. Remove the foil and place the pan back in the oven. Bake for 10 additional minutes to brown cheese.

Cool - Let it sit for 15 minutes before serving.

Love Letter Lasagne Wine Pairing: Sonoma Coast Pinot Noir. It's the balance of juicy red stone fruits and peppery vanilla spices that compliment the umami of cooked Italian sausage and herbs. The medium acidity and silky tannins cut through the richness of the three cheeses. While the velvety texture washes down the delectable dish, leaving a savory finish. A beautiful relationship forms when you marry the labors of cooking fresh ingredients with a sexy bottle of wine from quality terroir. Who knows, you might just fall in love too.

ooo

SEAGULL SOUP

February 16th, 2021

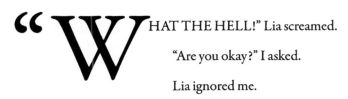

"**W**HAT THE HELL!" Lia screamed.

"Are you okay?" I asked.

Lia ignored me.

"What is it *now*?" Ella questioned sleepily.

Ella approached me on the navy and cream runner behind the island. She pulled the ties on her white waffle cotton robe tightly and bit her lip as she gazed up at me. I grinned as I handed her my untouched, fresh cup of coffee.

Lia was stoic on the deck, with the floor-to-ceiling sliding glass doors open. She continued gaping at the jacuzzi spa. Ella glanced at me with a flat mouth, her eyebrows furrowed.

"Shit, did we, did I, leave you-know-what, in there?" I whispered to Ella.

She shook her head furiously. We walked over to Lia together.

I don't remember leaving the cover off.

"Seriously? How could this happen?" Lia asked impatiently.

I walked out onto the deck and continued past Lia. Narrowing my eyes in on the jacuzzi, there were three seagulls floating on the surface. My stomach tightened.

"Oh, shit," I said, stumbling backwards. "Ella, stay back. There are, there are birds in there. Um, seagulls," I continued.

"How could this happen?" Lia asked again.

Ella joined us and peered over Lia's shoulder to observe the dead birds. She jolted backwards and spilled coffee on her bare feet and the wood deck.

"Wow, oh my god. I can't, sorry," Ella shrieked. She retreated into the house.

"Maybe they flew into the windows this morning? One probably followed the other and so forth," Lia suggested. Lia tilted her head; she brought her feathered brows together and frowned. Her dark shoulder-length hair with teal highlights shimmered in the morning sun.

"Well, whatever it is, I should probably clean that up before V and Logan get here. I don't think she would be happy to see that in her jacuzzi," I offered.

I returned with single-use gloves and a black garbage bag. Pulling the large gray and white birds with salmon pink webbed feet towards me. There was a white square of paper at the bottom of the jacuzzi spa. I tied the plastic bag and set it down. I glanced back at Lia, and she left me alone to comfort her older sister. I pulled up my sleeve and grabbed the metal hand skimmer off of the teak towel storage. Stretching my arm through the chlorinated water and feathers, I scooped up the card. Saturated and soft, but thick, and the ink remained intact. I turned around to face the ocean and read.

'The lies we tell ourselves.'

God, no.

I pursed my lips so tightly that my short mustache met my trimmed beard and stuffed the despicable wet card into my pocket. I met with Lia and Ella back inside.

"What is it, Lia?" Ella quizzed her sister's gloomy nature.

"I don't know, just like a weird flashback. Remember the summer before we moved? We celebrated Logan's birthday at Oisín's. We were playing on the lawn by the shore in his backyard. And a seagull pooped in your hair, Oisín. Ahh, you were so red. Claire proposed it was good luck, but you ran to the lake to clean it out. Someone else at the party, made a comment. Something like, your luck is countered because three seagulls flew directly over our heads, and it was a warning of death, soon. That *always* stuck with me. Now, I always look up when I'm by the sea," Lia recounted.

"Lia! *Come on*, enough with the superstitions. *Please*," Ella cried. "Sorry, Oisín, for this craziness. And thank you, for helping," Ella voiced softly.

I nodded with my lips still pursed and carried the bag to the front to dispose of it in the trash. Quick to return, I washed my hands inside and ran up to Ella's room to make a call.

"Hey Murph, how's it going?" Charlie answered.

"Hey Charlie, I was just calling to, uh, see if you remembered something really quick," I insisted, rushed.

"Oh sure, I have a minute. Shoot."

"Um, when we had Logan's twelfth birthday at my old house, do you remember everyone that was there, could you recite that?" I requested.

"Huh, that's a fairly odd question, Murph. That was some time ago. I imagine it was all of us, all the parents, some of our friends, maybe some neighbors. Your father made it a point to make sure everything went well. He was very involved with you kids, back then. It really helped me out a lot. He took care of the party decorations and barbecue. Your mother baked Logan's favorite cake," Charlie recounted.

"Ah, well, I wanted to call you earlier, actually. I tried my best to put the Pearl Point Murderer out of my mind, like you insisted. But I am certain now that they didn't convict the right man. I wholeheartedly believe that someone is haunting and taunting me to prove that. Look, the man in Florida, before he had a heart attack, he said that evil is following me. It enraged me at first, but someone *is* stalking me. Now, this thing with Gertie, an elderly woman, from the bank massacre, she was special to Ella and Lia. Lia told us she thought it was odd that authorities found an antipsychotic medication in Gertie's room. Same medication that they found on that old man's Knotty Red. They *both* suffered from a sudden cardiac death? Now, we found three seagulls *dead* in Ella's jacuzzi spa, with a note similar to the one from my birthday. I just, I'm trying my best here! This is *far* too coincidental," I confessed.

Charlie was silent for the longest five seconds of my life. I stared out the French doors, waiting for his answer. A pressure built in my head and chest.

"Son, I don't want to be insensitive to what you've experienced during your vacation. But I talked to Michaels, he doesn't suspect foul play. I know it's tough trusting the justice system. Hell, at the end of the day I'm still a black man. I understand, son. But, without evidence, you ain't getting no where. You have got to let the ghosts of your past go. They're messing with your head, which is far more dangerous than being physically assaulted. You're alive, but they're killing you, on the *inside*. You've let them pitch a cozy tent inside your mind. It doesn't matter how far you travel to get rid of them, they're always with you. So, when anything negative arises, it feels like they're following you and your logical explanation is to blame it on that. Look, Murph, it affects everyone else around you, for as long as they live too. It's best to talk to a professional about present trauma," Charlie finished.

"Alright, Charlie. I understand what you're saying, and I will talk to someone when we get back. Sorry to take up your time about this *again*," I said, vacillated.

"No, no. That's what I'm here for, it's better that you express your concerns instead of holding them in. We're all excited about your return. Devon has a full menu for y'all to try out when you get back. Stay safe and see you soon," Charlie said.

"Yeah, we're looking forward to being back. See ya Charlie," I said.

We hung up, and I shook off my distress, staring out at the modern deck. The dark ocean line married blue skies just beyond it.

"So, were you just going to withhold all of this information, for what, forever? Or lie? Because you knew we wouldn't see each other again?" Ella whimpered.

Shit.

I turned to face Ella; she was standing in her doorway with her arms crossed.

"Ella, no. I, um. I wasn't sure how to open up about this in the right way. I don't know what you heard, but it's troubling to explain. Even I don't know for certain what is going on," I stammered.

"Okay, I wouldn't know how to disclose that to someone, either. After the bank massacre, I started imagining that the robber was alive. But with therapy and friends as a solid support system. It has been lessening. Trauma is haunting Oisín, and it's *our* responsibility to reach out for help to recover. Doesn't change how hurt I am by this, though. I was engaged to a liar, and I've questioned my judgement ever since. Now you're leaving soon... I thought we had something, but now I don't know what I thought. Maybe last night was a mistake."

"Ella, it wasn't a mistake. It was incredible. But I care about you past the sex, and I should have disclosed this madness. I am so *sorry*," I professed.

"Yeah. Well, I don't know. It's like we went from being in strict quarantine to reuniting after almost two decades. We both went through distressing events. Maybe we just need time to work on ourselves," Ella proposed.

"If that's what you want, I respect that. I would never try to hurt you. Space would be better than throwing this away. I can stay at Bonnes Bay Lodge, just down the road. We can talk when you're ready. Is that okay?" I implored.

She nodded her head, got back into bed, and threw her comforter over her head.

I whispered, "I'm sorry."

How could I find the woman of my dreams and *leave?* Unafraid of the emotions she evokes. This is a woman comprising seaside treasure. Ella is the delightful expansion of lungs when taking a breath of fresh air during a crisp fall morning in New York. She radiates like the strengthening fireball of sunsets across the Florida sky. And she feels like the cool coastal sands of California, comforting and essential to the soul.

I messed up. The card is right. The lies we tell ourselves. Will come back to bite.

I collected my belongings and packed my luggage before heading to Woodsberry for a stun gun and any other types of defense weapons I could get my hands on.

ooo

THE JOURNAL

June 4ᵗʰ, 1989

I'M STAYING AT Johns tonight. I don't even know if I should write entries anymore, but they're the only way to remember. I like to relive the notable moments. To unscramble the letters from the words, from the numbers, to the absurd. My brain is a ticking time bomb. It has to be undone to become done. I have to get this down, but I'm shaky from the events that took place tonight. John will have to write for me as I recite and smoke a fat one. Here it goes…

The girls were already at the after party and I imagine they had no intention of waiting for me. Even though the cabin was mine and John's discovery. As usual, I was completely invisible to the Colombo family while I was getting ready. They had no clue that I was even home and started talking about celebrating such a victory. I was the victory. They chatted about how I was the goldmine that they gained by taking in my grungy sob story to pay for Sofia's tuition. Tuition?! Sofia is going to UCLA. California.

SHE LIED TO ME. She had lied to my face for months. She stole my admissions letter, the best I had, and her daddy pulled some strings out there for her. Of course, her daddy did. Privileged users. Here I thought she appreciated my efforts, all the hard work for her. But she wanted more. She always wants more. She thinks she's the epitome of class, strength, elegance, beauty. Hell, I may have seen her that way before, but I was blind. Taking off these heavy shades, man. And now, she's a succubus for love, for attention, for gifts. A straight up bitch for screwing over a loyal best friend. ME.

(I told you so dummy, John)

I was played. Hard. Harder than the slap of rough hands on the bare cheeks on my face. Harder than my mother's sharp eyes laid in on me as I took father's beating, each strike for each second that passed.

Your body will heal from a wound. It is the mental that pierces me.

Shakes, pierces me...

I had to confront Sofia. She wanted to leave me after she sucked me dry. But I was out of control. I needed a drink. I snuck out of her window to avoid exposing what I found out. John picked me up. I told him everything that had happened, and then we headed to the party, late at the pines.

John waited in the truck, half a mile away. I snuck around the front. Everyone was shit faced, high, or boning. Mullets, middle-fingers, and motors crowded our forested playground. All the football players in their letterman jackets, with the accessory of cheer bears on their arms. As I passed the cabin, I saw Jackie and Mike making out and dry humping on the lawn. Naughty cheaters. I half joked, well lied, that Mike's house was on fire. Mike and Jackie were so drunk and so stupid that they couldn't identify the sarcasm in my voice. They raced off to her beamer and the next thing that I heard was a car horn, then back to crickets, katydids, looping drum sounds, and a bouncing bass.

I didn't want to go inside the cabin and be seen by the barf bags. Instead, I poked around in the back. Walking through the dark and looming trees, I could hear Sofia's voice say, "Damn it, shit, shoot." I found her faux fur coat spread out like a picnic blanket on some flattened grass. I had to squint but saw that Sofia was alone by the river, throwing up what looked like some food, various liquors, and the deception she chewed on so eloquently this semester. I brought her coat to her. She was wearing tight, high-wasted blue jeans, an even tighter white shirt that showcased her immaculate boobs. She was barefoot. Moonlight reflected off the water and shined on the vampire vixen that she was. She even got chunky vomit in her pretty big blonde hair. But it was repulsive.

She struggled to get up from being on her hands and knees, tumbling slightly as she gathered her balance. She turned to face me. Vomit flowed down the stream in the shadowy water behind her. Her eyes, they were so glossy and red; I fought to identify her. I did not know where her Jupiter eyes went, the brown that turned orangish yellow in the right light. So hard to acknowledge that this was once my lovely Sofia. She looked annoyed that I was holding her coat, and that I was present. Through tears, snot, and something mustard yellow on her bottom lip, she belted out, "I had sex with Mike, okay? Stop following me like a damn puppy all the time! You do not know what it's like to be me, you just wouldn't understand! And we're never going to be more than friends!"

She unclasped my mother's strand from her neck and threw it at me with effort. But it was more of a toss. I shouted forcefully, "Oh no, Sofia, that was a gift. And a gift of pearls, means mother-fucking misfortune for you!"

I looked at her with pure disgust for the first time in my life. She jerked her head back, judging me in shock.

I dropped her coat to the ground and shoved her left shoulder. Not even hard! It sent her into a wavy unbalance, her body swayed in slow motion, yet her arms remained near to her sides. She gasped boisterously, inhaling. The little weight of her body buckled beneath her, but she didn't even put her arms out in front of her. She was SO drunk. She pivoted towards the water, falling violently on a large, angular, sharp rock; it pillowed her neck. I heard the strangest crack and squirt noise; it was the snapping of her neck as it melted into the jagged shard, puncturing it further. She was staring me down, pointing to her killer, awaiting someone to rescue her from this fate. Dispersed dark blood oozed continuously through her delicate throat. It trickled out of her agape mouth, glistening out of her body, over the rocks.

I watched the life leave her Jupiter's eyes. In that moment, I wasn't a meager dragon, nor a pathetic red devil with a pitchfork. No. I was God in that moment. I was God. It electrified me with delight, pain, and sensual relief. I understood my father, his blood, their blood, my blood, her blood. Sweet sagaciousness.

Even now, sitting here with John. It's still relieving. But back to Sofia...

The bubbling waters near us went silent. The sight of her captivated me. I imagined her as she was, but on Mr. Rossi's massive clock. Her body, lubricated, dripping wet in blood. Limbs serving as clock hands, slick legs folded over each other elegantly. She wanted me to take her, lying there directing me, imploring me to use her right back. Because as impossible as she was, she will always be my number one.

Oh, to die so gracefully by the peaceful waters, I'm such a good friend.

John found us and broke my trance. That was probably for the best. I picked up my mother's necklace and used my knife to cut the strand before a knot to free one perfectly round white ball. I poked the lone pearl into her jean pocket. On the back of my rough middle finger, I could feel the warmth of her body.

Still, I frowned and uttered, "There bitch, now you are pearlized."

John found this dramatic because it was. After my prolific Shakespearean performance, we booked it. Undetected in the dark of midnight, through maddening gray fog, past the cabin and out to the dirt road. We raced as fast as we could to get to his *truck, adrenaline running high, high, high. Past Jackie's beamer. John detailed that Jackie and Mike hit the towering elm tree. But there was no movement from their bodies, just stillness, and no one even came to their rescue. Deceiving sloppy seconds by his best friend and lover combined with tanked-up mishaps will now leave David forsaken. Mission accomplished, and I didn't even touch a soul.*

"A sweet type of pleasure derives from the conclusion of calamity."

- Me

ooo

THE CALM

February 20ᵗʰ, 2021

I AGREED TO GIVE Ella space. For one simple fact, I can't endanger her any further. We ended up texting each other every day since I checked into Bonnes Bay Lodge. Weather and pandemic updates produce little depth, though. Small talk is hellish.

Speaking of hell, *Hotel California* by *Eagles* has played over and over in the room next to mine. To interpret the song as the band members intended, I had a taste of excess self-indulgence and pleasure in California. And now I crave it. I could also interpret the song literally, as if my California hotel room was Hades. Because it *is*.

My impartial solo endeavor has spun me into a frenzy of obsession with a murderer that is dead. Researching public archives for murdered women from 1989 to the present, that involve pearls and numerals. Scribbling clocks on hotel notepads and trying to piece together who the other women are and *why* them.

Every time I hear a noise now, I flip the stunners on and whip out the heavy-duty collapsible baton. Ready to defend and ready to take down this psycho. Add the task of tracking my dad down, but I'm met with one dead end after another. All it will take is *one* look at Aidan's face and I will know if it is or isn't him. So, I have to get back to Foggerton to confront him, *unless* he's already here.

I also have to tell Ella how I feel. Bad timing, but the thought of dying expedites the desire. Even if she might not feel the same. The tension was there. The touch, the kiss, the sex. It was *so* good. It could just be lust. But the pros of the prose. We expressed how we felt through her choice of writing. Ella's nimble light started a wildfire in me. Maybe because it isn't about me and my demons anymore, it's about *her*. Her protection, her happiness, her wellness. It allows me to feel something other than dread on the backburner. Something untainted and virtuous. And that... is something worth fighting for.

The air was still. My hands felt clammy. Fluffy cotton ball clouds moved in, puffy against the darkening sky. The cows laid down on the hill, beside the lodge, and the birds have retired to their nests in a variety of trees beside the sea.

ooo

THE JOURNAL

November 22ⁿᵈ, 1989

Happy birthday to me.

DISTRACTION, NOT SATISFACTION. I can always count on the arms to extend to what they want, and they never stop. Brave little seconds, methodical minutes. I get lost in the curves of the three often. Imagining what it will be like to be me in three minutes... what might occur in six increments of 30 seconds each. Will I become weak, am I going to get lost as I dwale in a musing about the pines, or will I miss the entire lecture in Professor Depew's class because of staring down time. It's the envisioning of a more horrific future that eases my current condition. Because it's never as bad as I predict, not really. I think I'm journaling again because I miss the melancholy of what was going on around me back in the day. That made me want to write. Do I miss all the sickos, the bullies, and the users (Jackie, Mike, David) now that they're gone?

No, no, no. It's probably homesickness for the isolation, the abandoned beach, the little to no responsibility.

All that glitters is not gold.

It's much colder up here in Foggerton, same pace in life, but a lot more people. So many faces and spaces to explore, to touch. College has been just as I expected. Life is alright, just missing something, an appetition if you will.

On that note, happy birthday to me! John visited me last weekend, it was rad. It was gnarly how we both dropped our grunge looks for adult attire. I gave him enough funds to go to college. I refuse to go back down to Venoice, though I'd die to go to the pines, lie down in Sofia's spot one more time. The thought makes me hot, but I can't risk making a mistake there. The Colombo's called this morning to wish me a happy birthday. We are still in contact, despite my leaving them in grief over the untimely but timely death of their daughter. It's so lame down there that they're even using the cabin grad party as an example to not drink alcohol in high school, as if that was the cause. Gag me.

ooo

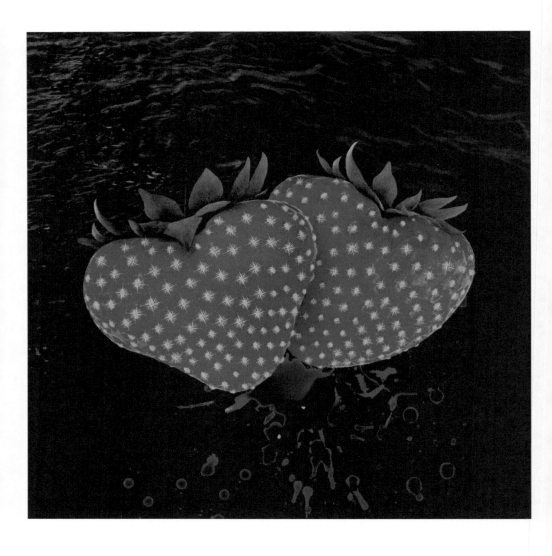

THE STORM

I OBSERVED THE MARVELOUS, spacious living space for a last time. The white on white, combined with the cool colors from Ella's new artwork, blending the kitchen blues impeccably into the living room. Memories flooded my mind when I grazed my fingers over the piano fallboard. How we lived easily in ecstasy days ago. Glancing at the jacuzzi spa, I reminisced about Ella being topless in there. A daunting image of three dead seagulls spanned across the top of the water, replaced my pleasant memories.

"Lia is upstairs, unwrapping some new fabric. She already hugged Logan. I think she's just, kind of moody because of her crappy co-worker, Tammy," Ella explained.

I can tell that Ella is just being polite about her sister's absence. I suspect Lia can't stand me after learning of all the things I withheld from Ella.

Pinot barked loudly to an undulating growl, the pitch rising and falling. A bolt of lightning struck the beach-access stairs. We all jumped. I reached into my front pocket of my hoodie to feel for my steel heavy-duty baton. Pinot ran to his bed in the room's corner by the lit fireplace, where he remained bug-eyed. The rain picked up and pitter-pattered violently against the floor-to-ceiling windows and sliding doors.

"Aww, Pinot, it's okay!" Ella assured. V and Ella walked over to the whimpering pup to comfort him. I maintained my distance by the piano.

Ding-dong.

Logan walked fast to the front door. He unlocked, opened it, and walked out to the entryway. I followed behind him.

"Ay, I think it was that teen, Leo! Someone just hightailed it from the front yard by the road, towards the left," Logan said. V joined by his side.

"There is no one else around here for miles. It is probably Leo, bored from hanging out with his mama. We could call the police on the brat," V proposed, joking.

"Lure the po-po out here for a prank?" Logan responded.

"I mean, I could check around back, if you guys want to head over and talk to his mom," I suggested.

"That would be good, actually. She's been avoiding all of my phone calls and texts for weeks. It isn't like her," V said.

V and Logan got dressed for the rainstorm and left the house.

"Did you want to join me?" I proposed to Ella.

"Yeah, yes," she said, breaking into a smile.

We gathered flashlights and ponchos from the garage. She put short black rain boots on over her tight black leggings. She took off her white pullover and slipped into her favorite worn gray hoodie with flat and wide drawstrings. I helped her put a translucent poncho on. I put one on myself as well.

We left the house to look around outside, using our flashlights as we scanned the wet, dark, sandy hill to the right of the house. Ella shook her head. So, we didn't press to go further. We trailed back around the front of the home, and I stopped walking. I pulled my plastic hood back, and I stood there for a moment, hesitating, letting the rain pour over me. The raindrops were sharp and heavy, darting down my cheeks, through my short, boxed beard. Down the back of my neck and back muscles.

Ella walked back towards me from the driveway.

"What is it, Oisín?" Ella asked sternly.

"Ella, I am *so* sorry for not being upfront. I now see that there were opportunities to say something. But I can't change the past. I would not want to change a thing, though. Especially what we have experienced together. I know this might sound corny, but I feel like I gained my best friend again. I cannot leave without telling you that... that I am falling in love with you," I admitted.

Ella pulled her plastic poncho hood back and came closer to me, examining my face. She wrapped her arms around me, clinging to my wet poncho. I hugged her tightly back and put my chin on top of her head. Through my facial hair, I could feel that her hair was soaking wet. I pulled back to put her hood back on, but she swatted my hand away.

"I'm falling in love with you too, Oisín," Ella whispered.

She gazed back at me, as if I were the very last person on the planet.

Ella continued, "I never imagined, in my wildest dreams, that we would be here, in Bonnes Bay, like this. But now, I can't imagine my life without you. I don't want you to feel guilty for not saying something sooner. But it *wasn't* safe. Please tell me exactly what is going on. I want full disclosures, the good, the bad, the ugly. To plunge into the unknown, to unearth and heal, together. Anchor through all types of weather, right?"

"Right. I want that with you too Ella. And I will explain everything. I'm sure you have a million questions after hearing my end of the call with Charlie," I suspected.

"I do, but first, this," Ella said in a breathy, strained voice.

She leaned towards me and tilted her head slightly, resting her cheek in my bare palm. She won't open her mouth for photos, but oh, how she parts them for me. Slowly at first, as she closes her sultry hazel eyes. Ella shares the warmth of her widening mouth, releasing her sweet berry breath. And then comes the soft, wet, stinging arousal. Jellyfish kisses. Then she pulls back, flexing her tongue up and down in my mouth, like a whale swimming at a lethargic velocity. She teases me and I surprise her by sucking on her lower lip. The only thing in the world to make me irresistibly weak in the knees is Ella clinging tightly to me. Is her tongue caressing mine. When time is no longer a thing.

As the storming sky released heavy drops of sea spray and rain dust upon us, the pelting washed away any remnant of existing reservations we had. It intensified the affection that we professed to one another. And it also pressed a profound matter at stake.

I could not leave her now, not ever.

We ran across the short lawn and dried off inside the foyer. We hung up our ponchos. I kept the flashlight in hand, in case of a power outage.

"I wonder how it's going with Logan and V," I commented.

Pinot sat at the bottom of the stairs, sniveling heavily.

"*Aaah*!" Lia screamed, followed by another shrieking scream and a loud thud.

I ran ahead of Ella, slapping each stair with my wet and heavy soles.

We found Lia lying on her back on the floor by her bed. She was wearing black slouchy sweatpants and a black band hoodie. Her right hand cuffed the right side of her neck, while her left hand gripped her right forearm.

"Oh shit, shit," I muttered. I lowered and slid on my knees across the smooth floor, stopping just before Lia's side.

"LIA!" Ella shouted.

Lia was bleeding badly on the floor, a small pool of blood formed next to her. Blood was oozing from an area on her throat, though I couldn't see the specific location. I noticed the slash marks through Lia's hoodie sleeves. Ella's utility knife was sitting next to Lia, with blood dripping off the short blade. A loosely strung pearl necklace lingered on the handle.

The necklace.

"Ella, I don't want to die, not like this please," Lia choked.

Ella struggled to breathe affectively. She shook her head in grief, the tears from her face splattered against the dark vinyl floor next to Lia.

"I tried to be strong like you, Ella, I tried."

Tears streamed down both sides of Lia's face and into her short, dark hair.

Both Ella and I winced, piercingly.

"*Breathe*, Ella. You got this. Take off your hoodie," I prompted.

Ella adjusted her breathing and pulled her gray hoodie up over her head.

I could see that Ella was experiencing a terror beyond her worse nightmares. However, she regained strength with the responsibility of preserving her sister's life. I pointed to Lia's wounds. I lifted Lia's head and gently placed the bulk of the gray hoodie underneath her head and used the sleeves to tie and dress the wound on her neck.

"Keep pressure here, to stop the bleeding. Make sure she stays awake."

Ella took my place on the floor. She scooted next to Lia and put her head in her lap to hold her.

I used Ella's flip smartphone to dial the police, lowered the volume, and switched to speaker mode. I placed the phone on the floor next to Ella.

"911, what is your emergency?" the emergency dispatcher answered.

"We need paramedics and police, now! Someone stabbed my sister. 1604 Silverstein Drive. Last house on the right."

"Where did they go Lia?" I whispered.

She lifted her head ever so slightly, shifting her eyes towards her bedroom door that faced the hall leading to Ella's room.

"Hang in there Lia, last thing. Where did you get this?" I requested and picked up the loosely strung pearl necklace off the knife.

"She's bleeding, Oisín! Why does it matter?" Ella whispered forcefully, raspy.

"From Gertie, someone gave it to her, she left it to me," Lia sobbed.

"It matters. Hold her, keep the knife. I'll be right back," I whispered firmly.

I leaned in to kiss Ella's forehead and exchanged a painful glance with Lia. I neglected to mention the Roman numeral twelve drawn in blood on the floor under Lia's head.

I stuck the necklace in my pocket and sprinted across the hallway. Trailing a mess of filth into Ella's Victorian room. There was an additional trail of sandy shoe prints. Quickly moving from Ella's walk-in closet to the bathroom, and ready for anyone to pop out, prepared to smash my flashlight on their dome. Ella's French doors were wide open, the curtain drapes whipped wildly in the wet wind. I flipped the switch for the porch light. Someone smashed out both bulbs. I sustained forward; glass crunched under my weight on the deck. Reaching the edge of the railing, I flashed my light down. I could see someone running in the distance near our bonfire spot, then seawards.

How the hell?

"HEY!" I bellowed.

A flicker of light, reflecting off the balcony bar beneath the wood, caught my attention. Two large silver metal carabiners secured to the bar, they held up a white rope ladder with reflective yellow steps. It lengthened past the lower deck and down to the sand, about twenty-five to thirty feet below.

"Shit, shit, shit," I mumbled to myself.

I slid the long black flashlight into the front pocket of my navy hoodie underneath my dark puffer vest. I swung my leg over the railing and lowered to the ladder, climbing down as fast as I humanely could. I jumped into the sand at five feet. A dense, grayish white fog rolled in, a fast-approaching clam chowder. The rain stopped, but the wind violently spit on my face with a fine mist, it stung my eyes. I sprinted across the beach, running further than I thought I had to. I was now on a beach portion I hadn't been on before; it was low tide. Walking towards the sound of the crashing waves, I clutched the flashlight.

The fog dispersed as I finally reached the shore, where white foam tickled the land. I could make out a tall outline of about my height. My flashlight illuminated a pair of combat boots, dark jeans, and a solid woodland green flannel.

I raised the light to their face. They held up a blood-splattered hand, attempting to shield their eyes. I recognized the chef's knife in their other hand, from Ella's birthday, but bloodied.

"*DAD*? What are you doing here?" I shouted.

"Oisín, come quick! It isn't safe!" my dad demanded, holding his blood-stained hand out towards me.

I was deteriorating rapidly.

"Dad. Jesus, please tell me you didn't do this," I begged.

I shuddered, astonished at the sight. Dread crept up from the pit of my stomach.

"No, Oisín. It's not my blood, and this isn't my knife! We've got to go! *NOW*!" my dad commanded persuasively.

I shifted, a sight of movement in my peripheral possessed me to rotate my head. Raising my arm to the right of us, I illuminated the motion of someone dressed in darkness, dashing towards us along the shore. The sound of crushing wet, grainy sand drew closer. My dad seized my puffer vest with impressive force and shoved me hard back behind him. My arms flailed out in front of me, faltering in the darkness.

"God damn it," I fumed.

Angry waves smashed down onto their receding counterparts nearest to me. The saltwater singed my eyes further. I grew impatient and furious with my disabled sight. I rose and sunk into the sand, seeking a more compact surface again. I picked myself up from the melting seashore below. Two steps forward, one step back.

"Look at the little deer, *all* grown up. Now a big, mad buck," a gravely voice said.

I pulled my dad back towards me and moved to the side of him. The tall bulky person pulled back their heavy black hood, uncovering their face in the full moon. White skin, thin chapped lips, a large beaked nose, beady black eyes. Shoulder-length sandy blonde hair thrashed in the sea air. It was the woman that I thought I saw in the vineyard.

"Dad! *Who* is this? What the hell is happening here!" I thundered over the violent wind and vulgar waves.

"My, aren't you playing the brawny and handsome dumb-dumb well? Embarrassing, really. Thirteen is my favorite number, tried to do it justice, by inviting you to play on your special day. I spelled out everything that you needed to know. South. Key lies in the stone... As in south of New York, the Keystone State. Pennsylvania! *Aidan*, tsk-tsk, this *cannot* be your seed," the woman ranted in a heavy and deep voice.

"Oisín, it's..." my dad started.

"Pu, pu, Pearl Point Murderer. Also known as Sandra, your friendly next-door neighbor," Sandra sneered.

My father kept quiet, frowning in pain, keeping his knife fixed on Sandra.

It came back to me, like playing with a child's retro binocular toy. Flashing through photographic reels of my past. It was Sandra, standing in her kitchen window on December 12th, 2002. Watching me, no, smirking at me with an evil in her eyes, as I franticly panicked in the snow. Sandra was wagging her index finger back and forth, as I foolishly demanded her attention. Until she lifted a long, shiny, and sharp blade to her paper-thin lips, maliciously motioning, to keep my mouth shut. She then ran the blade in the air, across her neck. Keeping her lifeless stare fixed on me.

I didn't forget, I blocked it out.

"I remember... it was *you*... You threatened me!" I shouted.

"*Dun, dun, dun.* It's called dissociative amnesia. The lies you told yourself, to comfort yourself. It worked out lovely in my favor. It has been *so* entertaining to watch you go mad for so long, with no one to turn to. The kitty cat was priceless, *meow*. Oh yes, and you destroyed my artwork on the ice. William Campbell also assisted me, with his pathetic idolizing. All the naughty men that have preserved my career. But it wasn't in vain. Sofia was technically an accident. My number one, but not my first victim. But Lia will be my last... Twelve girls, twelve pearls. All *pearlized*, by yours truly. The only mistake I ever made was attending your mother's memorial because I, too, loved her. Aidan followed me, to my second cabin. Has been on to me ever since. TWELVE years of chasing me through mountains, riverbanks, coastal towns. If I played for the opposite team, I'd say that it was tantalizing foreplay," Sandra snickered.

"You disgust me. But Oisín, it's true. I found your mother's scarf with the deer embroidery and her watch in Sandra's cabin. There was a disturbing journal as well, revealing, who Sandra *really* is. I had to hunt her. I couldn't risk losing her trail by alerting the authorities. If they found her first, she would never tell us. She had been elusive for so long. Oisín, I've always monitored you, from afar. I had to come here, I had to protect you, I couldn't lose you *too*. I'm sorry I lied, son," my dad agonized.

"All that time, dad? How, *how*? Why don't you have a gun!" I screamed at him.

"This is fun, boys. He *had* a gun, quite a few. But you forfeit your ticket to play if you choose that weapon. Your mother was special. An unbribed friendship, until you were born. She fought me tooth and nail to get back into his arms and to hold *you* once more. You didn't deserve the time you had with her, but you'll be seeing her again real soon!" Sandra sang.

"You, you had my mom. *Next door*, all that time, while we grieved?" I wailed.

My muscles tensed and my throat tightened. Sandra might as well had already killed me, choked me, stabbed me.

"*You* took Claire from me. And you don't deserve the Russo girls. Their blood is on *your* hands!" Sandra hissed.

"Oisín, move back behind me!" my dad demanded.

The adrenaline brought me to life, erupting my shell with ferocity. Blood boiled, rushing through my veins like a horror slip and slide. I savagely blinked my tears away.

"Fuck *you*!" I exploded.

I whipped the heavy-duty baton out with force, extending its length and lunged towards her; she dove towards me instantly, staggering dagger in hand. I pivoted my body at the last second, whilst smashing the steel baton on the top left side of her temple with intense vigor. She continued forward; her pointed blade sliced through my dad's shoulder like butter. She retracted it from his flesh and clothing. He shrieked in agony.

"*DAD*!" I cried.

Simultaneously, thick blood streamed into Sandra's eyes. Confused and desperate to see, she stumbled on the shifting ground, towards the ocean. She hysterically scooped water, bringing it up to her face. Blinding her further. I dropped the baton to sit my dad upright in the sand and applied pressure on my dad's shoulder.

I counted four furious rolling waves.

"Murph! The neighbors, they're dead! V is wit-what the hell? Is that your dad?" a familiar voice shouted. I turned to acknowledge Logan's shock. A tangibly thick fog persisted just past him. Red and blue lights swirled in the haze, at the top of the hill.

"Logan, hold my dad, here. Now, please!" I implored. Logan acted without question. I picked up my dads knife and charged towards Sandra. Penetrating cold water gnawed at my calves. Sandra stood precariously knee-deep in the ocean, with her back to the moon, and without her dagger.

"Come on! I can see that you want vengeance in those *Oisín* eyes. I've waited to destroy you, since the moment you were born. Now, fight like a man!" Sandra shouted, her voice like a foghorn.

She raised her hands, moving her fingers up and down, insinuating a fist fight. The water line was now thigh high on her, the surface so dark, except for the faint glow from the moonlight. Spindrift caused her to blink rapidly with frustration.

"OISÍN! Don't give your life up for her, *path to righteousness*!" Logan hollered.

I counted six waves. I switched the knife from my right hand to the left and pulled out the pearl necklace from my jean pocket.

"The world believes that you're dead, so *stay* dead!" I roared.

I pitched Sandra's menacing necklace as hard as I could to her.

"*NO, NO, NO!*" Sandra screamed stridently.

Her brows dug into her wicked and masculine face.

Even in the evening dusk, the lustrous pearls shimmered immensely under the moonbeam. Glistening as they soared high mid-flight. Sandra overextended her arms up with her palms upright. I lost sight of the pearls, backing up rapidly to the shore. She trudged rearward, fighting the pull of dark waters. In a matter of seconds, she was wading with the waterline up to her throat. Horror battered her face as she lifted her head to witness a colossal sleeper wave before it swallowed her whole. The seventh wave.

ooo

THE JOURNAL

December 10th, 1989

I T'S HARD TO believe that almost a year ago, Sofia kissed me with her cherry red lips. The deception tasted sweet, it's the aftertaste that was sour. Now, I'm maintaining a home and dating. It feels odd, normal? I have a craving to kick it up a notch, it's a little too normal. Gotta get the blood pumping again, get the blood running again.

A college women's bathroom, no other place in the world that a woman willingly spills her life out onto the floor. In the men's you get piss, plop, flush, and sometimes the sink will run after. With women, you get home addresses, vacation spots, favorite bars, phone numbers, gossip about who's hot, who's doing who. Weekend plans, hiking trails, protection against predators. This is public. Do they not understand they expose the goods that lead to their demise? These are the right bitches, 18 and pristine, liars, users.

These girls are not selling their bodies on the street. I know because I listen, I'm a creep. Yet, they still make the 5 o'clock news about them. It's all, "oh my God, that could've been me!" No bitch, the murderer is in the county over from us, in Monroe, he's doing sex workers and he's sloppy. The pigs haven't even strung the gems together. Honestly, I kind of delight at the thought of giving him a countdown until I anonymously call the piggies about a strange man by the river. He's predictable and easy to follow. There are well over 70,000 miles of streams, lakes, and rivers in this state and this dumbass sticks to a general area, the easiest prey, and doesn't hide their bodies in remote portions. Genesee River, if the elements don't destroy a body, the commercial contaminants certainly will. Prostitutes and hookers are the true epitome of used and abused, the ill-informed, owned by many, owner to none. The ones without the luxury of mommy's credit card, daddy's connections, and best friends to sabotage. Most of them, anyway. How could he take out those women? That's not a real hunt. He's weak.

I get it though; I can't help myself either. Sofia started this fixation. I slit the throats from left to right, severing the jugular and windpipe. A sea of blood flows from the deceptive. The point is... there is no point in just a point, but you can make a point within the collective of points. Swine follows swine, but over time they go where they're fed. Is the artist influenced by the subject or is the art seducing the subjects into taking the part? You can not copyright time. You can not own numbers. But you can make an immortal point with the points in a line.

This past summer was a recklessness stirring and brewing in my bones. I surely left chaos at my work sites. They will not find their bodies, but it was messy. Now I have to lie low for a while. John was in awe that I rampaged. He said there is no room for that type of behavior in this business. But he's confident that I'll correct myself and address my purpose once again. He volunteered to cover my tracks. I can always count on John to help me. He took care of father by leveling my house down, after all. Loyal. Devoted.

Maybe I need to start a family and lay down some roots of mine. It is the perfect alibi. Father pulled it off so well. Why can't I?

The woman next door is absolutely divine in every way, Claire. She's become an amazing friend. We sip wine by the water, and she bakes me the most amazing muffins. Claire reminds me of my mother, without kids. (Well, my mother before she became wretched. Before my father corrupted her. Before he shot and killed her.) It's worth a try to pursue Claire. She married young, but Aidan isn't a problem. I could give her some time while I craft my hunt for others.

It's not like she could run and hide. She sleeps soundly, within arm's reach. Approximately fifty-three feet.

ooo

PRECIOUS PROPOSAL

December 12th, 2021

ELLA, MY DAD, and I spread my mom's ashes in Foggerton bay, today. Charlie used connections to pull records of everything that Sandra owned. She buried my mom behind one house that she owned in Venoice, Pennsylvania. That's where a team brought my mother's remains up from this past summer. It wasn't legal. But what part of this journey has been? I never cried so hard in my entire life. Before, I suppressed it, in fear that if I let go, then it would be real. It is real, it's unfair, grueling, and devastating. I will always love my mom. And somehow, the chemicals in my brain have adjusted to the knowing. Somehow, my heart still beats with the loss. She feels closer now, yet free. Finally.

Therapy. *Lots* of therapy. My dad is in intense therapy and in an alcohol rehabilitation program. I've enjoyed getting to know him again and supporting his health plans. All of us have invested in therapy while Ella is seeing a trauma psychologist. She's doing exceedingly well, considering the year from hell. I surprised Ella with billboards in Foggerton advertising her work. Ella's latest abstract art collection sold in a matter of minutes at her virtual fall gallery. It has been a plethora of prosperity for her, and I couldn't be prouder. A flashback to the night at the vineyard crossed my mind. I guess it isn't *so* bad to profit from the public's fascination with killers. Her case was clearly in self-defense, but some buyers specifically sought her art because of the bank massacre. Life has not returned to total normality yet, but what is normality? Some of us have been masked, *far* before the pandemic.

Both Logan and I left our roots to live in California temporarily with the girls. In efforts to support Lia's recovery after *that* stormy night at the beach house. It thrills Ella and V that we are moving to New York next month. Logan and I sold our ranch-house to Devon and upgraded our living arrangements with our own homes on Foggerton Bay. Devon is still dating Vanessa. We've convinced him to partner with Cake Chest and Ocean Scoops and open a concept combination of the two in Foggerton, with his cuisine spin on it. He's also going to offer single servings of Ella's Love Letter Lasagne. Ella declared we are now The Paralian Club, her playfulness invigorates me. She has also made me into a man of words, well, more than just a previous basic vocabulary. We have continued to express how we feel by slipping printed poetry pages in hidden spots around the rental. She has introduced a youthfulness that has also convinced me it isn't *too late* to pursue a career in oceanography. I'll be starting with a few college classes.

The happiest thing to have happened this year is Logan proposing to V about a week ago. All of us, Ella, my dad, Charlie, Gloria, Devon, and V's parents, are joining to celebrate the couple. We arrived at the restaurant early, to shake off any jitters left from spreading of my mom's ashes. The Logan and V party should begin soon...

ooo

I glanced down at my *Omega Seamaster 300* watch; the clock displayed seventhirty. I took a sip of my *Midleton Very Rare Vintage Release* over a single cube of ice. The homely notes of caramelized honey, oak spices, a hint of ripe summer fruits and hay put me at ease.

I could see Ella exiting the restroom across the restaurant. She strutted towards me, sitting at the bar. I stood up and adjusted my maroon tie against the white collar. And smoothed my tailored black suit jacket. She enthralled complete strangers; jaws dropped on bright white porcelain dinner plates. Her satin burgundy gown grazed the Brazilian walnut floor beneath her black stiletto heels. Ella's dress draped softly from her body; cleavage gleamed from the plunging neckline. Luscious lips remained nude, while dramatic makeup played up her seductive cat-like eyes and sharp cheekbones. My girlfriend is the essence of poetry in motion. She's lawless, intangible as air, beaming with rhythm and complexity. Spellbinding.

"You are, *so* gorgeous," I said, as I pulled her barstool out for her.

"Thank you, handsome," she purred in my ear, and kissed my cheek above my short, boxed beard. She set her rectangular black marble clutch on the red oak bar top.

"I commend you for wearing those," I said, motioning to her interlocking brass G flower and classic white pearl drop earrings.

"You're the one who bought them for me," Ella exclaimed and giggled.

"Well, you ask, and you shall receive," I assured, chuckling.

"Oisín, you insisted we do gifts early. I have no regrets about our extravagant picks. We did almost die... twice. I love you and I love these. They are not unlucky gifts, though. The Pearl Point Murderer, I mean Sandra, inflicted pain on others and forced a narrative by driving fear into communities with a timeless and precious gem. My philosophy is, if someone gives a pearl in love with a clean heart, it *will* exude purity and wisdom. The joke is on her, anyway. She didn't complete her crazy clock of death. They may not have found her body, *yet*. But I have faith that the ocean served her a subzero dish of karma. I honestly believe that Mother Earth cleansed herself of Sandra's sinister presence," Ella denoted.

"I agree and they look amazing on you, my star warrior," I complimented.

"*We* are both warriors. Your mom would be really proud of you. You're basically fulfilling your name's origin, Oisín, the poet warrior," Ella giggled and grazed my muscular bicep with her small hand. "By the way, I am an unrestrained poppy in the wind over our trip coming up. I can't wait to see County Cork, Ireland."

"You're adorable," I laughed. "I'm happy to go anywhere with you. But... hell yeah, I am stoked about our trip next year! Then we have to plan a trip to see your nonna in Bergamo!" I replied with a wide grin.

"Cheers," we said in harmony.

We held our glasses up and clinked them together and took a sip.

"Are you an Oysin and Ella?" a server asked from behind us.

He wore a black face mask, matching black bowtie and vest over his white dress shirt. The server extended a round black tray between the Ella and me. A glossy mahogany box sat on a black cloth napkin in the middle of the tray.

"Oh, yeah, that's us. Thanks," I said, accepting the box. I set it on the bar top.

"Are, you proposing to me?" I questioned Ella, scanning her hazel eyes.

"Would that be so wrong? I happen to love you, Oisín Benjamin Murphy..."

"And I love you, Ella Marie Russo-Redhouse, more than *anything* in the world. I fully intend to make that commitment to you. I just sort of, want to make it out of this insane year first and give you the proper proposal that you deserve. No offense to Logan's impromptu proposal to V. I couldn't be happier for them. So, is this what I think it is?" I quizzed.

"Lighten up, love, I was kidding. All for equality, but I'll never propose to a man. And I totally agree, the new year can't come soon enough. It isn't from me, though, so open it already!" Ella shouted and began giggling.

The air shifted. It felt heavy, humid, stagnant. The smooth Christmas jazz music, muffled. Clinking of silverware and chatter came through as distorted. Warped shadows and shapes played off the walls of the fine Italian restaurant, inducing a growing paranoia. I watched Ella swirl her little black straw leisurely around a large, square ice cube in her cocktail. A bead sized berry lingered, frozen on top of the ice cube. Cranberry cocktail sloshed up over the ice, spreading a crimson wash. A bitter taste invaded the back of my throat. I brought my gaze back up to her. She smiled and mouthed, *open it.*

I lifted the top to the glossy mahogany jewelry box. My heart froze, my veins ran ice-cold. I brought my eyes back up to Ella's, shuddering as I turned the open box towards her. Inside, a brass compass screamed of the past. The engraving read, *My Little Deer, May you find yourself on the path to righteousness. Love, Mama.* Someone drew the number one and two on the plastic dial cover, in a deep vivid shade of red.

Bloody fucking twelve.

ooo

"My hour is almost come,
When I to sulphurous and tormenting flames
Must render up myself."

— William Shakespeare

ACKNOWLEDGEMENTS

Thank you

True friendship heals what time cannot. It inspires, it protects, it loves. For that, I am indebted to those who have blessed me with camaraderie. Thank you to those same people who listened to me talk tirelessly about my story and vision. Who helped me to identify loose ends and refine my work with this novel. And last, thank you for allowing me and *encouraging* me to thrive as a writer.

Sizzle, Robert, Mary, Amanda, Megan, Savion, Richard

o

Additional & deep gratitude to...

Tammy, Frank, Editors, BookBaby, Followers, Readers, Booksellers

IN MEMORY OF...

May the bodies of murdered Indigenous children, because of residential schools across the USA/Canada, be recovered and brought home.

May their souls dance under the stars of their homes.

May they receive justice.

B. K. SWEETING

B.K. Sweeting is an author living in Northern California. Although she is a native to the Golden State, she went to school in New York for psychology and film. Upon returning to the wine country, she went back to school for culinary arts and wine studies. B.K. is a proud member of the *Redwood Writers Club* and is an active Advocate for the *American Foundation for Suicide Prevention*. She's a thriller enthusiast, wine connoisseur, and lover of the sea. B.K. has firsthand experience working behind the scenes as a background actor in a popular *Netflix* mystery-thriller series and has acted in an indie horror film. If she isn't watching thriller films, she's aspiring to write them. She believes thrillers should always thrill the audience, but should also sprinkle a light of morale in the darkness that creeps around the edges of our souls. She is the author and illustrator of "Bubbly By The Sea". Her other work includes poetry and prose, fiction, mystery-thriller short stories, and lifestyle blogging. She enjoys baking, landscape photography, traveling, oil painting, and spending quality time with loved ones.

Learn more:

Bksweeting.com o Facebook.com/BKSweeting o Instagram.com/bksweeting